I0579183

AMBER R. DUELL

The Award-Winning Author of Dream Keeper

WHEN STARS ARE BRIGHT

Thumbelina Like You've Never Seen Her Before

WHEN STARS ARE BRIGHT
Copyright © 2019 by Amber R. Duell.

Published by Crescent Sea Publishing.
www.crescentseapublishing.com

Cover designed by Cover A Day
www.coveraday.com

This is a work of fiction. Names, characters, brands, trademarks, places, and incidents either are the product of the author's imagination or are used fictitiously. Any resemblance to actual events, locales, organizations, or persons, living or dead, is entirely coincidental and beyond the intent of either the author or the publisher.

All rights reserved, which includes the right to reproduce
this book or portions thereof in any form whatsoever
except as provided by the U.S. Copyright Law.
For permissions contact: amberrduell@gmail.com

For Mom
Thanks for crying over this one!

CHAPTER I

There's a certain thrill in doing something forbidden. Sneaking out past curfew, dancing freely to a jazz band, stealing kisses in a dark corner. Any one of those things will send my mother into hysterics. I'm not sure what she'll do if she finds out I'm doing them all at once. *When* she finds out, because she always does.

But, if I want to see Christian, it's my only choice.

The band electrifies the air with each note they play. At least fifty strangers twist and turn around us in the empty barn, and the lingering scent of hay tickles my nose. Christian doesn't seem to notice the lack of marble floors or fancy wall sconces. His eyes haven't left my face since we got here, except for the kissing.

His arms cocoon me near the wall, and I lean into his chest. He's warm and sturdy against me, and I close my eyes. The soft thump of his heartbeat beneath my palm dulls the sharp edge of missing him, but it never stops cutting. It won't as long as we're forced to sneak around behind our parents' backs.

"Are you tired, Lina?" Christian twists one of my curls around his finger. "We can go."

"We've only been here an hour." *And there's no telling how long until we can meet again.* I stretch up on my toes, the hem of my yellow skirt tickling the back of my knees, and kiss the fine stubble on his cheek. "Come on. I love this song."

Pulling Christian behind me, I find a free spot in the middle of the barn. Dozens of worn, dusty boots and Mary Jane's slam down on the planked floor, sending bits of straw and dirt into the air. The music vibrates against my body, and we join the rhythm.

The band wears worn slacks and checkered shirts like the rest of the crowd. Christian's the only one here without patched clothes or any idea of the work that will go into filling this barn with hay tomorrow. No one will have the energy for dancing after a day of haying. They'll be lucky to drag themselves to bed before collapsing, my mother and I included, though it will be a different field we work in the morning.

Sweat trickles down Christian's temple as we kick up dust of our own, and a wide grin breaks out on my face. I'm not the best swing dancer, far from it, but I don't care. Giving myself over to the music makes me feel weightless. Free. No one pays attention except Christian, and he's not much better. When the trombone sounds its last note, I laugh and collapse into his arms, breathless.

"Want to get something to drink?" I ask over the start of the next song.

He nods and leads me back through the crowd. His cotton shirt clings to his skin, showing off the muscles in his arms and back, and gray suspenders hang down from his waist. After more than a year together, it's the most I've seen of him, and it would be a lie to say I'm not enjoying it. If we didn't have to sneak around, I'd make him go dancing every weekend for the view alone.

"Wait here." He slips under a slanted support beam at the back of the barn, and kisses me. When he steps away, he keeps hold of my hand until he's too far to reach. "I'll be right back."

I scoot farther under the protection of the beam until it grazes my hair, and watch his head bob above everyone else. A lantern burns beside me, casting a warm glow, and the band plays their own version of *Puttin' on the Ritz*. There's no singer tonight, without a microphone it would be impossible to hear one anyway, but I know the words. I hum along with the smooth sound of the saxophone, my foot tapping in time with the bass and, before I realize it, I'm singing.

It's a cheery tune, but I keep my voice quiet. My mother is the only one who's heard me sing since I was little, and she insists I keep it that way. Being known as the infant abandoned in a tulip field, I'm used to whispers behind my back. Going steady with the heir to the Van

Buren petroleum fortune only makes things worse. I don't mind being thought of as an unlovable gold digger —not much anyway—but I'm tired of standing out. I especially have no interest in drawing a crowd tonight like I did when I was five. Twelve years later, I still get chills thinking about the people that closed in on me as I hummed in the marketplace.

A heavy man inches along the wall, hunching over to fit beside me. His eyelids droop over dark eyes, and his round face is close enough that I can count the pockmarks. His breath wheezes over the music. "You have a lovely voice. Where did you get it?"

I slam my mouth shut on the last line of the song. Naturally, the one time I sing in public someone's listening. Though it's only one person, this is somehow equally unnerving.

"Have you thought about a career?" The strange man leans closer. From his dialect, it's obvious he's from a different part of Holland.

"A career?" I shift away, and scan the crowd for Christian. When I don't see him between here and the water barrel, I step away from the wall.

The man bobs his head up and down, his jowls shaking, swallowing the yellow-stained Marlboro collar. "In show business. With that delicate face of yours, the blond hair and blue eyes, it would be easy to make a name for yourself. I've never felt an addictive quality as strong as yours either. Of course it's rare. Where did you get it?"

"I have no idea what you're talking about."

"Keep your secrets, little Symric. Fairy folk always do." He inches closer still. "But what do you say? You want to make it big in America with me?"

My laugh is quick and high-pitched. *Where are you, Christian?* "No."

"You should."

"She should what?" Christian asks from the opposite direction. He steps up beside me without refreshments and wraps an arm around my shoulders. I lean closer.

The man eases out from under the beam to reach his full height. He's on the short side—five-foot-three, perhaps—but still over a foot taller than me. "I was complimenting her voice. No harm intended."

"I see." Christian raises an eyebrow and steers me toward the exit. "Let's get some fresh air."

My lungs scream for it, but mostly I want to be away from the stranger. Away from the way his eyes burn holes into my back. I snuggle into Christian's side.

"Do you know him?" he asks. I shake my head. "Well, I'm sure he's just a harmless drunk. Don't worry."

Outside, the leaves show their backs in a promise of rain, but the moon shines down from a clear, starlit sky. The cool night air kisses my damp skin. I tilt my head back and take a deep breath. "I'm not worried," I lie. I can still feel the man's gaze roaming over me despite the wall between us.

Christian leans me against the only car on the property: his brand new 1930 Bentley. He's driven it for about two months now, and I've never seen him more excited to venture further out than our usual haunts. It's not so different than his last vehicle—it has the same curved fenders, chrome grill, and brown leather interior. This one is green.

"Good. Because I want all of your attention tonight," he says.

I fight a smile. "How greedy."

"Only when it comes to you." He wiggles his eyebrows and leans over, his mouth hovering directly above mine.

The familiar scent of mint leaves fill my senses, and my chest tightens when he closes the distance between us. His lips move gently against mine, and a tingle runs down my back when he cups my face. I clutch his neck, soaking him in. My fingers itch to move to the bit of exposed collarbone where the top buttons of his shirt are undone. But we agreed if we're going to betray our parents with our relationship, we would at least keep things respectable.

Sort of. Secret late-night rendezvous aren't exactly on the up-and-up.

"I should get you home," he whispers.

I groan. "Just a little longer?"

"We both have an early morning tomorrow." His bronze hair falls limp against his forehead, the gel spent after a long day at his father's office and a night here with me. He traces my jaw line with a finger. "We're already pressing our luck."

"Please?" I pull him against me and peek up from under my lashes.

"Don't look at me like that." He turns his face, rubbing the back of his neck. "You know it tears me up to take you back there, not knowing when I'll see you again."

I sigh, and look up at the stars twinkling overhead. He has more to lose with our relationship than I do. My mother will give me an earful, but his parents might disown him if he pushes too far. "I'm sorry. I know."

"I'd stay here with you all night if we could." He kisses my cheek and moves a piece of hair behind my ear. "You know I would."

The barn door opens, releasing a louder blast of music. The man from under the beam steps outside and strikes a match. I can't tell if he's watching us from beneath the brim of his flat cap, but it feels like he is. Ducking under Christian's arm, I scurry into the passenger seat without more prodding and force myself not to look back at the bright flame.

Christian steps to the front vehicle and grabs the crankshaft while I fidget, keeping my eyes away from the windows. The engine rumbles to life. I rub my sweaty palms against my knees as he lowers himself behind the steering wheel.

"Don't be upset with me," he says.

"I'm not upset." I've never been angry with him before, and I'm not going to start just because he's being sensible.

My willpower snaps, and I glance over my shoulder. Empty wagons stand along the front of the barn waiting to be hitched to teams of horses in the morning. A single tractor sits near the barn doors where a line of bicycles lean against the building. Smoke trails upward from the man's lips, and he wanders idly between them, the red cherry blazing his path.

My mouth runs dry. "Let's go. Please."

"Should I say something to him?"

"No. I'm sure I'm overreacting." My voice wavers, and he shifts into first gear. Bits of gravel crunch beneath the tires. We pull away from the dance, and I twist in my seat to watch the building grow smaller behind us. It isn't until the last bit of the barn vanishes behind a dark wood-shingled farm house that I exhale.

Christian gives my hand a quick squeeze before shifting gears again, and the speedometer climbs to twenty-five kilometers. Usually I would be glad he was taking the trip so slow to give us an extra few minutes together, but not tonight. Not anymore.

"He's gone. We won't go back there."

"We're running out of places to go," I grumble. "I hate having to sneak around like this."

He swallows hard. "I know it's not ideal…"

"It's better than not seeing you at all." I fiddle with the brass buttons running down the front of my dress and kick off my scuffed suede pumps to stretch my toes. The situation is wearing on me more than I'll admit to him—I don't actually *like* lying to my mother—but I don't want him to think I'm calling it quits. I'll keep this up the rest of my life if it means we can be together. "Maybe our parents will come around one day."

"Sooner than you expect, I hope." He winks. "Which reminds me, I've been meaning to ask you about something."

"Oh, no. The last time you said that, you wanted to go on a drive with your friends. Remember?" That day is the reason Christian has a new car. A cyclist had sped around a bend, forcing us off the road, straight through a fence, and into a cow pasture. The wooden slats cracked both headlights, and sent us spinning across the field. "We ended up knee deep in mud. I can't even say with certainty that's all we were standing in."

His laughter fills the car. "You were up to your knees. It was only up to my ankles."

"Christian." I swat his arm at the short joke. "It's not funny. My mother barricaded me inside for a month after that. I'm surprised she didn't throw away the key."

"No mud this time. I promise." He shakes his head, his face sobering. "My parents are hosting a garden party next week."

"Oh, well in that case." I pause. The nervous twitch in the corner of his eye tells me he's perfectly serious. My jaw drops, and a choked noise escapes my throat. "What? No. Have you met your mother? She's worse than mine. I'll be chopped up into little pieces and served as an appetizer."

"That was...vivid." He looks over at me with his big brown eyes. "Please? I promise everyone will behave."

I roll my eyes. "Don't make promises you can't keep."

We drive in silence then. Christian gnaws on the corner of his lip, and I study his silhouette. Each time feels like the last time I'll be this close. The thought sucks the air from the car, from my lungs. One day it might happen. One day I might wake up and realize this was all a dream. The car comes to a stop at the top of a hill, and the engine drones.

My cottage, a brick structure with a thatched roof and peeling white shutters, is nestled at the bottom between a creaky windmill and an empty tulip field. A candle glows in the front window, which means my mother's awake. She must have checked on me and found the bed empty. I crinkle my nose. The lump of blankets I arranged beneath my quilt was convincing tonight too. *So much for sneaking in.*

"I wouldn't invite you to come if I thought there would be trouble," Christian says, pulling my attention away from the window. "They'll never see our side of things if we don't make an effort to show it to them."

The way he's leaning in, holding eye contact, I almost believe him. He does have a point. Maybe if they see us together, they'll understand what we have is real, but his entire family is terrifying. They also take their parties very seriously. If anything happens, things will only get worse for us because, whatever it is, it'll be my fault.

"I don't have anything to wear," I say as an excuse.

"Wear this." He touches my puff sleeve. "It's a pretty dress. You don't have to doll yourself up to please anyone."

"I don't know." It's easy for him to say, but I know the looks I'll get if I show up in the house dress I wear to milk cows. I don't own a pair of shoes without dirt stuck in the seams, my hair is long and out of fashion, and I don't own a stitch of rouge. "Did you ask your mother if I could come?"

His cheeks burn bright, and he picks at the steering wheel. "I didn't want to give her the chance to say no. If you're there, she can't do anything about it without making a scene in front of all her friends."

"Does that really sound like a good idea to you?" It sounds more like a death wish to me.

"I'll beg if I have to," he warns.

I shake my head and slip my shoes back on. "I'll come if she says I can. I don't want her to hate me more than she already does."

"Please." He takes my hands. "For me?"

Every piece of my body warns me not to go. Instigating trouble with his parents is about the worst thing we can do, especially when they have enough money to force things to go their way. Our landlord is senile, his children eager to sell the tulip farm. It wouldn't take much to press the issue. My mother and I might as well move now before we're thrown out with the clothes on our back. But the Van Buren's wouldn't go that far if I went to one little party.

Right?

"Fine," I blurt. "Against my better judgment, I'll go."

His face lights up. "You won't be sorry."

Yes, I will. I already regret it. His world is closed off and confining, but he doesn't see it like I do. Even if he doesn't agree with all the rules, he's used to fine food, polite conversation, and proper manners. He can't throw an outsider like me at his society parents and expect them to be okay with it. They're looking for a proper daughter-in-law, not some spinster's charity case.

"I'll pick you up right here in nine days," he says.

I sigh and glare across the car at him. "This is a mistake."

"Wait for me at eleven," he continues, pretending not

to hear me. "It'll be fine, and when I bring you home, I think your mother will finally believe in us."

"The only way my mother will believe your intentions are true is if we—" *Get married.* My heart thunders. An engagement won't win my mother over; they can be broken. We'll have to be legally wed in front of multiple witnesses before she trusts a single word out of his mouth. Even then, I doubt she'll do more than tolerate him. When she makes up her mind about something, that's it, but if he does propose…"Are you trying to tell me something?"

He gives me a coy smile. "It's been hard not seeing you every day. I want to fix that."

I lean across the seat and rest my head on his collarbone, listening to the rhythmic sound of his pulse. *Engaged.* If he means it, if he proposes in front of his parents' guests, all this lying and sneaking around will end. No one will be able to keep us apart. I'll be Mrs. Van Buren, and we'll be able to spend every day together for the rest of our lives.

"All right." He kisses me quickly. "Get going. The sooner your mother yells, the sooner it'll be over."

I grunt at him and push the door open. "She's terrifying when she's upset."

"Be careful you don't end up an appetizer." He pulls me back across the seat. "One more for luck." He's smiling so wide, his kiss is barely more than a touch of the lips. "I'll see you soon."

"If she doesn't eat me first." I slip from the car, sticking my tongue out.

He shakes his head. "I'll wait here until you get inside."

I stare down the hill at the soft glow in the window. Without seeing her, I know my mother is at our small, round table, her elbow resting on the lace tablecloth. When I walk in, she'll be the first thing I see.

"I love you," Christian calls out the car window in a hoarse whisper.

I blow him a final kiss over my shoulder and race down the dirt road with the emptiness of the field nipping at my heels. The darkness glares at me, taunting me for my fear of the never-ending black void I was left to die in seventeen years ago. I hold my breath until I reach the low stone wall around our property and fly through the gate.

CHAPTER 2

Two years ago, my mother painted our front door orange. She said it was different. Fun. That it gave a bit of cheerfulness to the cottage when tulips weren't in season. I laughed at her then, secretly thinking she lost her mind. It's just a door, and we don't have disposable funds for something so senseless. Staring at it now, surrounded by the night, I'm glad she did it. The splash of color offers a promise of better, safer things on the other side.

Of course, actually going inside will make the dark less scary, too.

But it's exchanging one frightening thing for another. I can practically feel my mother's anger churning on the other side of the painted wood. Behind me, the night pricks at my back. I glance over my shoulder at Christian, and he waves from his car at the top of the hill. Puffing out my cheeks, I exhale slowly. I can't stand out here all night. It's better to get it over with, but my hand refuses to do more than grip the doorknob.

One more time, nine days from now, and she'll never have to yell at me again.

I cringe and push inside. My mother sits exactly as I thought: in a chair between the brick fireplace and table, facing the door. A white nightgown hugs her small, hunched frame, and a heavy shawl is pulled tight over her shoulders. Her gray hair is flat on one side—she slept at one point tonight. The tea kettle hangs over the fire pit with only orange embers glowing in the hearth, and our aprons hang on coat hooks nearby. Her fingers hit the tablecloth like tiny hammers, over and over.

"Hello." I shut the door quietly, lowering the wooden latch in place, and walk across the multi-colored rag rug. "I thought you were asleep."

"I know you did." She presses her lips together to give me *the* look, and sets her glasses on the table with strained gentleness. Dents remain on either side of her nose where they dug into her wrinkled skin.

I shiver, my nerves on edge. "I didn't want to wake you to let you know I was leaving."

"No." Her low pitch makes me cringe. "I would've stopped you, and you couldn't have that."

I lower myself into the rickety chair across from her and weave my fingers through the frayed lace tablecloth. "*Moeder*—"

"Don't you *Moeder* me. Where have you been?"

I swallow the lump in my throat. Her calm fury is

worse than screaming. A brewing storm. "Dancing," I squeak.

"Dancing? Where on earth would you be dancing at this hour? It's not proper, Lina." She stands, wisps of thinning hair swaying around her face, and points to the window. "That boy is destroying you. Do you know what people assume when they see you together? Do you realize how hard it will be to find a decent husband when he's finished with you?"

A fire burns its way up from my toes. If I can't marry Christian, I won't marry anyone at all. She never found a husband, and we're doing fine on our own. We might have to prove ourselves capable more often, but there's food on the table and clothes on our backs. If she doesn't need a man, then neither do I.

But I want one. I want Christian.

"We haven't done anything wrong." I focus on tiny brown tea stains dotting the lace. "I don't care what people think."

"You don't care?" Her voice quakes, but doesn't rise. "I'm not going to be around forever. What will you do when I'm gone? Hm? You need someone to take care of you, and you'll never find anyone if the whole town thinks you're a trollop."

"*Moeder*!" I gasp, my eyes wide.

"I'm not saying it's true, Lina, but you need to realize fairy tales aren't real." Her voice drops and falls flat. "I know he's rich and charming, but you're too trusting for your own good. You always have been. I'm an old woman —when I die, I need to know you'll be okay. You're worth more than this."

"Worth more than what?" I ask, matching her tone. "I think I'm worth falling in love with. I deserve to be happy."

"Yes, you do, but you won't find happiness with Christian Van Buren. Men like him don't marry women like us. They marry other socialites, not field workers. Not—" She catches herself and shakes her head. "Not... you."

"The first time Christian saw me, I was covered in dirt and sweat after spending an entire day planting tulip bulbs," I tell her. "He doesn't care about that. If you get to know him, you'll see he isn't how you think he is."

"That doesn't mean—" My mother flops against the back of the chair and holds her forehead. "Let's pretend for a second his intentions are good. His parents will never allow you to get married; his father came by just this afternoon."

My stomach lurches. "Why would Mr. Van Buren come here?"

She sighs, looking more tired than she has in a long time. "I debated mentioning it, but it might do you well to have some tough love. You need to end it with Christian, or they will."

"Why did he come here?" I ask again. My heart races, my palms sweaty.

"To get you to stay away from his son." She slams her fists down on the table, and I jump. Her mouth turns into a frown, and a familiar, faraway look enters her eyes. "In fact, he wants to preserve the family's reputation and his wife's mental state so badly that he's willing to pay us off."

My heart shatters, a million pieces scattering around me. Christian will never be able to bring me to the party, let alone propose. His parents have too much to hold over him. If they force him to choose between his inheritance and me, what will he do? "Did... did you take the money? We could use it, and I know you hate Christian, but please tell me you didn't."

"What kind of mother do you think I am?" She huffs. "I kicked him out of here faster than that fancy auto of his could take him. That doesn't mean I disagree. This relationship can't go anywhere, Lina. It won't. He's going to marry someone his parents choose, and you'll be cast aside. I don't want to watch you go through that. Things have gone on long enough. You *have* to end it."

"End it?" My throat tightens. Does Christian know what his father did? Is he really just toying with me? *No.* I can't let people plant doubts in my mind. We love each other and we will lead a happy life together. Everyone will see how well we fit. We'll prove them wrong. "You don't know him. He'd never do that—he loves me."

"Lina, you're barely seventeen. There are a lot of things you don't understand yet." My mother stands with hunched shoulders. Her eyes glisten, but she holds firm. "I'm sorry, but this isn't up for discussion."

She's right—it isn't up for discussion. No one can tell me who to love, and there's nothing she can say to make me change my mind. "I'm not giving him up," I say quietly.

"You don't believe me, but this is for your own good, *meisje*. You may see him once more to tell him goodbye, but that has to be it. I've lived a long life so you need to trust me on this. You don't know what the consequences of your match could be." She stretches her back with a small grunt and retreats toward her bed. "The wash is still on the line. Bring it in before it rains."

I open my mouth to beg her not to make me go outside, but there's no talking to her tonight. She snaps the hanging floral sheet across her corner of the one-room cottage. Looking out the back window in the direction of the clothesline, I grind my teeth. She doesn't understand; she's never had someone like Christian.

I spare a glance at my own bed, at the blankets heaped at the foot from my mother's search, and ball my hands into fists before heading out the back door. There's no one to watch my back this time, but I can always grab a chicken from the coop, and throw it at anything trying to eat me. At least I'm not under house arrest again. If I behave for the next nine days, I'll still make it to the garden party for one of the most important days of my life. Because Christian *will* come for me.

He will.

I could leave now. If I went to him, he would run with me. We could come back after we're married, and then there's nothing they can do. Except his family could still disinherit him. I wouldn't mind; hard work doesn't scare me, but he's never been poor. I don't want him to resent me later when times are tough.

Wind rattles the window beside me, its bitter talons slicing through the thin fabric of my dress. I shudder as the gust howls across the empty field and disappears. More than the darkness, more than the creaking trees, the unnerving stillness bothers me the most. I try to remember animals are more afraid of me than I am of them, except maybe the wild boars, and there's no such thing as the boogieman. For some reason, my brain can't reconcile that as truth. Any number of things can hide in the dark. When people say there's nothing to be afraid of, they're only fooling themselves. No one can ever be sure of what's lurking in the shadows until it's too late.

I press my lips into a straight line, and hurry off the back stoop. A fat raindrop splats against my arm and thunder cracks in the distance. I grab the large wicker basket beside the door, dragging it across the lawn in a near sprint.

"Please don't rain yet," I say, looking up. Clouds eclipse the stars now; it won't be long before the sky truly opens.

Standing on my tiptoes, I pluck round wooden clothespins from the line, and drop them into the basket. A new gust of wind whips the first sheet around my body. I bat it from my face, and tug it away from my legs, but the wind keeps me trapped. I spin around, my back to the fabric, and wad it into a ball against my abdomen. Once it's safely stuffed into the basket, I hurry to free our dresses. Another drop of rain lands on my cheek, then another on my neck.

I fumble with the pins holding down my mother's stockings and lightning breaks the sky. I pause, my fingers curling around the clothesline, and let the rain pelt against me. Let it wash away the words my mother said and the doubt that clouds my thoughts.

Nine days. I quickly pluck the stockings free. Then I'll be the future Mrs. Lina Van Buren. I smile, my giggle lost to the storm.

CHAPTER 3

The orange glow of dawn illuminates the cottage. I want to grip the sun and foist it higher in the sky, skipping the next few hours until I meet Christian. *Only a few hours.* I grin into my pillow. *Finally, finally, finally.*

"Rise and shine," my mother says from the other side of my curtain.

I pull the covers up to my chin and force a pained groan. "I can't."

"You can't?" She whips the curtain back.

I groan again and curl my legs up to my chest. The last three days have been spent planting the seeds of a faux illness. A cough here. A sniffle there. Leaving half my soup uneaten and going straight to bed. It twists my insides to orchestrate such an elaborate lie, but I can't meet Christian *and* work the Bakker's farm.

"What's wrong?" my mother demands.

I fidget, keeping my back to her, my face half hidden beneath the covers. "I don't feel well."

"I suspected as much. You've been sluggish for days

and that cough…" She leans over and places the back of her hand on my forehead. "You're not warm."

"I don't think I can go today," I grumble.

My mother is quiet for a moment. "I'll send word to Mr. Bakker that we won't be over today."

My heart races. It never occurred to me that she might want to stay to take care of me. I haven't missed a day a work since I was a little girl, and surely now she knows I can take care of myself. "You have to go." I fake a small cough. "The Visser widow and her daughters are looking for work, and if we aren't there, he might take them on instead. Then what will we do?"

My mother smoothes hair off my forehead. "But who will look after you?"

"I'm just going to sleep, *Moeder.*" The words are bitter on my tongue. She will need to manage both our workloads without me, and the years are already taking their toll on her bones. After Christian and I are married, she'll never work another day in her life. Even if things don't go well with the Van Buren family and I have to work twice as hard, she'll retire in comfort.

"I'll make you some tea before I go." She tucks the blanket around me, and I wince against the comforting touch. "If you're not better in the morning, we'll ask after the doctor first thing."

"I'm sure all I need is a day of rest," I say.

She pats my shoulder and shuffles away. *I'm sorry,*

Moeder. But she gave me a choice: lie or give up Christian. It isn't really a choice at all. She hums as she moves about the kitchen, an old tune she always uses to help me sleep. I stare at the knot in the wood beside my bed and will away the burning in my eyes.

She will be furious tonight but not forever.

Not forever.

I WATCH my mother disappear around the bend in the dirt road through the window beside my bed. I take a handful of breaths. My feet slap against the floor. The fire burns low in the hearth where she made my tea, and I move the heavy metal iron onto the brick base to heat.

My Sunday dress drapes over a chair to be pressed for church in the morning. I lift the orange fabric and shake it out, scowling. The color isn't my first choice, especially being as faded as it is, but it's the best I have. I arrange the skirt on the ironing board and carefully arrange the pleats.

A soft knock on the front door makes me jump. It can't be my mother—she's too far gone to be back so quickly and she wouldn't knock—but we never have visitors. "Who is it?" I call.

"Lina, open the door."

My lips part, my brows low. "Christian?"

He told me eleven, but it's barely eight. *His father...* Does Christian know what happened? If his father finally drew the line...*Oh, God.* I cross the room with shaking hands, my pulse thundering in my ears, and lift the latch. Christian pushes inside the moment the door cracks. I snap a knit sweater off the hook and throw it on to cover how thin my white nightgown is.

"What are you doing here?" I ask, my voice too high, and cross my arms over my chest to hold the sweater in place.

"I'm fairly certain your neighbors think I'm up to no good." He ducks down and plants a swift kiss on my lips. My chest loosens at the ease of his kiss but only a little. "I've been parked over the hill for ages now."

"Why?"

"I had to wait for your mother to leave."

He scans the cottage, seeing the inside for the first time. I shift my weight as he takes in the moth-eaten curtains, the cracked mantel clock, and scuffed cupboards. Bits of straw I should have swept away last night still litter the floor. All the while, he's in a crisp black and white pinstripe suit that's easily the nicest I've ever seen him wear. Finally, his eyes fall back to me, and my face burns.

"You said to meet you at eleven," I say before he can comment.

A smile tugs at his lips. "I brought you something."

He brings his hands out from behind his back to reveal a navy blue dress hanging from his fingertips. A belt runs along the seam at the waist and white lace travels across the neckline, ending with a bow on the left shoulder.

"You said you didn't have anything to wear." He clears his throat. "You don't have to wear it, of course. Anything is fine, but I want you to feel as comfortable as possible today. So, I thought… I mean, if you want it…"

"It's perfect." A knot loosens in my stomach, and I scoop the dress into my arms. The fabric is smooth against my burning skin. "Thank you."

"You'll be there then?" He shoves his hands in his pockets. "On the hill at eleven."

My breath falls in quick disbelief. He was worried about *me* not being there? If he only knew the doubt that's been swirling through me since we last met…"Have I ever stood you up before?"

He shrugs. "No, but I know it's intimidating for you to be around my family."

"Unless my mother comes back and finds you here, I'll be waiting." I push up onto my tip-toes and kiss his cheek.

His breath skates along my cheek, shaking. "In that case, I better go. I need to pick something up in town anyway, then I'll come back for you."

"Good idea." I lean back and hold the dress out

between us, eyeing the fine detailing. It's the first present he's given me. The first time we don't have to worry about my mother finding something that could be considered a token of his affection, sending her into a fit. I grin up at him from beneath my lashes. "Go on, then. I have to get myself ready."

He cups my face and gives me a second kiss. When he tries to pull back, I grip his blue tie. He showers kisses over my face, laughing. "I'll be back." He presses a final kiss to my nose. "Don't be late."

"Never." I release his tie, pleased with the slight crook my grip put in the knot.

Christian eases the door open and winks without fixing it. "I love you."

"Love you too."

I twist my hips, letting the smooth fabric of the skirt swish against my calves. Christian won't be along for another twenty minutes, but I can't stand another second inside. After I drank the tea my mother made, a stone settled in my gut. I've never lied to her like this before. Sneaking around with Christian doesn't count, exactly. She knew, and I never promised to stop so it was always more like willful disobedience. Not a *lie*.

But this is one worth telling.

The sheep slowly graze their way across the distant mountainside, dots of white among the bright grass. My mother and I helped pick the last of the tulips from the surrounding fields weeks ago. Now the landscape is brown and barren all the way to those emerald hills.

The hum of an engine purrs in the distance, and my excitement sparks anew. I stare down the hill, waiting for the first glimpse of chrome, of a green fender. Suddenly, I'm practically humming with nerves. This isn't a good idea. Christian's father tried to pay us off! What am I doing, waltzing into their house, into their world, and throwing our relationship in his face? I have to tell Christian about the offer before the party—it isn't too late to back out for either of us.

I blow out a breath and pluck at my curls. Maybe I should wait inside so the humidity doesn't ruin all my hard work. The pins holding my hair out of my face will only do so much. I drop my arms and drum my fingers against my thighs. I can fix it in the car if he still wants to go through with it.

The whirling of a wheel draws my attention. I lean onto my toes to peek over the incline, praying none of the neighbors that saw Christian told my mother and leant her a bicycle. The wheel crests the hill and flies straight for me. I lock eyes with an overweight man pedaling furiously and leap off the road at the same time he jerks the handlebars in the opposite direction.

I stumble into the empty field, my arms outstretched, and catch myself before I land on my face. Staring at the tilled earth, I press a hand against my chest and take a deep, steadying breath. The bicyclist groans from the opposite ditch. I shake off my shock and step out of the field.

"Are you all right?" I call.

I take another step and a familiar warning rings in my head. *Don't,* it says. *Run.* But, in all good faith, I can't turn my back without checking on the man's wellbeing. The spokes on the back tire spin round and round in the middle of the road.

"Help," the man calls, his body hidden in the steep slope of the trench.

I shift backward. "I'll go get someone."

"Wait." He sits up with his back to me and slowly trails his fingers through his dark hair as if searching for a cut. Then he reaches into his breast pocket and snaps out a handkerchief. "Can you help me up?"

Just then, Christian rounds the bend. Relief sings through my body. "My boyfriend is much stronger," I say.

The man's face hardens as the car rolls to a stop, and he tucks the fabric back into his pocket. Christian steps out of the vehicle with a puzzled look. "Are you well, sir?"

"Fine," the stranger grumbles and climbs to his feet.

It isn't until Christian helps him retrieve the bicycle

from the road that I recognize him as the man from the dance. My heart skips a beat, and I race into the passenger seat. I believe in coincidences, but this is too much. The dance took place in another town, for one. Everyone around here is a familiar face, even if I don't know their names.

Christian finally joins me in the car with a giddy smile. "You're beautiful."

I swallow my fear and force a smile. Today is a big day. If anything's going to ruin it, it won't be this. "Thank you."

"Are you ready?" He grabs my hand and kisses my knuckles.

I eye the man walking beside his bicycle as he returns the way he came. Christian maneuvers his car back and forth until we're heading away from him and my house. The further we get, the more my nerves switch back to the party.

"Christian."

He stops talking midsentence, though I hadn't realized he was talking before.

"Your father came to my house last week." I twist my fingers together and will them to stop shaking. "He offered my mother money to keep us away from each other."

His head whips toward me. "What?"

"She didn't take it," I assure him quickly.

Red sweeps up his neck, coloring his face with quiet rage. "I'm sorry, Lina. I'll take care of it."

Take care of what? I want to ask, but can't bring myself to. "Maybe I shouldn't come today?"

"No. This is all the more reason for us not to back down."

It's practically a growl, a sound so different than I've ever heard come from his mouth that I ease away. "Christian…"

He kisses my hand again. "I'm sorry. I'm not upset with you, okay? I'll deal with my father."

There's no arguing with Christian so I don't try. This whole party, the pending proposal, all seems tainted. It's like fate is stepping in to warn me away. My ears ring as we pull up to Christian's house. No—house isn't right. It's a mansion. Stone railings lead up a wide staircase, and huge arched windows interrupt the creamy white exterior on both floors. Staff in dark suits and dresses line the bottom of the steps.

"This isn't going to work," I say quietly.

He stops the car and two men rush forward to open the doors. "Of course it will."

"I don't think I can walk in there," I admit.

"You're nervous." He looks up at the man holding his door and motions for him to wait. "It's okay, Lina. Trust me."

I do trust him. That isn't the problem. It's the sudden,

overwhelming fear that I'll be thrown out before I even reach the gardens, and, if I'm not, that this could become my life. Feeling inferior forever, hearing even more whispers at my back. At least the people working the fields don't pretend to be my friend. I've heard about the socialites from other workers, who heard from maids. How the girls act one way to someone and another after they leave. I may not have friends now, but I have my mother. Who will I have in a place like this?

"We can leave if you really want to."

The sound of disappointment in his voice pulls my attention to his face. *Christian.* I will have him, if no one else. "We're already here, so we might as well go in."

I'm rewarded with a bright, relieved smile, and he hops out of the car. Rounding the back of the vehicle, he waves off the man holding my door to help me out himself. Even the gravel lining the drive appears perfect —all rocks and no dirt. I squeeze Christian's hand and let him lead me toward the house.

We don't go inside but around the side. To get there, we pass through a courtyard with a large fountain. The water spewing from the giant fish's mouth appears cleaner than what we cook with. I'm so transfixed that I almost don't notice the copious amounts of rose bushes lining our path or the ivy hanging from a trellis overhead. Tiny yellow flowers peek through the foliage while the roses give way to rows of bright pink flowers. A white butterfly flits from one flower to another, dancing elegantly in the air.

"It's magical here," I say in awe.

"You haven't seen anything yet," Christian promises. He's watching me with the same admiration that I feel for our surroundings, and I blush. "The actual gardens are fit for royalty."

I skim a flower with my fingertips. "I don't think they could be better than this. Even a fairy king would feel at home here."

He blanches, but before I can ask why, a man bellows Christian's name. I jump and immediately attempt to pull my hand out of Christian's on instinct. He tightens his grip and stops at the very end of the trellised walkway.

"There you are," the man continues.

"Father," Christian replies.

A man in a well-fitting suit with perfectly combed blond hair strides up to us with authoritative steps. Everything about him exudes power from the shine of his shoes to the thin mustache above his lips. He resembles Christian so much that there's no doubt they're related.

"Your mother's been looking for you everywhere. Where—" Mr. Van Buren stops in his tracks. His face is expressionless as he takes me in, but there's a storm in his eyes. "You brought her *here?* Have you lost your senses, boy?"

Christian straightens. "Have you lost yours? I know you offered Ms. Holt money."

"She would've been wise to take it," he seethes. "There have already been enough issues with this party today, so take her home before your mother sees."

"I will not," Christian insists and leads me around his father to an enormous yard behind the house.

White linen canopies flutter in the breeze with nearly fifty people socializing beneath their shade. More guests sit in chairs beneath their parasols or walk beside friends while small children race around the perimeter of the party. Their gleeful shouts fill the air. Beyond the jubilant party-goers are hedges, a second fountain, and a rainbow of colorful flowers that stretch on and on. A gasp escapes me before I can stop it.

"You will not ruin this day with scandal," Mr. Van Buren growls behind us.

My stomach twists. I don't belong here among these happy, carefree people in their light color dresses and callus-free hands. Even the wait staff carrying silver platters look as if they know nothing of hard labor. Perhaps they do, but they don't *look* like it. Even in the new dress Christian gave me, I stand out.

"Take me home," I agree. "It's okay. Let's just go."

"At least one of you has some sense," Mr. Van Buren spits.

Christian ignores us both and tucks my hand in the

crook of his arm before striding out toward his peers. We've barely made it three steps when I'm ripped backward by my other arm. Mr. Van Buren shoves his way through a partially opened glass door, dragging me along with him.

Floor to ceiling windows let in the afternoon sun. The rays bounce off the gold décor situated around the room. Sweat immediately beads on the back of my neck from the heat. Colorful flowers grow in pots all around the room, filling the room with an almost cloying scent. The furniture situated at the center doesn't look like it's ever been used, and a small chandelier hangs down with amber-colored sconces.

The door vibrates when it slams shut, and Mr. Van Buren twists a lock. My heart bangs in my chest. "What are you doing?" I ask desperately.

Christian screams to be let in from the other side of the door. His father ignores him and calls for someone named Cobus.

"Let go," I demand.

"Listen here," he barks. "If I see your face again, I'll make your life so miserable that you have to flee the country. No! The continent."

A man—presumably Cobus—enters through a heavy, ornate door on the other side of the room. "Sir?"

"Prepare the car."

"Cobus?" A woman slips in behind him. "What's all

this?"

Christian skids into the room, practically shoving the butler out of his way. Fury paints his fair cheeks bright red. "Release her."

"Go back to the party, dearest." Mr. Van Buren speaks in a somewhat softer voice. "We'll join you in a moment."

The woman flicks open a fan hanging from her wrist and uses it to cool herself. If she is Mr. Van Buren's *dearest*, she must be Christian's mother. She's wearing a white dress with small pastel flowers and layered sleeves. A strand of pearls circle her neck three times and a large-brimmed hat protects her face from the sun.

"Mother," Christian says. "May I introduce you to Miss Lina Holt?"

She pales and grips the doorframe to keep from collapsing to the floor. The pressure leaves my arm as Mr. Van Buren rushes to his wife's side. "She's leaving, dearest. Don't worry yourself."

"Don't worry myself?" she asks, shrill. "This… this creature you call a son brought his floozie into our home. And today of all days!"

Christian clenches his fists. "Mother—"

"I am *not* your mother! You are not the son I bore!"

The blood drains from his face, but he says nothing more. He simply holds his hand out for me to take. I rush to him, reveling in the safety of his touch.

"Get her out of here," his father roars.

"Trade him back," his mother weeps. "I don't want this one."

Mr. Van Buren shoves Christian's chest. "Now!"

Still, he doesn't move, so I tug him back the way we came. Every step we take back to the car seems surreal. I don't understand all of what happened, but I do understand one thing. Christian and I are fighting a losing battle.

THE HOUSE IS dark when Christian pulls to a stop atop the hill. It's expected—there's another hour before sunset which means another hour before my mother will head home. For once, I'm disappointed. A lecture would be a welcome distraction tonight. The intense silence is more than uncomfortable and walking into an empty house will give me too much time to reflect on the day.

"Lina," Christian starts quietly, then pauses.

"It's okay," I assure him in a flat voice that's entirely unconvincing.

"No, it's not." He tightens his grip on the steering wheel. "I have no excuse for the way my family behaved…"

I deflate. That should be the least of his worries—his mother just told him he isn't her son. Whether it's true or not, there's a lot to process. "It's not your fault."

"Isn't it?" He faces me, the pain clear on his face. "You were worried about this very thing when I asked you to come today, but I brushed it off. I was so sure she wouldn't make a scene."

I set my palm against his cheek to silence him. "Please stop blaming yourself."

Christian turns his face so he can kiss my palm. His eyes flutter shut, his right hand covering mine. The tension inside the car calms at his touch, and my chest fills with a new emotion. What more proof do I need that my mother is right?

Panic scratches its way up my throat. I don't want to lose him, but I don't know how to keep him. The only action I can think of is to step back from the relationship. There's no replacement for family, no matter how they treat you, and it will save us both heartache. He will eventually resent me if I allow him to choose between me and them.

"My mother..." Christian hesitates. "I should've told you about her obsession with fairies. She's usually better at hiding it, but I suppose I didn't realize it would be so stressful to..."

To see me at their house.

"I was a sickly baby," he continues. "I caught a horrible cough when I was only a few weeks old. The doctor told my parents I wouldn't survive more than a day or two, but the next morning, the cough was gone completely.

Everyone tells me it was a miracle, but my mother thinks I was switched with a changeling."

That explains why he looked so upset when I mentioned fairies in the garden. I can't imagine what it was like growing up with a parent that thinks you're someone else—some*thing* else. The only mother I've ever known is loving and kind, but none of this changes the fact that we're on a path to disappointment. "I love you," I say, barely audible.

"I love you, too," he says, solemn.

"But—" My chin trembles as I pull my hand away. "We should stop seeing each other."

Christian's eyes go wide. "You don't mean that."

I don't *want* to mean it, but I see no other choice. At least for now. "I do."

"No." His voice is hard, but his eyes glisten with the threat of tears. "*No.* We belong together. We're going to get married."

I shake my head and twist my skirt in my hands. Surprisingly, my own eyes are dry, but a thick lump in my throat keeps me from speaking.

"Please, Lina," he begs. He searches his jacket pockets with trembling hands. "I... I have a ring, and you'll be of age soon. We don't need their permission."

"I have to go," I say in a rush. His warm hand closes gently around my upper arm, and I freeze. "Don't make this harder than it already is."

"Please."

I fumble with the door handle. "It's for the best."

"I love you," he pleads. "Don't do this."

The door finally opens, and I swing my legs out. "I love you too, but this isn't going to work. We both know it. I'm simply the only one admitting it."

"You're hurting," he reasons. "I understand that. But… but if we just give it time—"

I push his hand off my arm without making eye contact. If I did, I'd cave. "We've given it time." His ragged breath fills the car. I have to get away before he cries because it will undo me, and I have to let him go. "I'm sorry."

His voice cracks on my name, and I sprint down the hill to my house. The tears don't spill until I'm safely inside with the door bolted. *What have I done?* I slide down the orange wood and bury my face in my knees. We fought so long and so hard to stay together before this, and now I can't breathe. I will never be able to breathe again. *What have I done?* Maybe Christian hasn't left the top of the hill yet. If I hurry, I can take it back and—

"Don't cry, little one," comes a masculine voice.

I jerk up with a gasp to find the man from the dance crouching in front of me. My heart nearly stops. "Wh— what are you doing here?"

He smiles, strangely sincere. "I can't leave without my treasure, can I?"

I shove up to my feet, only for him to mimic the movement. His body shimmers. A side effect of the fear, most likely, but it sends me into a frenzy. I lift the latch on the door, muscles tense and ready to flee. A scream rips from my throat despite there being no one nearby to hear.

A flash of white flies into my peripheral vision. A hand slams down on my mouth. I scream again, so hard my throat burns, but the muffled sound is lost behind a clammy palm. A sickly-sweet smell invades my senses when I inhale for a second scream. The man loops an arm around my waist, pulling me against his wide chest. I kick back at his legs, but he only presses the cloth down harder. I dig my nails into the broad forearm. Wetness blooms under my fingers, but if anything, he holds tighter.

My feet dangle in the air and each kick holds a little less oomph than the last. My eyelids are heavy. So heavy. *No*, I scream at myself. *Stay awake.* I have to stay awake. I have to get away. The world tilts, my vision blurring. *No, no, no.* I can't lose consciousness. I scream into the hand again, but it's the last thing I do before pinpricks sear their way across my skin.

A deep, pulsating, terrifying darkness swallows me whole.

CHAPTER 4

My stomach churns, pulling me, gagging, from unconsciousness. My legs tingle, ready to cramp with the slightest movement. Acid sears its way up my esophagus, and I groan. When I pry open my eyes it's to a darkness so complete, it throbs. Or maybe that's my head pounding. I press my eyes shut, and open them wide, but there's still no light. My pulse roars. *I'm blind.* I pant, my lungs begging for air. This has to be a dream; it can't be real.

I shift, pushing up on my elbows, and my head thumps against something hard. Sliding back down, my elbows bump a wall on either side of me. There isn't enough room to straighten my legs. My chest feels as if it's being ripped open and a piercing ringing fills my ears. I press my hands above my head, running them along the smooth surface. Using the side walls for leverage, I push. My arms and shoulders scream with pain, but I keep going until I'm dizzy from the effort.

"Remember," I whisper. Hot tears roll down the sides of my face, pooling in my ears. "No boogieman."

There wouldn't be room for one in this box anyway. *Box... Coffin.* I've been buried alive. Bile coats my tongue. "No, no, no, no, no," I whimper. I can't be underground. I *can't* be. I won't die like this, leaving my mother to wonder what happened to me.

"Help," I scream. My throat feels like sandpaper, and I bang on the roof. Pain shoots down to my elbows. "Someone help me!"

Metal clanks on the other side, and I freeze. I'm not buried; not yet. There's still time to get out. I resume my assault, pressing against the ceiling with both hands and my forehead. A cramp burns its way up my calf. Fresh tears stream down my cheeks, but I ignore the stinging muscles and claw at the surface above me.

"Please," I scream again. "Let me out!"

The lid cracks, a thin line of light spilling inside. I shove my way free, gasping for air, but a pair of arms wrap around my waist as soon as I'm standing. They keep me from climbing out of my prison. Before I can shout again, a hand clamps over my mouth. My lips scrape against my teeth so hard I taste blood, and my calves grate against a sharp edge as my captor pulls me from the coffin.

"Stop squirming," a man hisses in my ear. "I'm not going to hurt you."

Liar. I swing my elbows back in quick succession. They bounce off his abdomen without loosening his grip.

I kick back, my cramp blazing with the motion, and I jerk against the pain.

"Stop or you're going back in there."

Fear lances through me, and my gaze darts around the tiny room. A set of bunk beds attach to a white steel wall dotted with rows of rivets. Wide industrial pipes run overhead, and a small cracked sink is tucked into the corner. My coffin isn't a coffin at all—although it smells like something died in there—but a large black steamer trunk with the name 'Ackerman' painted on the lip. It takes up almost the entire floor, leaving just enough space for one of us to stand outside it. One circular window about the size of my head is the only source of light. The door must be behind me because I don't see another way in or out.

My kidnapper must take my stillness as agreement because he lets go, and shoves me forward. I land on the bottom bunk, barely missing the edge of the sink with my forehead. Nausea rolls through my body and saliva floods my mouth. I inhale, ready to scream, when he steps forward with his hand raised. I choke down stifling air and press myself against the wall. His hand falls back at his side without striking, but the threat still leaves me breathless.

"I know you," I say before I can stop myself. I'll never forget the shaking jowls, or sunken eyes. He's in a polo shirt now, his gut hanging over his belt, and his thinning hair is greased back. Not like it had been when he crashed the bicycle, but like it had been that night in the empty barn. "You were at the dance. That was… that was you on the bike."

"It's nice to know I'm memorable." He extends a pudgy hand to shake. "Name's Walter."

I recoil. How did he find me after I left with Christian? Did he follow us home? He could have kept up on a bicycle, but I don't remember seeing anyone behind us on the drive. As soon as the barn was out of sight, I had put Walter out of my mind. I was sure I'd never have to see him again. I should've watched longer, should've paid better attention; he gave me such a strange feeling… I should have asked Christian to drive faster. *Should have.*

"What do you want?" My voice cracks. "Are you going to kill me?"

"Kill you?" He laughs. "If I was going to kill you, I wouldn't have gone through all this trouble. What do you take me for—a fool? This took a lot of planning. I didn't know until I saw you at the dance that I would need you. Luckily, I already had some chloroform, not that I intended it for you, of course, but it took so long to get you alone. When I saw your mother at the farm without you, I transmitted to your house as fast as I could, but you weren't there. Without knowing where you went, the quickest way to travel was on the bicycle, and we both know how that turned out." He shakes his head. "No matter. I got you, didn't I?"

It should reassure me that he needs me. It means he won't kill me, but my mind is spinning with other reasons for being here. With the possible motives he would have to carry chloroform. I grip my skirt. "What do you need me for exactly?"

Walter steps into the trunk to close the distance between us. "You're going to use that voice of yours to make money in New York. Behave yourself because you can benefit from this, too. You could be as big as Jean Harlow one day. Imagine!"

His rancid breath churns my stomach, and I stop inhaling until he's finished talking. He wanted me to go with him that night at the dance… But this still doesn't make sense. "I don't understand."

"It's not important right now." Walter reaches up to the top bunk without looking away, and a coil of rope falls, pooling on the edge of the bed. He winds one end around his fist. "What's important is how the rest of your trip is going to go."

I inch down the thin mattress until my back hits the wall. "Don't put me back in there," I plead. The thought of being trapped in the trunk, tied up or not… Cold sweat beads on my face.

"I won't have to if you do as you're told." He sniffs, running his arm under his nose. "I've talked with the captain, and he's agreed to give you free passage as long as you stay in the room. We don't need you upsetting the other passengers with crazy tales, and I don't have the funds to pony up if you try to escape."

"Captain?" I forget to breathe as the word sinks in. The nausea. The world moving under my feet. It's not a side effect of the chloroform. "We're not..." Pushing to my knees, I press my face against the window. A bright blue sky stretches out over a darker blue ocean—ripple after ripple, as far as the eye can see. There isn't a single bird in the sky or speck of land on the horizon. "No." I push away from the glass. "No, no, no. Tell me that's not the Atlantic Ocean."

"Of course it is." He slides the trunk in front of the door, and stands between it and the sink. "There's nowhere for you to run, so let's make a deal. Promise to stay quiet and I'll only tie you to the bed."

Only tie me to the bed? I'm not going to let him tie me to anything, and I'm definitely not going to keep quiet while he tries. There may not be anywhere to run on a ship, but that doesn't mean I can't find help. Getting away from this lunatic is step one. Finding a way home comes later. "You kidnapped me," I say, my voice rising. "And you just expect me to be okay with it?"

He picks at a skin tag on his neck. "That's exactly what I expect because if you don't, you'll go back in the trunk. Then, if you're still too noisy, I've got an entire bottle of chloroform left. I'd hate to keep you drugged for the next couple of weeks. Honestly, you wouldn't survive it, and I rather like you. You're pretty, talented, and magic —the whole package. Even if you weren't a Symric, you have star quality. It would be a shame to waste such a rare talent as yours. You'll get the audience addicted to your voice in no time, and we'll never have to worry about filling chairs again. In fact, there will be so many people clamoring to get a dose of your magic that we'll need a bigger theater in no time! So let's try to be good, hm? Besides, a girl has to eat, right?"

My stomach growls at the mention of food, but it's the last thing I want. It will just weigh me down anyway. Walter has at least two-hundred pounds on me and, with his talk of magic, clearly unbalanced, so I'll need every advantage possible. I can't push past him. Even if I could, the trunk is up against the door. I eyeball the window but it's too small, even for me, and I'll never survive the open ocean.

"What's your plan then? Keep me tied up and hope no one notices?" I snap.

He grabs my arm, yanking me forward. "Like I said, the captain knows."

"Does he know you kept me locked in a trunk for two days?" I shout. *Two days.* My breath falters. My mother and Christian must be going crazy by now. Almost as crazy as Walter was with all his nonsensical ramblings. A sharp stab of pain hits my chest. *No.* Christian might not even know I'm missing now because instead of getting engaged, I left him.

"I opened it while I was in the room so you didn't suffocate." Walter shrugs, calling my attention back to the present. "The captain said to pass along his regards, and he hopes you're feeling better soon."

"Feeling better?"

His clammy hands set to work tying a knot around one wrist. It's tight but not so much it cuts off circulation. "I told him I was trying to get my sister to New York to see a specialist. Top of his field. There's a new treatment that's rather promising, you see."

My brain strains to put the words into useful context. "What?"

"Guess you're not as smart as I thought." He moves on to tie the other end of rope to the metal bed frame. There's enough slack for me to move about the room which doesn't say much. "No matter. No one really listens to insane folk anyway. Not that they'll get the chance," he adds, meeting my gaze. "Because you're not leaving this room, Symric."

There's a glint in his eye cautioning me he means business. He thinks he's won. He's confident in it, but confident people get lazy. They make mistakes.

"My name is Lina," I say helplessly.

He chuckles. "A Symric is what you *are* though and that's much more impressive."

"I'm just a girl."

His jowls wobble as he takes me in. "Hasn't anyone told you before? Do they have a different name for it where you're from? I've only ever heard Symric, but it's not as if it's a common topic around here. Mostly, Symrics are the subject of idle chatter from the people up north who deal with the fair folk. Rumor has it that the fairies keep your kind hidden from the rest of the world so aren't I the lucky one?"

"Please." I choke back a sob, not understanding a word of said. He's mentioned *Symric* more than once, but it means nothing to me. Combined with his apparent belief in fairies, I can only assume it's part of his delusion. "Just let me go. I won't tell anyone what happened. I'll just say I ran away—"

"That's likely what they're thinking anyway." He gives the rope one last tug. "I was standing outside when you fought with your mother after the dance. I heard everything. I'm dying to know how you came to call someone so nonmagical your mother, by the way. Symrics can only be born to two Syrmic parents."

My bones feel as if they're full of iron. I ignore his mention of magic and focus on what he said about my mother. Will she think Christian and I eloped when it became clear we wouldn't get their blessing? When she realizes I did the exact opposite of that, she'll never believe he had nothing to do with it. She'll be convinced he killed me in a fit of rage and start looking in every ditch she walks by.

"Not feeling chatty, eh?" He shrugs, unbothered. "We have a long journey ahead of us. Plenty of time for us to get to know each other."

"You don't understand. My mother's going to be devastated. I'm all she has. Let me go back. Please, Walter."

He grunts. "It's too late for that. Once my destination is out of sight, there's no way to transmit anymore. My mother can, mind you, but no one is powerful enough to make it this far off shore without a ship of their own to go part of the way."

"What?" I ask between heaving breaths. It's partially a rhetorical question as I'm sure he's simply lost his mind, but my own head is spinning so fast that I can't stop the word from tumbling out.

"I'm a Transmitter. Obviously." He speaks as though I'm stupid for not understanding. "I can travel large spaces in a single step thanks to some fairy ancestor generations ago. Diluted magic, but magic nonetheless."

A sudden burst of rage burns its way from my throat. "There's no such thing as magic!"

"I'll get you something to eat. See if we can't curb that attitude with a full stomach. If I hear a peep out of you, back in the trunk you go." He motions under the bed. "There's a pot tucked under there if you have any business to take care of."

I glare at him as he backs away, slides the open chest away from the door, and leaves. If he thinks I'll sit here and wait, he's got another thing coming. There's no telling what he has planned for me in New York. This is someone who admits to carrying chloroform with him on what sounds like a regular basis and believes in fairy magic so whatever it is, I don't plan on finding out. I've heard stories about girls that go missing and are never found. I refuse to become the next cautionary tale.

With one hand untied, I pick at the knot around my other wrist. My short, brittle nails aren't much help, but I keep working until they bleed. It takes longer than I hoped, but I finally dig the end of the knot out of the loop, and toss it aside. My heart explodes in my chest. *Please don't let me be too late.*

I crawl to the end of the bed, avoiding the trunk, and step gingerly onto the cold floor. My shoes are gone, but running will be easier, quieter, without heels anyway.

My hand quivers on the metal knob. *Please.* Hopefully the dining rooms are on the other side of the ship because it's now or never. My teeth clatter as I swing the door open and dart from the room. A long, narrow hallway of doors stretches out on either side. The walls are the same as inside in the room—white-painted steel

—only with a stripe of red across the middle. The dim lighting flickers and I stumble into the wall. The stench of vomit does nothing for my own stomach. I debate pounding on each door as I pass until I find someone to help, but I can't be sure Walter doesn't have an accomplice staying nearby.

Instead, I run to the right where more artificial light filters down a set of stairs. My bare feet slap against the floor. I launch myself up the narrow staircase, clinging to the railing for support. Knotted hair whips around my face each time I hit a landing and turn toward the next set of steps. Each heavy door has a large painted number, each number getting closer to one. I consider hiding, but can't stop until I'm free. If enough people see me, maybe one will believe me. Or, at the very least, I'll be missed by someone if Walter decides to throw me overboard. I'm hoping for the first option.

At the fourth landing, the letter "D" replaces the number. Real sunlight shines through the window—a small patch of blue against the clinical white of the landing.

I stumble into open air. The breeze carries a light hint of salt. I squeeze my eyes shut against the sun as it bounces off the water. "Help," I call in a hoarse voice. I force myself to squint into the brightness, and find two men in tailored suits puffing on cigars. They turn away from the railing. "Please, help me."

They exchange a cautious glance before the one on the left steps forward. His fedora shades his eyes against the sun, but he still squints as he scans me from head to toe. "What's the trouble, miss?"

"I was kidnapped." I sway as the exertion of my escape creeps in. "He locked me in a trunk and—"

"There you are." Walter's voice booms behind me, although I think he's actually speaking in a normal tone. "I've been looking all over for you."

I back toward the two men with my hands held out in front of me. "Keep away."

"What's going on here?" the second man asks. "She says someone kidnapped her."

Walter's eyes never leave mine. "I'm sorry to trouble you, gentlemen. My sister is ill." He taps his forehead. "We're going to see a specialist as soon as we arrive."

"I am *not* going to America," I scream. "You can't force me."

Walter moves to grab my arm, and I slap him across the face. The crack freezes everyone in place, myself included. I flex my stinging palm.

"I'm not crazy," I say in a measured voice. "My name is Lina Holt and this man is a stranger. He drugged me and stuffed me in a trunk."

Each breath is heavy. My lungs fight against it, telling me to give up. The four of us remain still, each taking in the other's reaction. The men don't seem to know what to do or who to believe. My appearance can't help my case. Layers of oil cake my face, and I know my hair is a snarled nest. My new dress, the dress Christian gave me, is torn and wrinkled. I must be the portrait of insanity.

I turn toward them and reach out. They shrink away. "Please. I'm telling the truth."

"Our mother died recently," Walter says. He snaps my wrist up before I can slap him again. "It worsened her condition. The captain knows all about it."

The first man clears his throat. "You should get her below deck before she creates a bigger scene."

"Of course." Walter drags me back toward the staircase, and I hear the men mutter, "It's going to be a long trip."

I can't let Walter take me back to the room. To the trunk. The darkness. "Don't let him do this," I scream. "You can't let him."

But they can, and Walter does. The last thing I see before going back through the door is the two men turning their backs on me. I kick at Walter, screaming as loud as I can. At one point, a woman rushes by with a nervous glance, but a hand lands across my mouth. I bite down until I taste blood, and he pulls away. I call after her, but she's either gone or pretending she can't hear me.

Walter shoves me against a wall the moment we're alone. "What did I tell you?"

"I—"

His fingers dig into me, and my vision grows fuzzy. I try to blink it away. If I faint here, I'll wake up in the trunk for sure. The ground disappears for what can only be a handful of seconds before my feet slap into a puddle of warm liquid. A bowl lays shattered on the floor in front of Walter's room, the liquid assumedly soup with bits of carrots and peas. My jaw opens and shuts. We weren't this far down the stairs a moment ago. I must've blacked out before... The thought sits wrong, but what other excuse is there?

"Hope you're not hungry," Walter sneers.

Yes.

No.

It doesn't matter.

He lifts me over the mess, tossing me inside. The door slams behind him so hard the pipes above my head vibrate. His hand closes around my neck, cutting off another scream before it can begin. Fire dances in his eyes, and my blood runs cold. Just because he isn't planning to hurt me more than he already has doesn't mean he won't if he feels the need to.

"I'll kill you," he hisses, almost as if he's reading my mind. "I'll toss you overboard, and let the fish pick your bones clean."

My breath wheezes as I try to suck in air. Murder is worse than kidnapping, but he'll do it. It's obvious with every strained muscle in his arm, each tight tendon on his neck, and the bulging veins on his forehead. The consequences mean nothing to him. Not when no one knows I'm here and everyone I love probably thinks I ran away.

"Do you want that? A slow, painful death, freezing in shark-infested waters?"

I shake my head as much as I'm able, tears welling. Nothing could be worse than that. Almost. He could lock me in the trunk before throwing me over. My bottom lip trembles, and I loosen my grip on his forearm.

"Listen closely, you little hussy. Stay put."

Walter's hand falls from my neck, and air whooshes into my lungs so quickly I fall into a coughing fit. He pinches my wrists together until my bones feels as if they'll snap and ties the rope tightly. My fingers curl under the pressure, but I don't fight him. Even if I wanted to, I'm too numb.

"Keep your trap shut." He waves a wad of cloth, a sock maybe, under my nose. "Or you'll be eating this."

The edges of my vision blur. "Why?" I wheeze. "Why are you doing this?"

He squats in front of me and grabs my chin. "I told you. I need your voice."

"You heard me sing one song. Less than that." I swallow and wince against the new ache. My neck will be bruised before the day is over.

"It was enough to feel the power of a Symric." He

drops my chin and pats me gently on the shoulder. The sudden kindness in his voice twists my insides. "I'm sorry for the way it had to happen, but it's worth it. We can experience New York together for the first time. My mother's written all about it and secured me a job with her boss. I haven't seen her in years so I'm rather eager to get there. It will be an adventure, don't you think? So many people would kill for a chance like this, and *we* have one."

"I just want to go home," I whisper.

"That's not the right spirit. You're a *Symric*. The world will bow at your feet for a small *taste* of your voice, and with me at your side, we can go anywhere in the world. Once the troupe is secure, I can transmit us into any city you want. You'll get used to the quick hops, or maybe my mother can transmit us the longer distances. No matter. One thing at a time."

He's cracked. Completely cracked.

Walter stretches up on his heels. "I've got to clean the mess outside. Move so much as a centimeter while I'm gone, and I'll lock you back in there for a week. I don't want to do it, you know? We can be friends, but I won't let you ruin everything."

Walter leaves, and I fold in on myself. Between the rocking of the ship and hysterical tears, my mind shuts down. I fall asleep on the crisp white sheet.

CHAPTER 5

"Get up," Walter snaps.

I pull my knees under my chin where I lay on the bottom bed and continue staring at the whitewashed wall. There's no point moving. I can't bring myself to make the effort. I've been stuck in this tiny room for so long I've lost track of the date. The sleepless nights blur one day into another. Walter belches constantly when he isn't rambling on about magic and snores like a bullfrog. While I have no choice but to debase myself by using the chamber pot with him in the room, he hasn't shown any qualms about relieving himself in the room. The only thing he *does* leave for is food.

If Walter threatens to toss me overboard again, I'll almost certainly take him up on the offer. Dying now would be better than slowly rotting away tied to this bed.

My captor yanks on the rope. The knots dig into my raw flesh, and I cry out. I'm angry with myself for giving him a reaction, but the feeling doesn't last. Nothing lasts anymore except the hollowness that's taken up residence in my core. The empty hole in my abdomen keeps me company after everything else faded.

"I said, *get up.*"

The trunk creaks open, and my muscles stiffen. I'm afraid to roll over and see it, but I'm even more afraid not to listen to him. Four days into the journey, I thought he was asleep and made another break for it. I didn't even make it to the door before he caught me and tossed me inside. The time locked in there broke something in me. Rolling over, I look up at Walter's scruffy face with a tight chest.

"It's a shame I'm not able to clean you up first." He looks me over with a sigh and gives the ropes a final tug. "I suppose they'll have to look for your potential. We've docked, and there's no time to waste. My mother promised someone would be waiting to give us a lift."

Tremors rattle my body, starting at my head and reverberating in my toes. I push myself to my knees, and clutch the sink for support while the room spins. My hunger strike hasn't accomplished more than giving me a dozen dizzy spells a day. When my vision returns to normal again, I peek out the window.

A planked wall stands in the way of my seeing anything but heavy coils of rope holding us in place. Men shout at one another in the distance. The water I forced down earlier freezes in my gut. If I leave this ship, I'll be leaving behind everything connecting me to Holland.

Walter hauls me back by my neck, holding me against him. "I'm sorry, but I need to see my destination so we have to transmit from the dock."

There's barely time to blink before another chloroformed cloth soars toward my face. I hold my breath, and kick out at him as it hits my face. I won't go under. Not again. Not in that trunk.

"Be a good girl," he says in a strained voice. "We don't have time for this."

I kick, elbow, and scratch until my lungs scream for air. The more I struggle, the harder he holds me. My eyes flutter. I can't hold on much longer, but I can't give in either.

"There you go," he whispers.

I still haven't taken a breath, but my body is shutting down all the same. I wrestle against the fog threatening my mind and will myself to fall limp. My muscles fight it. They remember the cramped box as well as I do, but if I want to stay conscious, I have to let it happen.

Walter catches me with both hands as I collapse against him. My face slides down his stomach, and he hauls me over the lip of the trunk. I let myself flop, hard, into the bottom. He grabs at my limbs with sweaty palms, stuffing them haphazardly into the confines of the box.

"There," he says again when nothing is left over the side. He brushes the hair from my face as if he's tucking a child into bed. As if my arms and legs aren't screaming at the odd angles he left them in. "Sleep tight."

The top slams down, and I wince. I wait for the click of the lock, sealing me in, trapping me, but it doesn't come. My eyes fly open. There's nothing to see except the blackness, and I cover my mouth with both hands to keep myself from crying out.

Wait. I have to wait. Because it's not locked.

One, two, three, four.

Walter lifts one end of the trunk with a grunt.

My eyes close, squeezing silent tears from the corners. The trunk smacks into something, a wall maybe, and the force makes my ears ring.

Five. Six.

Walter whistles as he walks. A bright, happy melody.

Seven. Eight.

The trunk bangs to the ground and stars burst in front of my eyes.

Nine.

Metal clatters and knocks. Two loud rings sound. The ground shifts. My heart leaps to my throat.

Ten. Eleven. Twelve.

We jerk to a stop, Walter still whistling cheerfully. There's another clatter of metal. He lifts the end of trunk with my feet, and I brace myself against the sides.

Thirteen.

I take a deep breath.

Fourteen.

A seagull caws.

I kick out at the heavy lid, and the trunk tips, spilling me on the rough deck of the ship. Walter gapes, too stunned to move, and I shove myself up. My feet pound against the polished wooden planks before his shock wears off, and the lightheaded sensation from before claws at my vision.

"Help!" The scream comes out as a hoarse croak.

Scanning the vivid white railings all around the deck, my eyes focus on the first person they see: A man in a white hat and dark blue suit with a bushy brown beard. Two rows of gold buttons run down the front of the jacket and four stripes embellish each cuff. "Please," I call. "Please, you have to help me."

He frowns and looks me up and down. "Help you with what, pray tell?"

Walter's voice carries across the deck, and I grab the man's arm. "Please, sir. I was kidnapped and held hostage downstairs. You have to help me."

He presses his lips tight. "What's your name?"

Lina sticks in my throat. My name shouldn't matter. He has to see that I need someone to save me. "Help me. Please."

"Lina," Walter shouts.

"Ackerman?" The man huffs. "I expected as much. Your brother was supposed to keep you out of sight."

"What? No—Holt. Lina Holt, and I don't have a brother." I shake his arm. "I'm running out of time. *Please.*"

"All right, miss. Let's remain calm." He squints over his shoulder then back at me. "Mr. Ackerman, I thought we had a deal."

"Sorry," Walter pants. "I'm sorry, Captain. She got away from me in the lift."

The middle-aged man nods solemnly and checks the gold pocket watch attached to his jacket. "I thought you were on your way already. Make sure you two go directly down the gangway. I understand your troubles but, even with the other passengers gone, I don't want my crew upset by an outburst. This line has a reputation to uphold, and I have an example to set."

"Of course." Walter grips my upper arm, digging his fingers in tightly. "Thank you, Captain. I'll just grab our things and we'll be out of your hair."

The captain turns his back to us. I jump forward, reaching for him, but am wrenched back to Walter's side. I had to try. We nearly trip over each other's feet as he drags me back the way we came. "I told you," he whispers in my ear. "The captain knows."

"What he knows is a lie," I hiss.

Walter lugs me toward the elevator. "Don't make me regret keeping you alive. Your voice is important, but not as important as my life."

I suck in a breath. He may have beaten me down on

the trip over, but now there's a real chance to escape. Without thinking, I let my body fall limp again. Walter trips over my free arm, and I spin to land on my bottom. He flails, his hold on me slipping. I leap to my feet and race across the deck.

"Stop her," Walter screams.

My legs pump nearly as fast as my heart. The shore isn't far with its long docks and crowded wharf. If I'm leaving the ship, I'm doing it on my own terms. I refuse to let Walter drag me away to do who knows what. He kept his hands to himself on the ship, but there's no telling what he'll do when we're away from potential witnesses. I'm not going to find out. Not if I can help it.

"Grab her," the captain shouts, his voice urgent

I'm so close. Only two more steps until I reach the railing. Something heavy slams into my side, knocking the air from my lungs, and my body crashes to the floor. My elbow stings where the skin scraped off. Stars dance in my vision, and I reach up to touch the egg forming on the side of my head. A young sailor keeps me pinned down, his eyes wide with concern. Whether it's for my wellbeing or fear I'll fight him, I'm not sure. All I know is I won't be moving at all if given a choice. My body has reached the end of its tether.

The captain hovers over me, his face a blur. I only know it's him because of the thick brown band of facial hair topped with the white of his hat. "Are you all right?"

"Swell," I wheeze.

"Let's get you up then." He extends a hand and the sailor slowly eases away. I roll away from him. "The sooner you're at the hospital, the sooner you'll recover."

Anyone listening might think he means a hospital for the injuries I got when his man tackled me instead of the asylum Walter lied about. I drag my knees beneath me and push my torso up with shaking arms. "I'm not crazy, Captain. He's lying to you."

He leans down and pats my back gingerly. "Sane people don't try to swan dive off my vessel."

"I know how it looks but I swear to you, I was kidnapped. Please, don't let him take me," I beg.

Walter limps into view. His lips pull back from his teeth, and he cracks his knuckles. "Enough," he growls. "Stop embarrassing yourself."

The captain helps me to my feet. "Don't be too hard on her." He tugs my skirt back into place. My stockings barely have enough material left to be considered stockings at all. "It isn't her fault."

"Thank you for all your help. I really do appreciate it," Walter tells him. He lifts me over his shoulder and storms back toward the abandoned trunk.

"Captain, please," I screech. "Anyone!"

Walter tosses me into the elevator. My shoulder bangs against the yellow wall, sending pain shooting down my arm. He lugs the open trunk in behind us and kicks it into the corner. His nose whistles as he drags in rapid breaths. In one quick movement, he slides the metal grate across the opening and pulls the lever to go back into the bowels of the ship.

"Walter?" His name scrapes my throat. I press myself into the corner. "Walter, you don't have to do this."

The elevator is still moving when he rounds on me, his face scarlet. "You. Stupid. Little…" A hum rises from his chest, and he slams the cloth over my face again. This time I'm not ready. I claw at his sleeve but within seconds, my fingers merely skim the fabric. Then they fall to my side and my feet slide out from beneath me.

"Come on." Walter's voice calls through the fog. He taps my cheek. "Snap out of it."

I groan, and my chin rocks back and forth against my chest.

"I'm not carrying you," he growls.

An engine purrs in the distance. Laughter. The stench of rotting fish and urine. I gasp and snap my eyes open. Walter holds me off the ground, shaking me like a rag doll. Bile rises, and I nearly vomit all over him.

"Took you long enough." He drops me on my feet.

The shock of the fall shoots up my shins, and the hot pavement scorches my soles. I stumble back into a brick building nearly identical to the one on the other side of the alley. They reach into the sky, straining toward the heavens. Tears rush to my eyes, but I blink them away. I need clear vision if I'm going to get out of this. *I have to get out of this.*

Walter grips my hair, pushing me forward. The ground rocks beneath me despite my feet being on solid ground, and I do my best not to stagger as we pass through a black iron fence. "Don't try anything else. I'm warning you."

People peer at us, but no one tries to intervene. I think one woman wants to. She steps toward us instead of away like everyone else and opens her mouth to speak. As we go further down the street, she looks away. I'm not sure what shocks me more: being kidnapped in the first place, or people's reaction to the obvious abuse I've endured. There are many people standing around—unlimited witnesses to a crime. Do they not know what they're seeing? Do they really not care?

"See?" Walter asks in a hushed voice. "Act like you're doing nothing wrong and no one questions you. For all they know, you're my daughter. Maybe my wife. I don't seem concerned with what they think so they assume I'm doing nothing wrong. It's all about perception."

I swallow a hiccup. "You need help."

"That makes two of us." He struts toward a man holding a sign: *Walter Ackerman.* I cringe. On one hand, I won't be carted off and disposed of without anyone's knowledge. On the other hand, I might be murdered by two people instead of one.

"You Nik?" Walter asks in English.

The man—handsome with a deep, tan complexion and dark hair shaved in an undercut—can't be much older than I am. He wears belted navy pants and a gray shirt with the sleeves rolled to his elbows. His eyes, the palest green I've ever seen, lock onto mine. He's looking at me. Really looking instead of a nervous glance. His features remain blank so I'm not sure if this is a good thing or not, but hope swells anyway. I have to maneuver carefully.

"I am," Nik answers in a light accent. "You must be Irena's son."

Walter pulls me closer to his side and releases my hair. "That's me."

"And who's this?" Nik asks slowly, as if the answer doesn't matter.

"A gift for Madam Augustine. It's my way of saying thanks for letting me join." He pinches my cheek with stubby fingers. "Not only is she a looker but she can sing. A Symric, if you can believe it. Found her a week before I left."

Nik tosses the sign into an open window of a dark blue steak-rack truck and inhales. "I'm not sure I understand. We weren't expecting two of you."

"Ma said the troupe is having trouble, and this one will turn all that around. She's the real deal. I'm thinking a duet with Ma to end the show."

I sigh, drawing Nik's full attention. He scans my body, eventually stopping at the rope burns on my wrists. I fight the urge to hide them; I have nothing to be embarrassed about. Let him see. Let him understand I'm here against my will and do something about it.

"Do you speak English?" His voice is strangely calm.

"Yes." Although my accent is thicker than his. I learned the basics in school then studied on my own after I met Christian. He promised we would travel the world after we're married so I wanted to be prepared. I swallow hard. None of that matters anymore—I lost him.

"Are you hurt?" Nik asks.

"She's fine," Walter snaps.

Nik quirks an eyebrow, and I notice a white scar running through it. It's small, nothing more than a little diagonal line toward the side. "I'd like to hear that from her."

Walter nudges me. "Tell him."

I narrow my eyes at my captor before turning to the first person who might believe me. "I'm not fine."

Walter laughs, clapping me on the back. His fingers curl over my shoulder, squeezing, and I bite the inside of my cheek to keep from reacting.

"In fact, I'd like to talk to the authorities as soon as possible," I continue.

Nik's other eyebrow shoots up to meet the first.

"Because." I keep talking before Walter can stop me and hold out my wrists as evidence. "This psychopath kidnapped me and dragged me across the Atlantic tied to a bed, all while claiming to have magic powers."

Nik blinks slowly at the red rings around my wrist. "He did… what?"

I pry myself away from Walter. "*Please*, help me."

Foreign words fly from Nik's mouth so fast I'm sure I wouldn't understand them even if I knew the language. He leans in, placing a hand on my lower back, and urges me next to the truck behind him. Whoever this person is, I'm not leaving his side until I talk to the police. Gratitude seeps out of my pores. I hope he feels it, because I don't know how to put into words what this means. Language, any language, fails me. All I know is that I'm safe now, or as close to it as I can be in this moment. He's a light at the end of my dark, dark tunnel. I want to jump up and wrap my arms around him.

Walter grabs the collar of my dress before I take the final step to safety, yanking until the neckline digs into my throat. I gag and almost fall backward over the curb, but Nik steadies me.

"Let go of her," he says in a low voice.

Walter huffs. "I'm not chasing her through the city.

There are too many people around to transmit, and she's more trouble than she looks."

Nik mumbles something in his language again. "Let go or I'll cut both your hands off."

Walter raises his hands in the air. "Fine. Have it your way."

"It'll be okay," Nik whispers in my ear. The truck door opens with a whining groan, and he helps me climb in the passenger seat. It smells of old tobacco and musty leather. "Don't worry."

"Hey," Walter says.

Nik slams the door shut. "You can sit in the back."

His tone makes me cringe, but being directed at Walter, I can't say I disapprove. He deserves everything he gets and more. I lean into the seat, close my eyes, and take a deep breath. *Finally.* I can go home.

The driver's door creaks open. When the bench seat shifts beneath me, I hug myself. "Thank you."

Nik mumbles a string of foreign words under his breath and pulls away from the curb.

CHAPTER 6

The truck jerks forward as we park alongside the road, the gears creaking. Nik pulls the brake in front of a blue L-shaped house, two stories high, with a long white porch. The roof is missing a few shingles and sparse shrubs dot the corners of the property. Four men load a crate into the back of a van across the street in a seemingly quiet neighborhood. It's a strange place for the police to have an office, but then again, I don't know what's odd in America.

I inch forward on the seat, ready for this nightmare to be over, and my breath catches at the sign hanging over the stairs: *Whitman Boarding House.* I stare at the painted words, held to the porch roof with small-linked chains and am sure I'm misreading them. Nik explained we were in New Jersey when we crossed over the Hudson River, but this is a residential area complete with shabby picket fences and small front yards. How did I not realize sooner? Surely New York has one of the larger police forces in the country...

"This isn't a police station," I say. Although, he never

actually said he was taking me to the authorities; I assumed. I never should've trusted him. I'm not this foolish. *No.* I am. My mother always says I'm too trusting. Panic picks at the edges of my newfound sanity, sending pieces swirling back into the void in my abdomen.

Nik cuts the engine without looking in my direction. His jaw clenches tightly and the joint bulges. "I know."

"I thought you were going to help me." My voice rises, bordering on hysterical. "You let me think you were."

"I know, I know." He drags a hand down his face. "I'm sorry. Things are... complicated. I *am* going to help you, I swear. Walter won't come anywhere near you."

I narrow my eyes. I feel entirely betrayed—mostly by myself for believing I could escape so easily. Fate is playing some sort of cruel joke on me and isn't done laughing yet. That's really the only explanation. So many people can't fall in my path and condone kidnapping. This is all one long, horrible nightmare.

"As if I'd believe anything you say now," I growl through my teeth.

"Augustine won't want something like this linked to her troupe," Nik says in a strained voice. "She'll likely send you home herself just to avoid the scandal."

"Likely?" I make a low, desperate noise in my throat. "Great odds. Probably the same as if I tried to run right now."

Nik's lips twitch. "You're welcome to leave whenever you want, but I'd caution against it. Strange city and all."

Walter opens the truck door and grabs my arm. I'm eye level with him for the first time. "Don't touch me." Swinging my feet around, I kick him in the groin, and he releases me. "Where do you think I'm going to go?"

Sliding across the cab, I follow Nik out the driver's side door. I spit in the grass, something my mother would scold me mercilessly for, and glare at Walter through the open vehicle. "Pig."

"Well, then." Nik fights a smile. "Let's get you cleaned up."

"Where's my little boy?" A woman with brown hair, streaked white, rushes across the lawn. There's no denying who her *little boy* is. The resemblance to Walter is uncanny, and they both speak the same dialect of Dutch. Their jowls, rounded nose, and dark eyes are identical. "Get over here." She sweeps him into a hug.

At least someone is getting a happy reunion.

"Come on," Nik says softly. "I'll ask one of the girls to lend you a dress."

I pick at the limp bow on my shoulder, feeling numb. The ends of the lace collar are frayed from weeks of constant fiddling. Rips mar the skirt, earned in different ways over the last two and a half weeks. All the detergent in the world won't be enough to remove the stench from the fabric, but I don't know what else to do so I follow Nik through a screechy screen door.

Inside is a small sitting room with a brick fireplace and faded green chairs. Gray medallion wallpaper is darker where pictures once hung, and the navy blue runner in the entranceway is worn down from years of footsteps. The hardwood beneath it is stained and chipped. Dusty crown molding circles the ceiling. It must have been a grand home at one point.

"Whoa." Walter swings the door open, following us inside the house with his mother trailing behind. "Where do you think you're going?"

"Where does it look like we're going?" Nik steers me toward a narrow staircase along the right wall. The pieces of rug here are just as threadbare, and the stain on the banister bubbles off. "Worry about yourself. It looks like you're good at that," he mumbles, more to himself than either of us.

I peek over my shoulder at Nik and find myself wanting to smile. But that's crazy because he's holding me here just as much as Walter. He may not appear happy about it but that doesn't change things—he's still going along with it.

We hit the landing, and he hesitates before pointing down the hall. "The bathroom is the third room down." He turns, knocking on the second door.

"You're not coming with me?" I ask.

"To the bathroom?" he asks carefully. "I… thought not to."

Heat blooms across my cheeks, reaching down my neck and beneath the stained fabric. *Stupid.* Of course, he isn't, but I suppose I hoped he would stand guard outside the door. The thought of going off alone with Walter lurking downstairs makes my breath stick.

"Walter won't bother you." Nik touches my hand, stopping me from digging unconsciously at my uninjured elbow. "Go on. Someone will be in with a change of clothes."

The door downstairs slams shut. Walter's voice drifts up the stairwell, and I duck through the third door, slamming it shut behind me. Sunlight filters in through a window over a mint green sink. Three-quarters of the wall is covered in pink tile with a stripe of black along the top. A white curtain covers an archway while an open door to the left of it reveals a matching green toilet.

"Walter, what were you thinking?" Irena's strange dialect floats up the stairs.

"You don't understand," Walter replies in a hushed voice.

"You're bringing the same problems here that you're running from back home," she says.

"But, Ma, she's a Symric."

There was a soft gasp right outside the bathroom door. "No! They're so rare. Wherever did you find her?"

Unwilling to listen to Walter's tale of my *magic*, I leap into the tiny room and scramble onto the toilet lid. I close the door as quietly as possible. The stench of bleach is overpowering but at least I know it's clean. Besides, any smell is better than the ship. Or myself—I'm worse. It was easy to ignore before, but now I'm not sure how I managed. I bring my legs up and bury my face in my knees. With shallow breaths, the combination of odors is a little more manageable.

The door to the bathroom opens and shuts with a soft click, and I stop breathing completely. I'm not sure what Walter will do if he corners me. What else *can* he do? The trunk is gone, left in the alley, and even though I told the truth, I'm right where he wants me.

A soft knock comes on the door directly in front of me, and I hug my knees tighter, refusing to look up.

"Are you all right in there?" asks a soft, feminine voice. I stay quiet, not ready to face anyone. "Nik asked me to bring you a few things."

I should tell her to leave them and go. I don't want to be social, but I don't want to be left alone even more. Staring at the silver doorknob, worn black from years of touch, I almost forget I'm not attached to a fixed object anymore. The burned soles of my feet hit the cool burgundy floor tile, and I push myself up. "I'm here," I say, and crack the door.

A woman in her early twenties with carefully pinned,

deep red hair stands on the other side. She blinks slowly with the longest eyelashes in existence—they aren't even fake. And she's tall, much taller than I am. I want to be jealous but the gentle, startled look on her face won't allow it.

"Hello," I say.

"Hello." She steps back, forcing a smile. "I thought maybe you ran off for a second."

The thought crossed my mind but not in any serious way. Nik was right when he said it's a strange city. I wouldn't even know which direction to go. I have no money, no connections... If there's a chance this Augustine person will help me get back to my mother and Christian, I'll wait things out a bit longer. I can always run later if I have to. I force my lips into what I hope passes for a smile and slip by her.

"I needed a minute alone." I paw at my hair. Hers is so perfect; shiny and flawlessly curled. Mine doesn't look like that on a good day.

She reaches out to shake my hand. "I'm Jackie."

I cross my arms, tucking my hands tight against my sides. It looks like this girl stepped out of a catalog; there's no way I'm going to touch her with my grimy hands.

"I brought these." She holds up a stack of folded clothes. "They might be a little big but they're fresh from the laundry."

"Thanks," I mumble. Judging by her height and the longer hem of her cream dress, the clothes will swim on me, but most things do until I alter them. With a tight belt and a few pins, it'll stay in place well enough. I take them from her, and hold them away from my body.

On her other arm hangs a tightly woven basket. "Soap." She picks a white wedge from inside. "Shampoo. There's a tube of Pepsodent, but I don't have an extra toothbrush. Sorry."

"It's fine." While a brush would have been amazing, my finger will do the job for now. Jackie sets the basket on top of the clothes. "Thank you."

"You'll need a towel." She spins to a door halfway up the wall. "The owner of the house keeps them here for us to use. The family is actually quite accommodating. Some of the boarding houses we stay at barely have clean running water. The one in Boston doesn't have a bathroom at all. I think we get such nice treatment here because of Madam Augustine's connections, but she'll deny it. They know talent when they see it, she says. Whatever the reason, I'm glad we stay here the longest. We're trying to catch our big break now. After ten years, I'm starting to wonder if it'll ever happen." She laughs and waves a hand through the air. "Not that I've been here ten years, of course. I didn't start dancing professionally at eleven." She turns with a stiff, folded towel. "I'm rambling, aren't I?"

"A bit." Even if I have no idea what she's going on about, it's a nice distraction from Walter's boisterous laughter in the hallway. "I don't mind."

Color rises in her cheeks. "I tend to talk when I'm nervous."

She's nervous? What could she possibly have to be nervous about? She didn't just get dragged off a boat and tossed at the mercy of strangers. "It's fine, really."

Jackie chuckles before tossing the curtain aside to reveal a green tub. "Well, I recommend a shower instead of a bath." She looks conspiratorially over her shoulder. "Everyone shares the bathroom, but not everyone knows how to *clean* it. If you do want a bath though, there's a trick to getting the right temperature."

I stare at the straight piece of pipe jutting from the wall. My mother and I had to drag a tub into the kitchen once a week and fill it with buckets from the well. It might be nice to experience a shower. And, considering the layers of filth coating my skin, I'd rather not sit in a pool of black water. "A shower."

"Right, then give it a few seconds to warm up before jumping in. I'll be right down the hall if you need anything else."

She steps toward the door. I lurch forward to grab her, stopping myself just before making contact. "Wait." I don't want to be alone. Not in the same house with Walter, and definitely not in the shower. Nik disappeared, and he's the only one to believe me so far. Maybe Jackie will, too, but I want the shower more than I want to explain everything. "Will you stay?"

She freezes. Her mouth opens and closes twice before she gets any words out. "Nik didn't give me any specifics and you don't have to tell me anything you don't want to, but I have to ask… What happened to you?"

This isn't something that will stay a secret, even if I wanted it to. A part of me wishes Nik had filled her in so I wouldn't have to. I can keep quiet and let someone else do it later, but will it be the truth? Or Walter's version of it? I've seen firsthand how convincing he can be.

I shrug, trying to make it less ominous. "Walter brought me from Holland against my will because apparently fairies blessed me with magic," I say with an eyeroll. "I'll be going to the police soon though, and they should help me get home."

"Irena's son *kidnapped* you?" she says in a high voice. "What... I mean, how...?"

A wave of exhaustion settles around me. I sigh. "It's a long story."

"I'm sure it is." She tilts her head. "And you want me to stay so he doesn't come in?"

I nod, grateful she understands. "If you don't mind."

"No, no." She hurries back to the tub and twists a knob. The pipe groans as water sputters from the faucet near the knobs. "I'll stay. Of course, I will. I just can't believe *Irena's* son—" She shakes her head and turns a lever, forcing the water out of the overhead pipe. "She's such a sweet lady."

I bet.

I eye the falling water, eager to wash off the weeks of grime. Setting the basket Jackie gave me down beside the tub, I unbutton my dress. The dark blue is now dull beneath a coat of grime. I don't know where the dirt came from—if he dragged me from my yard instead of carrying me, or if I was dropped somewhere along the way. The green streaks are definitely grass stains. Some of it is dust from the bottom of the trunk, and the black stains—whatever they are—is anyone's guess. The rip in the skirt, the result of wrestling against Walter during my second escape attempt, is bigger than I thought.

Jackie swiftly turns around as the ruined dress hits the floor, giving me the illusion of privacy. I hurry over the lip of the tub and pull the curtain closed. The water pressure takes me by surprise. The first few seconds sting but then it's actually nice. The water swirls brown around my feet, and my head falls back. Stepping closer to the stream, it hits my face, soaks my hair. A heavy breath wracks my body at the same time I lose control of my tears. I let them come freely, biting my lip to stay silent. No one can see me fall apart here. It's important not to give them an advantage by letting them seem me weak.

I'm not sure how long I stand there, using the hunk of soap to scrub away every speck of debris, but the water is freezing when I'm finished. I twist the knob Jackie used to turn the water on, cutting the flow.

"Here." Jackie's hand pokes around the white curtain with the towel. "Would you like me to help you do your hair after you're dressed?"

I wrap the towel around me for warmth and dab my cheeks with one corner. "Please," I say. My voice is a bit stronger now that I'm clean, and the thought of having my hair done doesn't seem like such a waste. Looking presentable might actually help when I insist I'm sane.

"I'll run across the hall for my comb," she says. She's through the door before I can stop her.

I dry off as quickly as possible and snatch the clothes off the edge of the sink. If Walter's going to burst in here and demand I go somewhere else with him, I'll be fully dressed when I punch him in the face. Now that someone, two someones, are possibly on my side, I'm not afraid he'll kill me. Not straight away, at least. He'll have to be more careful with people watching. Unless they're in on the whole thing. I tug the green wool dress over my head with shaking hands.

The door opens again. "He's still with his mother," Jackie whispers. "I checked."

I slide the shower curtain back and pull the wide brown belt tight around my waist. The dress is heavy on my shoulders and the wool scratches at the nape of my neck, but it smells divine. Like spring. "He hasn't come looking for me?" I ask, climbing out of the tub.

She shakes her head, pats the seat of a chair she must have dragged in, and sets another smaller basket in the sink. After I'm sitting, she uses a dry towel from the cupboard to rub the water from my hair. "Are you feeling any better?"

Being clean makes me feel human again, but it doesn't change things. On the ship with Walter, I learned what to expect—Walter would disappear in the mornings before I woke and return with food a short time later. Every day was filled with uncomforting words of security and dreams of the future. This is different. It's too hard to think straight right now so, instead, I shrug.

"It's a wonder what a good wash can do for the soul." She sets the towel around my shoulders and reaches into her basket. "You have great hair. I'd kill for a bit of natural curl."

"It never does what I want it to do," I say.

She laughs. "I suppose the things we don't have are always more appealing than the things we do."

"I suppose so." Although I'd gladly shave my whole head if it meant not being in this chair. In this house. This country. Everything I used to worry about, which wasn't much compared to most girls my age, seems so trivial now. Fashion. Hairstyles. Makeup. Boys. I already found my match and now he's probably lost to me forever. If I ever get the chance, I'll never hide our relationship again. Our parents don't have to agree with it—I don't care if they do.

"You're from Holland then?"

I pull my bare feet up to the edge of the chair as her fingers slip along my scalp. I close my eyes, the gentle tugs lulling me toward sleep. "Yes."

"So you knew Walter and Irena before all of this? They're from Holland too but I can't recall where exactly. Is that why he brought you? Because he knew you?"

"No, I didn't know him," I reply quietly. If she thinks he forced me to come along out of love or friendship, she's dreaming. "I saw Walter at a dance one night. I had such a strange feeling about him that Christian took me home, but he must've followed us." I rest my chin on my knees. "Honestly, I expected to be tossed off the ship in the middle of the night despite how much he claimed to need my magic. I'm convinced he belongs in an institution."

Jackie's laugh holds no humor. "I think anyone that forcibly drags someone away should be shot. Forget about their motives and all the talk about magic. Institutions are a hoax. Half the people in there aren't even bats. Their families just want to get rid of them because they're an embarrassment or won't do what they're told."

My eyebrows fly up. Being shot is rather extreme, not

that I would mind, but Walter is obviously in need of mental help. Lots and lots of it. I keep my mouth shut though. It seems like there's more to Jackie's words and I have enough of my own problems.

Jackie's hands still in my hair. "Nik said Walter called you a Symric," she hedges.

"Which means I have fairy blood apparently." I scoff. Just because I'm short doesn't mean I'm hiding fluttery wings beneath my dress.

"Anyway, I'm sure Madam Augustine will help you." Her voice returns to a light, airy pitch and her fingers begin to move again. "She's a tough woman but, deep down, she has a soft spot for anyone with special gifts."

"Special gifts?"

Jackie stumbles over a few vowels before finding her voice again. "I just mean… singing, dancing, and the like. Augustine knows a good entertainer when she sees them."

"Madam Augustine." I say, changing the subject. My voice is turning out to be more of a curse than a gift. The word *madam* sounds familiar, but I can't remember exactly what it means. "She's been mentioned a few times, but no one's told me who she is."

"No?" Jackie gently tugs at the back of my hair, tucking stray pieces away. "She owns the troupe. Madam Augustine is really her stage name, but don't let on I told you. She insists she go by it at all times. Rumor has it, she was married to a very well-to-do man before the depression hit but he killed himself when the market crashed. I think that's why Mr. Chamberlain—he's our patron—takes such an interest. His family was close to Madam Augustine's and he feels—"

The door opens. "Enough chit-chat," Walter grunts. "Augustine wants to see us. If I knew I'd get so much grief about you, I never would've bothered. That's gratitude for you, right?"

I tense under Jackie's fingers, and she gives my shoulder a squeeze. "I'm not sure who you think you are, but you're not about to barge in here barking orders."

He pushes himself up straight. "Move it, Symric."

Jackie inhales to say something else but I touch her arm. This will be the last time I have to see Walter, the last time I have to hear him call me Symric, even if I have to walk out of here and swim home. The sooner it's over, the better. And hopefully Jackie and Nik are right— Augustine will help me get home to my mother. And Christian, if he forgives me.

"Don't bother," I say. "I want to see Madam Augustine too."

CHAPTER 7

The hot, arid air in Augustine's room smells so strongly of orange blossoms that bile rises to the back of my throat. Walter nudges me from behind, forcing me further into the suffocating room until my arm brushes against a wall. I blink, dabbing moisture from the corners of my eyes.

Don't let them see you cry.

Nik steps inside, blocking my exit, followed by Irena. I don't understand why she has to be in here. With so many people crowding into the already tight space, I can scarcely breathe. There's nowhere to move when Walter presses against my side, and my pulse flutters.

A bony woman sits in the faded armchair angled toward the window, her snowy white hair bright against the dark walls behind her. She clutches a curved wooden cane in her left hand and looks me over from beneath heavy eyelids. She purses her lips, the lines around her mouth deepening, and snaps her gaze to Walter.

"Let's get right to it, then," she says in a surprisingly high-pitched voice. "I run a tight ship. This country has seen better days and folks have to be very careful where they spend their hard-earned money. The silver screen is making things harder for us by the day."

Walter nods.

"So, with the competition, it's reasonable to assume a scandal will only hurt my show." Her beady eyes narrow. "Scandals like kidnapping a teenage girl and keeping her like some sort of zoo attraction."

Walter blanches. "Madam Aug—"

"And you," she says, turning to me. "I'm not sure what kind of game this is to Walter, but going to the police isn't an option. People talk. The city isn't half as big as the mouths on some."

Moisture coats my palms. I'm not sure why I'm surprised, but I am. "You can't be serious."

"I'm never anything else, dear." She inhales. "You're a tiny little thing. How tall are you?"

I glance at Nik, desperate for a friendly face, an ally, then back at Augustine. "150 centimeters, but I'm not sure what that has to do with—"

"Translate," she snips at Nik.

"About four-foot-eleven, Madam," he answers.

She scowls. "Hmm."

"Madam Augustine, please listen," I beg. "I never wanted to be here. He chloroformed me, locked me in a trunk, dragged me onto a ship, and convinced everyone I was insane while keeping me tied to a bed just because he thinks I can sing. All I want to do is go home."

Augustine pinches the bridge of her nose. "Well, Walter. What do you have to say for yourself?"

He wheezes beside me. "With a Symric like her, we can land any gig you want. I recognized her magic the moment she opened her mouth and had to bring her."

"The next sentence you utter needs to be you asked her politely." Madam Augustine stands, crumbs falling from her ankle length pinstripe skirt. "Because I'm finding it very difficult to find a reason she would lie. I'm not blind—look at her. She's a mess."

My breath comes faster, and my entire body tingles in anticipation. There's no reason to lie if I wanted this. None. I don't want it, and she sees that. The sailor followed his captain's order to tackle me on the ship, but Augustine is a self-made woman. The owner of an entire... something. Actors? Musicians? I jolt with sudden realization. *Madam* Augustine. *Madam's run brothels.* My blood turns icy in my veins.

And I thought it couldn't get worse.

"I just thought... I...Well, I..." Walter stutters.

"You *stole* a girl from her home, gifted or not. I'm incredibly troubled you don't see a problem with this," Augustine chides.

The room tilts, and I rest my head against the wall. The stale air burns my nostrils and the wool dress bites at my skin. Sweat beads along my lip. I wipe it away and try to focus on the scene in front of me. The hum of Augustine's voice reminds me of a wasp, incessant and angry, but I can't make out the words. A hand touches my shoulder, and I twitch away from it.

"Are you okay?" Nik whispers.

I look up into his face. The edges blur. I try to speak but my balance shifts, and I fall back against his chest. The citrus scent of the room churns my stomach. I'm going to vomit. Or collapse. Something. My brain screams not to but my body isn't listening. It's shutting down, pushing away the new reality of things.

Augustine steps closer to Walter and points a crooked finger in his face. Neither of them bother to look in my direction. They don't notice that I'm leaning into a complete stranger to stay on my feet. A stranger who, from across the room, noticed my distress when no one else did. He's the first person I've met that didn't focus on the wrong end of the problem. Yes, bad Walter. Shame on him, lock him away for life, but get me out of here first.

"I don't." My voice comes out as a puff of air. "Feel," I try again. My tongue refuses to work. Am I dying? Will I wake up if the darkness wins? It doesn't feel like I will.

A clicking echoes in my ears. My teeth, I realize, as the shaking spreads down the rest of my body. My feet are numb. And my hands. My lips. My stomach lurches and I gasp. My knees give out. A pair of hands grip my arms as I fall.

A THROBBING PAIN behind my temples pulls me from sleep. I grimace, my back arching, but a hand on my forehead holds me down. My eyes snap open, and Nik hovers over me. "Shh," he says. "You're safe."

My racing heart says otherwise, but I attempt to relax against the lumpy mattress. I'm lying in a cannonball bed, covered to my chest with a blue quilt. A cane chair is beside the bed and a green slag glass lamp with black trim sits on a small table, taking up most of the tiny room. A broom leans against yellow and pink floral wallpaper. It must be a room at the boarding house but whose?

Nik dabs a wet cloth against my cheek. "Are you feeling any better?"

"Wh—" My voice sticks in my throat. I cough and try again. "What happened?"

He shifts to sit in the chair instead of on the edge of the bed. "You fainted."

"Well, yes, but..." I try to sit but another wave of dizziness throws me back to the bed. "Is there something wrong with me? How long was I unconscious?"

"Almost three days." He lifts his eyebrows, concern

etching his otherwise blank expression. "We called a physician and he promised you only needed some rest. You were severely dehydrated. Honestly, I'm not sure how you lasted as long as you did without collapsing. When did you eat last?"

I rub my temples. Three *days*? I should be on my way home by now. "I haven't felt much like eating."

He sighs. "I know it's hard to eat without an appetite but you can't let yourself starve."

He's right. I know he is but my time on the ship wasn't spent in what I consider the right state-of-mind. I mean, I tried jumping overboard. *I tried jumping overboard.* I groan. That has to be my worst decision to date. I can't see my mother or Christian again if I drown. I need to start thinking things through and form a plan.

"I brought you some breakfast." Nik grabs a bowl with tiny gold and pink flowers along the edge from beside the lamp. "If you keep this down, I'll bring you something better later."

I inch into a sitting position using the wall, and he sets the food on my lap. It's a small serving of clear broth. *Why bother?* But my stomach growls. "Thanks."

He leans back in the chair and extends his long legs. The knees of his brown pants are a shade lighter than the rest. "You don't want to force too much down at once. Not after you haven't eaten in so long," he says, crossing his arms. "Trust me."

Strangely, I do. We never had much at home, but I never went hungry. The way Nik's watching me makes me think maybe he has. Still, there are things more important than my diet. "Where's Walter?"

"Gone. Irena, too. Augustine fired them both." He sits forward again. My eyes lock onto his and for a brief second, I see something there. A small glimmer of something I can't decipher but then it's gone, hidden beneath a still face. "I'm sorry I couldn't get you the justice you deserve. I wanted to take you to the coppers, and I apologize for letting you think I was. It's just…"

"Complicated?" I ask, remembering his words. He stiffens. "You were the first person to believe me, so I'll forgive you this time."

His lips quirk wistfully. "This time? Do you plan on desperately needing the police a second time?"

"Yes." I grip the bowl, remembering the revelation I had right before losing consciousness. "If your boss tries to force me into prostitution, I'll most definitely need them."

His eyes widen. "Prostitution? Where on earth did you get an idea like that?"

I hesitate. Could I be mistaking the term? "*Madam* Augustine…?"

Nik's head falls back with a laugh so hard, his chest heaves. "No." He pauses to collect himself. "She runs the troupe. Not a… house of ill repute."

I press a hand over my breastbone and exhale. I should be embarrassed but really, I'm just relieved. "Thank goodness."

"I'll say." His eyes still shine with amusement.

"So what is the troupe then?" I poke at the broth with the heavy silver spoon. "Some sort of opera?"

He laughs again, this time quietly, and holds his hands out to each side. "Welcome to Vaudeville."

"Vaudeville?" I scowl. "What's that?"

He tilts his head. "Seriously?"

Heat creeps into my face. Growing up without extra money, I never went to a show. I remember the circus passing through a few times but I was generally too busy working to pay much attention.

"It's a variety show. Singers, dancers, comedians, jugglers, magicians. That kind of thing." He shrugs. "We're being phased out in favor of the pictures, but we're not gone yet."

"Oh." That seems less scary than the opera for some reason. I would probably want to see their show under different circumstances. I sip at the lukewarm, flavorless broth. "What do you do?"

"I'm multi-talented," he says with a wink. "Mainly I'm the piano man, but occasionally I fill in if a dancer or actor is sick. I was actually hired to do hard labor, moving props and things. When they found out I could read music and knew how to play, I got promoted." He briefly wiggles his fingers in the air between us like they're touching keys, then folds his hands on his lap and clearly his throat. "So, is it true?"

"Is what true?"

Nik looks down at his lap and chews his lip before clarifying. "You're a… that you can sing."

I press further into the wall and watch his face. "I enjoy singing, but I wouldn't go so far as to say I'm a great talent. It's just something I do for myself when I'm alone."

Nik checks the door over his shoulder. "Walter wouldn't have gone through all this to get you here if you weren't a— good. If you weren't good."

"Who knows what he would've done?" I swallow another spoonful and it hits my stomach like a brick. "Is he really gone?"

Nik inclines his head. "They left within the hour and aren't allowed back."

I exhale slowly. One nightmare down, one to go. I barely remember what normal feels like but it feels within reach. I can stop worrying if Walter will hurt me or what he has planned next.

"Jackie says you're Dutch."

I hold my hand to my mouth as saliva builds along with my nausea. "Yes. Where are you from? Not here?"

"Nowhere. Everywhere. My family never stayed in

one place long." He inhales, letting it out slowly through his nose. "Listen—"

A sharp knock stops him from saying more. Augustine shuffles into the room, her cane clacks against the loose hardwood floor.

"Good, you're awake," she chirps.

Nik jumps to his feet and holds the chair out for her to sit down. "For a few minutes now."

"Perfect timing." She falls into the seat with a grunt. "Wait outside."

Nik gives me a final look before stepping into the hall and closing me in with Augustine. All semblance of inner peace goes with him.

"Let's start again." Her smile is stiff. "I'm Madam Augustine."

"Lina Holt," I mutter.

"It looks like you're in a bit of a pickle, Lina Holt. We both are."

The orange scent from her room clings to her. It's not as overpowering as the source but a cold sweat breaks out on my skin at the memory. I focus on my bowl. Looking at her makes me more nervous. She sees too much, and she already has the upper hand. I need her help, that much is obvious, but I don't want her to see how desperate I am for it. I'll lose all power to negotiate if she knows.

"Irena and her horrible son are gone," she continues.

"You're welcome to recover here."

Recover. That gives me a day, maybe two, and then what am I supposed to do? She already made it clear she doesn't want me to go to the police. "I have nowhere else to go," I admit. If I run off on my own, without money, I could end up in worse trouble. Jackie and Nik both said she might help me so it's worth a try. "But, I wanted to talk to you about getting home."

"You look like a sweet girl," she says.

That's never a good start.

"So small."

Insults. The best way to win friends.

"But, the world has gone to pot. I don't have funds to spare to get you passage."

It was worth a try, but the disappointment still stings. "I understand."

She holds her hand up to stop me. "Is it true? Can you carry a tune? And I mean really carry it, not flounder about like a fish out of water."

I gape at her. Never have I met anyone so blunt. "I've been told I can." It's all I can think to say.

"Many terrible singers have been told they can sing." She leans on her cane. "Would you mind letting me hear a small sample?"

I glare at the door behind her, wishing Nik would come back and save me. "Right now?"

"It's important I hear for myself before we continue

this conversation."

"Why?" She already said she couldn't help me. What else was there to say? "I'm not interested in staying on."

She exhales sharply. "Humor an old woman, won't you?"

Willingly sing in front of someone? A stranger? My body shudders. Even if I want to, I'm not sure I'm feeling up to it. My throat is dry and scratchy, and I'm still weak but maybe if I sound horrible, we can put all this nonsense behind us. "I'll try, but I can't promise it'll be any good."

She waves her hand dismissively. "Go ahead. Something snappy."

I bite the inside of my cheek to stop myself from saying something I might regret later. Augustine may be pushy but I'm not in a position to make enemies, so I start singing the same song Walter heard in the barn. At first, my voice is tight and my diaphragm aches when I tighten it. I close my eyes against the discomfort, concentrating on the lyrics, and let my body take over.

I picture Christian pulling me away from the beam. Our kiss against his car. The way his eyes shone when I agreed to go to the garden party. His playful grin when he hinted we'd be engaged soon. It's easy to pretend I'm singing for him instead of a crabby old woman. If I ever see him again, I won't be afraid to let him hear me.

"Enough."

Suddenly I'm back in the small room wearing Jackie's itchy dress. "Sorry. I was a bit off."

"A bit off?" She laughs, her face morphing into something much friendlier. "If that's you *a bit off* then I dare say you'll be a star."

I blush. My life goals don't include a stage. "Thank you," I mumble. "But I—"

"Here's the thing. This whole situation is difficult. On top of your little scandalous affair, firing Irena left me without a singer for the show next week."

I try not to assume what she's hinting at because it can't possibly be what it sounds like. "I'm sorry. I hope you're able to replace her, but I didn't have any part of Walter's scheme."

"You have no money for a ticket home, and I have none to spare. Hopefully we can come to a mutually beneficial agreement."

"I don't think—"

"Stay on with Nova Troupe while we're in New York. I won't have to scramble to replace Irena, giving me time to find someone suitable. You'll be kept safe while you're here and can earn money to pay your way home."

I pause. The thought of earning money never crossed my mind, let alone a way to make it. That takes time and I've been gone too long already. Even if he hates me now, Christian will send enough to get me home if I can get him a message. That could still take days though. If I say no to Augustine, what will my next option be? To live on the streets? This could very well be the best offer I get. At least it will keep a roof over my head and food in my stomach.

"I'd like to make a phone call," I say cautiously. "So my family knows I'm safe."

"There's no phone here, but the theater has one. You can ask the manager when we go for rehearsals," she says.

I press my lips together at the mention of practice. I haven't agreed yet. I should. Why aren't I jumping at the chance? It's not forever. I can force myself to sing in front of an audience if it means getting back to the people I love.

"I'd like to send a letter, then." It won't be an instant connection, but I can't wait another day to send word to them. As long as something's on the way, I'll feel better.

Augustine fiddles with the curved head of her cane. "I'll have stationary brought to your room after lunch."

I bite the inside of my lip and clutch the thin quilt to keep myself from clawing my skin again. "Okay then."

"Splendid." She beams. "I'll start planning your act. Naturally, our patron will want some input on the matter." She surveys my head. "How do you feel about cutting your hair?"

My mother likes my hair long. *I* like it long. It doesn't matter what's in fashion—short hair makes me look ten years old. "No."

She grunts and pats the blankets over my legs as if I were a petulant child. "Rest up."

When she bustles out of the room, she leaves the door wide open. Nik leans against the opposite wall. Augustine smacks his chest with the back of her hand, laughing. "A Symric!" she cackles. My breath catches at the joke about Walter's fairy nonsense. "I have to tell John." Her laugh continues until a door opens at the end of the hall.

At the sound of it slamming shut, Nik lifts his chin to meets my gaze. His eyes are dull and haunted.

"Welcome to Vaudeville?" I ask with a quiver in my voice.

He pales.

"I kept the broth down," I say.

"Good." He steps forward and grabs my door handle. "That's… good."

A sense of dread tugs at my gut. I know Christian will help as soon as I talk to him. It won't be long until I'm able to bury my face in his chest and feel the safety of his arms around me. I have to believe he'll accept my apology. *I have to.* But, for now, I won't cry. I'll stay strong for him, and my mother. There will be plenty of time to breakdown when I'm home.

"Does that mean I can try something for dinner?" I ask.

Nik looks away, nods, and shuts the door without another word.

CHAPTER 8

"Knock, knock." Nik's voice floats through the door.

I straighten, letting the heavy curtain fall back over the window. It's been an hour since I first looked outside, watching people move about their town. Women hold their children's hand as they walk down the street and dogs wander about yards. A few older vehicles passed by in the morning but it's been mostly bicycles since. The other houses I see from my window are like this one—beneath the need for repair lay the bones of impressive homes—and the yellow house directly across the street has at least four families living under its sagging roof.

"More broth?" I call back. The dinner Nik promised me the night I woke up had been more of the same. A huge disappointment but for the best. Yesterday I graduated to crackers and cheese.

"Something better."

It's not hard to beat a bowl of flavored water, but I admit to feeling stronger now. Hopeful, even if the normal, everyday things outside put a cloud of jealousy over my head. Augustine took my letter to Christian, though, promising it would go out with the first post. My mother is too proud to ask for help, but Christian isn't spiteful. He'll let my mother know I'm okay even though I broke things off. It's a small weight off my shoulders—a pebble chinked away from the boulder.

I swing open the door. "Please tell me you've found some *kerrieschotel* in the kitchen."

"I have no idea what that is, but I do have these." He wags his eyebrows, holding up a white rectangular box in each hand. Three smaller ones, wrapped in brown paper are tucked under his arms. "Can I come in?"

I step aside, glaring at the boxes. "What's all this?"

"It's a surprise, Canary." He sets them down carefully on the bed and steps back to stare at them with me.

The bright glint is back in his expression and a little tension fades away knowing he's not upset anymore. Asking the cause of his sullen mood isn't worth risking its return, and I need a friend here if I'm going to keep my sanity. Jackie hasn't checked in on me all weekend so he might be all I have.

I keep staring at the boxes as if they contain unknown horrors. "I'm not much for surprises."

Nik crosses his arms, and I catch a whiff of his slightly spicy musk. "Who doesn't like surprises?"

I watch him shift his weight from the corner of my eye. Sometimes surprises are honest and good. Other times they come with strings or implications hidden behind shock value. If I have to guess which kind of surprise this is, I bet on the latter.

"Who's it from?" I ask, ignoring his question.

He shrugs. "Augustine, I assume. Jackie did all the shopping. I've never seen her so excited to go into the city before."

I glare at the boxes again, wanting to tell him to take it all back. Unfortunately, that would be rude, and I need Augustine. There has to be a hundred other girls able to replace Irena, but they'll have to wait until I'm gone. I need this. At least until Christian comes through. The voice in the back of my head needs to stop screaming at me and get on board with the plan—even if it does make a valid argument against trusting these people.

"Augustine didn't have money to get me a ticket home, but she had money to send Jackie shopping?" I ask.

Nik cringes. "Like I said..."

"Complicated." I can barely see through my anger. It feels like my body will explode into bits if I don't find a way to release it.

"Go ahead," he urges. "The anticipation's killing me."

"You're too excited about this," I seethe.

"I have a feeling it might make you feel better and if anyone needs it, it's you." He reaches for the first box. "Allow me."

Folded neatly beneath tissue paper are two dresses.

The first a deep blue cotton with tiny red rose buds. The v-neck is trimmed with white ruffles that reach to the hip on one side, on the other is a square pocket, and the same trim accents the sleeves. The second is a light pink day dress covered with tiny white polka dots. A matching piece of fabric is tied around the waist in a bow. Beneath them, edges of silky white undergarments are visible. I quickly pull the dresses back over them before Nik can see.

"Clothes?" I say flatly. My teeth clamp down on the inside of my cheek until it hurts. "Why did she buy these?"

"We tried to salvage your dress but it was too far gone, and you can't keep wearing that." Nik picks at the shoulder of the borrowed dress hanging limply from my body. "If you're going to be here for awhile, you'll need something to wear."

But that was the dress Christian gave me. I dig nails into my palm. "Where is it? My dress."

He has the good sense to appear regretful as he informs me, "Thrown away. I tried to save it for you, but it was too late."

Thrown away. My heart sinks. All I feel now is sorrow, heavy and foreboding. It's only fitting, I suppose, since I threw Christian away before Walter took me, but I want my dress back. I want Christian back too, but that dress... it's the last piece of home *here*.

"Canary?"

I swallow the lump in my throat. "I won't be here for awhile, and I can't afford this." I can't afford anything.

He meets my gaze for a brief moment before looking away. "I don't think she expects you to pay for it."

"How... kind of her," I say carefully.

"I wouldn't say it's purely selfless," he admits. "She'll want you to be presentable as part of the troupe. Appearances and all."

"A *temporary* part of the troupe." I chew on my lip. "So, it's like an investment, then." Maybe I should've asked Christian for a bit more than fare in my letter. I drag the second box to the edge of the bed, dreading what I'll find inside. "And this?" I ask.

"I'm not sure." He pops his thumbs joints inside his fists. "It's probably your performance dress."

"This is what I'll wear to sing?" I glare down at the box with a flutter in my stomach. I almost forgot the stage is in my near future.

"I've got news about that, too."

I take a deep breath and hold it. "I'm not sure which I'm more afraid of."

He cocks his head, and I flip open the lid. Bright white lace stares back at me. I lift it out by the shoulders and give it a shake. It reaches the floor with small silk roses above frilled sleeves. It's stunning, but it won't be on me.

"I can't wear this."

Nik takes the dress carefully, studying it. A silk under layer peeks through the lace. "Why? What's wrong with it?"

"I'll look like a child playing in her mother's clothes."

Nik laughs and lays the gown carefully on the bed. "You'll look great. And you'll *sound* great, especially working with me."

"What?" I can't peel my gaze away from the gown.

"I'll be your pianist. We start rehearsing tomorrow for the show on Friday so I hope you're a fast learner."

"Tomorrow?" A cool sweat springs up on my forehead. I'm not ready. I can't be prepared for a live performance in a handful of days. It takes time to build courage, and I've barely registered the situation. Will I even be able to practice in front of Nik? What was I thinking agreeing to this?

"Breathe, Canary." He takes my upper arms gently and waits until I'm looking him in the eye. "Don't worry. We're in this together, yeah?"

No! No one is in anything with me. They all belong here. They want to get up on stage and entertain people. None of them know what it's like to be here by force, but I hold back for fear of hurting Nik's feelings. He's been nothing but nice, even if he mislead me at first. I take a deliberate breath to show him I'm listening.

"Better?" he asks.

"No." *Maybe a little.*

He rubs at his chin. "Let's forget about all this for a little while and do something fun. We both need it."

"What did you have in mind?" I ask. Maybe burying my troubles will help—whether or not it's possible is another thing.

He bops me on the nose. "Get changed and meet me in the hall."

Just because I'm stuck here doesn't mean I have to be miserable. *Right?* There's no point moping around until Christian comes through. What will that solve? Nothing, and I need to get out of this room before I go stir-crazy. I hurry out of Jackie's green dress and fold it on the chair to return to her later. My skin drinks in the air, finally free of the scratchy wool.

The blue dress is feather-light in comparison. It fits perfectly, the hem hitting mid-calf. I've never worn such smooth stockings in all my life. Pulling the twine off the first smaller box, I tear through the brown paper and find a pair of tan heels with laces crossing up the front. Inside the second is a white cloche hat with satin trim and a pair of matching gloves. I push it aside and peek into the third brown box—cosmetics. Still paler than usual from my whole ordeal, I spare a few seconds to put a splash of color on my cheeks.

When I step out into the hall, Nik's lips part. "Wow, Canary. You look like a thousand bucks."

"Just a thousand?" Jackie comes up beside me, all

smiles, and sweeps me into a tight hug. "I'm sorry I haven't looked in on you. Things have been busy. Are you okay?"

"I'm better than I was." I pat her back, surprised at the quick familiarity. "Thank you for shopping."

Nik smirks. "You have good taste, Jackie."

She steps back and studies her choices. "I thought this one might bring out the blue in your eyes. Madam Augustine insisted on white for your performance dress; she wants you to shine up on stage." She shakes her head. "You don't need a dress for that. There was an amazing dusty rose gown I thought would be perfect, but my hands were tied. I grabbed the other pink dress to compensate. It'll be a good color on you. I had to guess on the shoe size. Do they fit?"

"They're perfect," I say.

"It was between those and a black pair. Tan can get dirty easily, but then I thought where would you be going to worry about mud? It's mostly concrete around here." She beams. "Black seems too severe for you."

Nik grins. "Jackie."

"Rambling again," she cries. "Well, I'm glad everything worked out. They're waiting for me downstairs to head to the theater. Oh, gosh, you should come down with me. Everyone is dying to meet you. The new girl Madam Augustine has stashed away in Irena's room. You're very mysterious, you know."

"Um." Meeting an entire group of people right now… I'm barely wrapping my brain around everything as it is. "We were just on our way somewhere."

"Oh." Her voice rises. "Are you heading to the theater too? Madam Augustine won't mind if you take another day to yourself. I think she's expecting it, actually. We rearranged the schedule for tomorrow, so I assumed…"

"No, you're right. We'll start tomorrow," Nik tells her. "We're going out for some fresh air and a change of scenery."

"Good. Get out of here." A car horn blasts outside. "I better run. Enjoy yourselves."

Nik and I watch her skip down the stairs without moving. When the screen door bangs shut, he points to my feet. "I hope those new shoes are comfortable."

"Why?" I follow him downstairs and out onto to the porch. "What are we doing?"

From the top step, I see Jackie jump in the passenger seat of the red and beige Chrysler waiting in front of the boarding house. The driver, a man with dark skin and a broad nose, waves. I wave back, my hand dropping when a girl with dark hair and puckered lips glares at me from the back seat.

"Who is that?" I whisper to Nik.

"Theresa. She's a real barrel of laughs." He shakes his head. "Poor Gus. He'll get an earful now that she's seen you."

I lower my brows and watch the white-wall tires roll around a corner. More trouble is the last thing I want so I don't ask Nik what he means. Smooth sailing back to Holland is my only goal. To get through this, I need a basic level of civility with everyone. It's not the first time I've gotten that look from other girls and it won't be the last if Christian forgives me.

"So, where are we going?" I ask again.

He heads in the opposite direction of the car and shoves his hands in his pockets. "You'll see. We're taking the scenic route so let me know when you need a rest."

AN HOUR LATER, I'm carrying my new shoes across smooth stone. It's hot against the soles of my feet but it's still better than pinched toes and blisters. The humidity frizzes my hair and my skin is sticky with sweat. Wherever Nik's taking me, it's worth it to be out of the house but we've had to rest five times. The walk probably is as lovely as Nik claims, but my eyes find the ground and don't look up again until we hit a populated area.

A horn blows behind us and I scan the crowd. Unshaven faces, disheveled hair, and bleak faces bustle by without making eye contact, but no one resembles Walter. My muscles coil anyway, ready to run. A bicycle rings its bell as it zooms around us and I jump, slamming into Nik's back. He stops at a low stone wall with his arms lifted away from his sides.

"What do you think?" He fills his lungs with air. "Beautiful, isn't it?"

I shake the sound of the bicycle bell from my ears and follow his gaze. We're standing at the edge of a river where a small boat sails along the dark water. Small caps of white appear on the surface as it crashes against itself. New York City rises up on the other side with harsh edges to every building. In its own way, there's beauty, an intimidating splendor about it, but I prefer grass under my feet. Trees, flowers, nature. And quiet. How I wished for a moment of silence.

All around us, someone hawks their goods or services: ice cream, vegetables, newspaper boys, shoe shiners. Some people wear sandwich boards as they walk along the paved sidewalk. When two horses clop by pulling a car without an engine compartment, I stare openly until a siren wails in the distance.

I can't help wondering who the police are after. Is Walter kidnapping someone else? Killing someone? He's out there somewhere. I look through the crowd again. He could be here. Watching. Waiting. Ready to finish me off for getting him fired and stealing his mother's act. There's no doubt in my mind he'll kill me if he has the chance. A man that kidnaps without remorse will almost certainly kill in cold blood. Especially when his sole reason not to is gone.

"Sometimes when I stare out across the water, my problems feel smaller," Nik says. "Like the city somehow makes them insignificant in the grand scheme of things."

No view can make my problems go away. It's just a reminder of where I am, or, more precisely, where I'm not. "How much do you think it costs to book passage on a ship?" I ask quietly. Goosebumps dot my arms. "Did Augustine say anything to you about how long it may take to earn enough?"

He takes two breaths before swinging one leg over the wall and sitting down. "I don't know. She doesn't tell me more than she has to but I suppose it depends on the ship."

He's right. Prices will fluctuate, but there has to be a cheap option. The country is in the middle of a depression so it only makes sense to have some kind of economic choice. A more solid backup plan will put me at ease—it doesn't matter what the plan is exactly. I'm willing to row myself across the Atlantic if someone gives me the oars.

"I came here with the hope of a better life," Nik tells me with an uneasy voice. "My family didn't have much of one before because of me." He rolls his shoulders and his eyes grow distant as he looks at the skyline. "Honestly, we moved so much I didn't mind leaving Europe. I never really put down roots so what was one more change? I came here with my younger sister to find work and a place to live while my mother planned on joining us later."

So he's not alone then. I'm glad. "Will your mother come soon?"

He shakes his head. "She's in Norway now. New York is big enough to get lost in… to hide in, which is why we chose it, but things went wrong. While she was waiting for word from us to come, she actually managed to settle for a change."

"What went wrong? Why do you need to hide?"

He inhales deeply. "Those are stories for another time."

Also, it isn't any of my business. I sit down beside him, keeping one eye on the people around us. "Is your sister in the troupe too?"

"No. Last I heard, she lives in North Carolina." He throws a pebble into the river. "We lost touch."

Without siblings, I can't pretend to understand how he feels. Especially when he wears such a blank expression. But family is family. "I'm sorry."

"Are you hungry?"

Without waiting for an answer, Nik sprints up to a weathered man in a tattered jacket selling apples for five cents apiece. He's only a few yards away but my pulse quickens. *Alone.* I'm alone. Walter can get to me. He can take me again, and I'll be gone before Nik turns around. All it will take is one shove for me to fall into the river. I'll hit my head and never resurface. I leap from the wall, backing away from the edge. Spinning with my hands in fists, I pause on every face. He's here somewhere; I know he is. The sweet smell of chloroform reaches my nose. I see the darkness of the trunk and feel the burn of rope on my wrists.

"Whoa," Nik says. "What's wrong, Canary?"

I whip around to face him, fighting for air. "He's…"

"Sit down." He shifts both apples to one hand and lowers me back down to the wall. I want to snap that I'm not going to faint a second time, but that requires being able to speak. Also, I'm not entirely sure it's true. "Hey, breathe. Okay? Just breathe. Walter isn't here. He can't hurt you."

I shudder. "How do you know?"

His palm rubs circles against my back, and he stares at into the distance through narrowed eyes. "I won't let him near you." His tone is somber, unyielding. "Tell me about home. What's it like?"

A pang reverberates in my chest. I want my mother to pull me into her arms and never let me go. To feel her fingers trailing through my hair as I fall asleep and the slightly wet kiss on my forehead before she retires to her own bed. "I live with my mother next to a tulip field." I press my fingertips against my temples. "Each spring everything smells like them. Inside, outside. You can't get away from it even if you want to. And, trust me, you don't want to."

"That sounds nice." He pauses. "Where's your father?"

I draw a short breath. It's strange to have to explain my life when everyone has always known who I am. "When I was about a week old, my mother heard crying behind the house and found me abandoned between rows of red and yellow flowers. She didn't think I'd make it but here I am."

"Here you are."

I recognize the look on his face. I've gotten it from nearly everyone growing up. *Pity*. But I don't need it. I grew up knowing nothing but love from my mother. It never mattered that she didn't give birth to me. She's the same as anyone else's mother. Better, because she's mine.

"Anyway." My voice sounds as worn as I feel. "She never married, so it's always been the two of us."

"You must be close."

I raise one shoulder in a shrug. We were before I met Christian but then things changed. "I hate to imagine what she's going through right now."

"You can't think like that. You'll drive yourself bonkers."

A laugh bubbles out of nowhere. Nothing about this is funny, but I can't stop. It just keeps pouring out of me. Each note feeds the next. Tumbling together. Blurring.

Nik goes still and watches me with his mouth slightly open. He must think I've finally snapped. He may be right.

"Sorry." I wipe away a tear and try calm myself. "I just imagined what my mother's going to do to Christian and the look on his face when she does it."

"Christian?"

I gasp for air, finally shoving the hysteria down. "We've been together fourteen—no, fifteen months but both our parents are against it. My mother hates him because he's a wealthy heir and rich boys don't marry poor girls." I shake my head. "His family hates me because I'm poor, which actually supports her theory. He's not like that though. I swear. He even hinted at a proposal on our last date, but I... I think I ruined things."

My face tightens. Things were just about to turn around for me. Why did his mother have to react so dramatically to my presence? Why did Walter have to take me? I can't fix anything from here.

Nik moves a piece of hair from my face. "Your mother will be so happy to hear you're okay, she won't hold anything against you."

"You don't understand," I whisper. "We had a fight a week before I was taken because I snuck out to a dance. What if she just assumes I left, that Christian and I eloped, and she's so frustrated that she lets me be gone?

It's possible no one will look for me for weeks. My letter might be the only thing to tip them off."

Nik studies me, his head tilted. "I'm no expert, but if your mother cares enough to yell at you for sneaking out, she'll care enough to look for you the moment she notices you're gone."

I hope he's right. He *sounds* right, but maybe I did one thing too many, pushed just a little too much. She might wash her hands of me and move on, happy with one less mouth to feed. What if she won't forgive me?

"What about your friends?" he asks. "Won't they miss you?"

Heat rushes to my cheeks. "I had to quit school to work. I haven't had time to see them lately." Or at all in the last two years. It doesn't feel right to call them friends at this point.

"Really? How is your English so advanced?"

I beam. "Is it? Christian travels abroad a lot so I practiced in case I ever went with him."

"He's lucky to have someone so devoted." Nik chomps into his apple with a loud crunch and hands me the second one.

I raise it to my lips. Devoted, yes, but it wasn't completely selfless. I did it partially so his family would hate me less. What will they think when they find out I sang on stage in a variety show? "Do you think I should've turned Augustine down?"

He pauses mid-chew and swallows while avoiding my gaze. "I think from your perspective, given the circumstances, it was a logical choice. Just don't be too trusting. Yeah?"

"Who shouldn't I trust?" The possibilities are endless. Before the kidnapping, I would've laughed him off like I did my mother. Now I know better. "You?"

He scowls, shaking his head. "I'm one of your safest bets, but you shouldn't take my word for it. If I don't earn your trust, it's not real."

"Well, I have to trust someone." I bite into the apple and juice flies into Nik's face. He jerks back, and I cover my mouth with a hand. "Sorry."

He wipes his nose with his sleeve, smiling. "Nice aim."

I laugh along with him. It's not the same hysterical laughter as before, but a calm, soothing one. A happy one. Whatever Nik's holding back, I still need a friend right now and being with him feels right. *Safe* despite how little I know of him. I'll give him the chance to earn my trust while I wait for Christian if it gives me moments of normalcy like this. Little pockets of sanity.

"Canary, listen." Nik pauses and takes a deep breath, his jaw tight. "I don't know how to talk about this or what to say to make you believe me."

"I believe that you'll help me."

"That's not… No. I mean, yes. I will help you but, you deserve the truth."

I tilt my head and wait for him to continue. It's at least thirty seconds before he whispers, "magic is real."

I fly to my feet. "That isn't funny."

"I'm not trying to play a gas. Sit, please." His voice is resigned, his shoulders hunched as if he were weary of everything, so I sit. "We both have it. Magic, I mean. You *are* a Symric and Symrics are extremely rare. It's dangerous for you not to know—both for yourself, as Walter proved, and others."

The world bustles around me, but I'm stone. Nik peeks over at me with such a raw look that I know he believes what he's saying. I start to stand again, oblivious to where I'm going, when he takes my hand. It's a gentle grip, the look on his face pleading, and that's the only thing that makes me sit back down.

"I know how it sounds," he admits.

"Do you?"

"I do."

"Prove it," I challenge, fully away he can't. "Show me this *magic*."

He pales. "You can't see either of ours."

"Convenient."

He runs a hand through his hair. "I'm an Amplifier. Whatever you're feeling, I can intensify it. That's why we're performing together. Your voice will dazzle the audience while your Symric ability will instantly addict anyone who hears, and I'll be there, making it ten times worse for them.

Augustine is risking a lot combining our magic. Addicts are unpredictable and we're going to create the worst kind."

I narrow my eyes in disbelief. "Do it."

"What?"

"If you want me to believe in fairies and magic, use yours on me."

He sighs. "You don't want me to do that. Not with the way you're feeling."

"Can you… read emotions?" I ask.

"It's more like a vibration, but I suppose you could call it that."

I shift uncomfortably. There are a lot of feelings inside of me right now—fear, relief, and grief—but they can't possibly be worse. My mind is consumed with worry. "If you don't prove it, I have no reason to think you're any more sensible than Walter."

We hold eye contact for a tense moment before his gaze falls and I'm sure he'll refuse again. How can he not when it isn't possible? But then I feel it. The same oppressive emotions I had on the ship cripple and crush me from the inside out. Every ounce of relief at being free of Walter is gone. *No. Nononono.*

"Lina?"

The feeling fades quickly, and I blink at Nik. Sorrow is written all over his face as he wipes at my tears with his thumbs.

"Are you okay?"

No. I'm hyperventilating, and my stomach churns like it did the first few days on the ship. The world blurs and wobbles like it did the first time I stood on solid ground in New York. Nik rubs circles on my upper back until my breath is under control. I grip the stone wall beneath me to steady myself. When I'm able to speak again, I ask, "You did that?"

"I'm sorry."

It's real—what he says he can do—and now I don't know *what* I feel except hollow. As if I'm waiting for someone to tell me what emotions to have. My hands tremble and the marks on my wrists burn as if the rope is still there. But the sun is warm on my skin and the ground stills beneath me. This isn't the ship. Nik isn't Walter.

"This is a lot," he says gently.

"What's a Symric?" I blurt, surprised at my own question. I've been called that over and over but no one has explained it outright.

"Like I mentioned, your voice is addictive. The more people hear it, the more they'll *need* to hear it. It's as simple as that, really. You can't stop it from working on anyone and you don't need to do anything special to use the magic. Just like I'll feel you if you touch me, I'll get a dose of Symric magic if you sing."

"I don't understand. How? How am I… this? Can I get rid of it?"

He winces. "You're born with it or you're not; there's no changing it. Symrics are actually something of a fairy tale because they're so rare. Both parents need to have the same magic to pass it on, but half-fae aren't commonplace. As quarter-fae, your children won't have the same gift. Unless, perhaps, their father is a pure-blood, but I'm guessing you don't know any fairies."

A laugh cracks in my throat. I can't help wondering if this has anything to do with why my parents left me in the tulips to die, but it only stirs more questions that I'm not ready to ask. "No," I answer. "I can't say as I do."

Nik leans away and draws a deep breath. "Maybe I should've kept my trap shut, but you have a right to know. People may come after you again, to hurt you or to hear you, and you have a right to save yourself."

"I'm glad you told me."

The truth is like oil floating on water. It doesn't work in the world I know and I'm not sure how to make it fit yet. Everything Walter said on the ship take on a new meaning. It's no wonder my mother forbid me from singing. *My mother.* Does this mean she knows what I am? How? Why would she keep it a secret from me?

"Do you see that police officer over there?" Nik asks.

I glance around Nik's shoulders, and my heart somersaults at the sight of the dark uniform with gleaming silver buttons and shield. "Yes."

He takes my apple with slow, calculated movements. "I'm going to stay right here so if anyone asks, I can honestly say I didn't see you approach him until it was too late."

All otherworldly thoughts vanish. I wipe my hands on my skirt, my breath uneven. "What should I tell him?"

"The truth. Maybe try to leave me out of it as much as you can." He shrugs. "I'll lay low for awhile either way."

"Thank you," I say, breathless.

He blushes. "Go on now. Fly away home, Canary."

I jump up from our seat along the river and rush down the sidewalk where the officer now faces the street. I grip his arm, and he jolts beneath the touch. "Help," I wheeze.

His eyes widen. "Are you all right, miss?"

My ears ring. *Finally!* "I need to get home. To Holland."

He blinks twice. "Well, if you head down to—"

"No, no." I swallow hard. My adrenaline pumps too furiously to find the right words in English. "I was... brought here by someone." I squeeze my eyes shut, willing my heart to calm down. "Walter Ackerman. He brought me here to sing for—"

"Miss." He pries my hand off his arm. "I'm sorry, but there's nothing I can do."

"But he—"

"I understand. You came hoping for your big break in showbiz, and now this Walter Ackerman fella has left you high and dry."

"But he kidnapped me. That's a crime, isn't it?"

"Hey, now," he scowls. "Don't go accusing someone of something serious like that just to get yourself a ticket home."

My jaw drops. "I'm not."

"I've heard all the excuses, Miss. You look rather well taken care of, so I suggest you keep doing what you're doing, and the homesickness will subside in time."

"I—"

"Enough," he snaps. Two children race down the street, looking over their shoulders guiltily, and the officer snatches the opportunity to chase after them, blowing his whistle.

I stare after him, my hope shrinking with every millimeter he puts between us. The foreign streets seem to narrow, the crowd swelling, and the strange scent of the city nearly bowls me over. I stagger back a step into Nik's side.

"Canary?"

"He…" My tongue feels numb. "He didn't believe me."

Nik is quiet for a long moment. Or maybe a short one. "You can use the theater phone tomorrow."

"Right." I sway on my feet, and he offers me a hand. "The phone."

"Come on. We don't want Augustine thinking you changed your mind and ran for the hills."

I take his hand, if for no other reason than to steady myself. It's warm and sturdy in mine. Kind. Maybe the boy next to me is one of the people I shouldn't trust, but I'm not sure how to tell the difference, not in this place. So, right or wrong, I choose to believe in Nik and his promise to help.

CHAPTER 9

Wind whistles across the empty field, its icy tendrils grabbing at my ankles. Rows of sheets whip back and forth on the clothesline, warning me. *Danger,* they scream. *Run.* But I can't leave them to the elements. I fight against the heavy blast, forcing myself forward, and grab the line. I pluck off a pin, then another and another. The fabric rips from my hands, flying over me like a ghost.

I turn to follow and my head bumps into a man's chest. I laugh. "Christian, I thought you'd be halfway home by now."

"Who's Christian?" the man asks.

I look up into a pair of solid black eyes. *Walter.* His lips curl into a snarl. I try to scream but his hand smashes over my mouth.

"Vaudeville needs you."

I bite down until I taste blood. When he lets go I try running but the wind comes at me from every direction, holding me in place. Mud sucks my feet into the ground and the harder I pull, the more I sink. A scream rips from my throat.

"Lina." The voice is different. Distant. "Lina!"

I blink and a white tin ceiling replaces the night sky. "Nik?" I croak as a pair of wide green eyes hover over me. It was a dream. *Just a dream.* My head thuds back onto the pillow, the hint of blood lingering from where I must've bitten my tongue. "What are you doing in here?"

He looks down at me with a creased brow. "You were having a bad dream."

"I know." I rub my eyes, trying to erase the image of Walter. Every night on the ship was filled with similar nightmares. I got a short break from them here, probably because I was unconscious instead of asleep, but apparently my respite is over. "Sorry. I didn't mean to wake you."

Nik slides from my bed and brushes lint off his blue shirt. "You didn't. Everyone's downstairs eating breakfast."

I reach for the curtain, my hand still shaking. "What time is it?"

"Nearly seven. Augustine wants to start rehearsal early so you and I have extra time to work on our act."

I sit up and tuck the sheet under my arms. He's respectfully not looking below my face but being alone with a man in my room while only in a slip is still unnerving. "Of course she does," I grumble. I'm still not sure I'll be able to do it. I can't sing in front of one person, let alone an entire audience. Maybe if I pretend everyone in front of me is my mother or Christian, I'll remember why I'm doing this. I have to try anyway. "I'll be right there."

When Nik leaves, I stretch across the bed. My heart races from the nightmare and my fingers tingle. *I'm safe.* Walter's gone. Augustine's given me shelter. Christian will send help soon. It's okay. Everything's okay. If I want it to stay that way, I have to get up, go downstairs and sing.

There. A new goal. I'll take it one step at a time.

I can and I will.

By the time I've repeated those words a thousand times, I'm standing outside the dining room, staring at the glass knob, questioning my new mantra. It sounds good, but not realistic. If a few shows will earn me enough money to get home, no one here would be pinching pennies, especially not the owner. No one specified how long the troupe is staying in New York. Maybe they'll be here six months; maybe they'll be here three weeks. If I can reach Christian on the phone at the theater today, I'll be long gone before either.

A blend of voices beat on the other side of the door. I swallow my doubts and step into the dining room. The chatter cuts off and I fight the urge to step back out. Sixteen people, ranging from children to middle-aged, pale skin to dark, are crammed around a long rectangular table. A chandelier hangs directly over the table with white glass cones on each arm. Bowls of boiled eggs and brown porridge sit on the off-white cotton tablecloth.

"Good morning," I say when everyone remains silent.

Nik places a platter of small sausages down and motions to the empty chair across from him. No one speaks; they hardly move while I inch between the wall and chairs. The click of my new shoes fills the silence. I'm an outsider here and I took Irena away from them. Her son they may not care about, but they liked his mother. Jackie called her sweet. Of course, they hate me. I would hate me, too.

Finally I squeeze into the seat between Jackie and a bald man in a striped dress shirt. To sit, I have to climb over the seat of the chair and pull it forward, wedging myself between them. Jackie wears a headpiece of jewels and feathers that takes up nearly half the side of her head. "Hi," I say, glad to be next to at least one person I know.

"Hello," she says. All trace of her bubbly personality is gone as she pokes at her breakfast with a spoon.

The short exchange triggers a change in the room. Someone asks for the salt and silverware clinks against plates as eating resumes, but no one looks in my direction. I glance at Nik and he fakes a cough. Still no one speaks.

"Everyone, this is Lina," Nik says loudly after a long,

uncomfortable silence. "Lina, this is everyone. Ben, Pearl, and their twins—Eleanor and Gilly," he motions to a young couple sitting at the end of the table beside two children, about seven years old, with curly blond mops of hair. "You know Jackie. That's Tommy next to you. Then Pedro, Will, James, Gayle, Mitch, Eddie, Etta, and Theresa." Theresa stares daggers at me again while everyone else seems nice enough, if disinterested. It's a handsome group of people. "If you feel anything under the table, it's Chester."

There's a boy under the table? *Who feeds people under the table?* Lunatics, that's who. I lift the tablecloth and gasp. A small yellow dog with wiry hair stares up at me with his tongue dangling, and I reach down to scratch his head.

"It's nice to meet everyone," I say. Half of their names are already lost to me, the rest I'm probably remembering wrong.

Silence.

"Eat something." Nik tosses a boiled egg across the table. By some miracle, I catch it before it smacks me in the face. "We've got a long day ahead of us and won't eat again until tonight."

"*Long* is an understatement. Why not move us into the theater with these hours?" Theresa scoffs. "Our acts better not suffer because you need extra rehearsal time."

Nik inhales sharply. "If you have a problem, take it up with Madam Augustine."

"All I'm saying is the rest of us have to practice too." She motions to the group with a hand full of rings. "I don't want to spend every second in the back room, especially not if we're kept there late."

"Theresa," Jackie says quietly. "Our acts are established and they have to start from scratch. We're going early to make sure everyone gets time."

"We're going early to watch this *thing* practice while we sit on our thumbs," she snaps. "As if she needs to practice at all. The audience will be addicted no matter how bad she is."

Nik slams his palms on the table and I wince. The air thickens, making it hard to breathe. I've only known Nik a few days but he seems to have himself in check. Judging by the shocked look on everyone else's face, they're just as surprised by the outburst.

"We don't need extra time," Will says, backing Jackie up. "Our routines haven't changed in months. They have five days. We've each got a slot on stage today and there's plenty of room to practice in the back if you really need it."

Theresa glowers, a storm brewing in her brown eyes. "You—"

Augustine steps into the room, banging her cane on the

floor. "Keep your ungrateful trap shut, Theresa. We all know you're an intolerant cow, but unless you want to find yourself out on your arse, you'll put a lid on it. Special gifts aren't a requirement here. There are plenty of dancers in the city and you'll be hard-pressed to find another employer so understanding." Augustine glares across the room, stealing a glimpse at Jackie before taking a seat at the head of the table. "Now, I hope you're all as excited as I am for the show this weekend. I've got some wonderful things brewing. No, no." She holds her hands up, warding off imaginary protests. "I won't tell you. You'll have to wait."

Tommy snaps his fingers and points at Madam Augustine with a grin. "You're a tease, Madam."

She giggles like a school girl. "Don't I know it? Now pass me the porridge."

The chatter slowly starts again, building until I'm wrapped in one large whirl of voices. They're either ignoring the tension or they're so used to it, it doesn't faze them anymore. For me, it's still very real. Even Christian's family hides their hatred behind social pleasantries in front of other people. I'm not sure how to process what just happened. I've gotten strange looks and heard whispers behind my back, but never such blatant resentment without reason.

"Canary?"

I look up from my empty, chipped plate, the boiled

egg warm in my hand, to find the room empty except for us. "Are they all... like us?"

"Not everyone, but everyone knows. It would be hard to keep that kind of thing a secret here."

"You aren't worried they'll tell someone?" This is a strange country, but I can't imagine the truth would sit well. Historically, people kill for less.

"Ah." Nik hesitates with his hands in his pockets. "No, not really. The twins can create illusions even though their parents have no magic, and they'll never betray their kids. Everyone has a reason to stay quiet."

"I see."

"Anyway, if you're not feeling up to practice, we can try tomorrow instead."

"No." I shake the cobwebs from my thoughts. If the act isn't any good by the weekend, Augustine might change her mind and toss me out on the street. "We have to go. I don't even know what song we're doing."

And I'm eager to test my voice. Despite Nik's demonstration, I'm still not convinced I have magic. The cows that came to hear me sing that day and my mother's no-singing rule tell me there must be something to the claim. Why wouldn't my mother tell me the truth if she knew? Things make sense, though I'm not sure I want them to. Suddenly, I regret not practicing on my own before this moment. Could I have? If my voice is addicting, logically I would need to sing around someone to test it and then ask if they felt anything. Their answer can't be considered proof though—they can maintain the lie.

I have so many questions that can't be answered. Who are my biological parents? Who gave me this skill set? What does it mean? The cycle never stops circling my thoughts.

Nik comes around the table to sit in Tommy's vacant chair. "What Theresa said... Don't let it get to you. The only thing she's ever wanted is to be a star but she doesn't have the spark or the gifts you do. Unfortunately, she *does* have a talent for making everyone's life miserable if she doesn't get her way."

"Are you siding with her?" If the only reason she hates me is because I can sing, I don't understand why she's so upset. I'll be gone before I can steal the show.

"No, of course not. I can't stand her but we have to pick our battles." He sighs and holds his hands up. "You and I, we both want something much bigger than this show. There are greater things waiting out there, but right now, we're stuck here. This is a stepping-stone. Possibly the last one before we get to where we want to be. I know it's hard but you can do this. We'll stick together, yeah?"

"Just a stepping-stone," I whisper to myself. A sharp, pointy one beneath already bleeding feet. "What is it you want, then? If it's not this?"

He gives me a half smile. "There's no time for that now. We have a lot to accomplish today."

Nodding, I set the egg down and scoot my chair back.

"I am sorry, Canary. About everything." He takes my hand and walks me from the dining room. "I'd do more for you if I could."

I believe he would. "I know."

"Then let's go show that *intolerant cow* what a star looks like." He tugs me onto the front porch, twirling me around.

I can't help but laugh as my skirt floats out around my knees.

THE LIGHTS AREN'T ON, but I can tell where the theater is between store fronts with peeling painted and boarded windows. Bulky white letters spelling out *The Den* are surrounded by large bulbs. Bigger lights outline the building and even more under the canopy facing the street. It must look like a magical beacon at night, drawing people in like bees to nectar.

"It's just a small theater," Ben says as he pulls up in front of it and pulls the break. "It's not even in the theater district, but maybe one day, huh?"

Maybe someday they will be somewhere larger, but I won't. This is plenty big for my taste. Too big. Hundreds of people must fit inside. My gut rolls at the thought of singing in front of so many. What if I can't pull it off? What if they hate me and I'm booed off stage?

Nik holds the door open for me. "You coming, Canary?"

I tear my gaze away from the lights in time to see the rest of the troupe disappear down a side alley. I scramble from the car and follow Nik through a barred door at the back. In the distance, a light glows, calling me. Nik places a hand on my back and guides me toward it. The troupe is silhouetted in front of me, practically running, and my adrenaline surges. By the time we emerge in a large dusty area, I'm sure I'll faint again. I really should have eaten but with my luck, my nerves would've brought everything back up anyway.

Ropes are everywhere. Tied to the wall, hanging across the ceiling, and coiled on the planked floor. To the left, a small set of narrow stairs are tucked into the wall. To the right is a wide hallway full of doors. It smells of sweat, sawdust, and fresh paint. Above, the ceiling is nothing but exposed beams and raised metal walkways with a pulley system.

"Upstairs are the offices," Nik tells me. "We aren't allowed up there without an invitation. The dressing rooms are down there"—he points to the doors—"but we aren't doing a dress rehearsal today so we'll just be using the stage and practice room."

We turn left. More ropes and levers surround a platform with a heavy red curtain. Painted sceneries hang overhead and I hurry out from under them. I've never seen anything so elaborate. So complicated. It must take a dozen men to work everything. Maybe more.

I lean forward to peek around the curtain. "Is that the stage?"

"Yes. We'll let the others have a go first while we figure out how we want to arrange the song." He motions further down the hall to a large, open room. "It was written for Irena but she never used it so we can take some creative liberties."

My steps falter and I look back at him. Can I learn to sing a new song flawlessly in a handful of days? Doubtful. If the song is a cover, I can feed off the original, but to create something entirely our own? There's no way. "I assumed it was something popular."

Nik smiles encouragingly. "It'll be popular when they hear you sing it."

"Flattery helps no one."

He laughs and we step into what he calls the practice room. Six panels of warped mirrors make up most of the back wall and the hardwood floor is covered in dings and scratches. There's nothing but the troupe and a giant crate in one corner. A couple of the guys pull props from it—cups, a hose, interlocking metal rings—and hand them out.

Chester bounces on his back feet while the twins imitate him. Theresa storms by us with a large feather boa around her neck, her shoes clacking against the wood. Jackie hurries after her with her head down and my chest tightens. I shouldn't let it bother me. Jackie will have to deal with Theresa long after I'm gone but it still stings. Having a friend would've been nice.

"Sorry." Will rushes after the girls with a slick black cane and pair of white gloves.

"Such a bearcat, that one," Pedro calls across the room. "Poor Will."

Mitch snorts. "Glad I'm not a hoofer."

"You shred it, wheat." James says. Etta elbows him in the ribs. "Oye, lay off. You know she's a pill."

I don't understand a word of the conversation but some of the tension drains away as they joke with one another. These are nice people just trying to hold everything together, and I'm messing with their dynamic.

"Let's sit over there. We'll be out of everyone's way." Nik produces a folded paper from his shirt pocket. "The song is only a few lines so we'll have to be careful how we spread it out. Most of it will be on me, I think, since we aren't sure of the reaction from the crowd."

"What do you mean?"

"Symrics have different potencies. If yours is too strong and they hear too much of it, things could get ugly."

I swallow hard. Why would Augustine take this risk? Surely the money isn't worth the consequences when she made such a fuss about avoiding scandal.

"Don't worry. Augustine promised to hire extra muscle until we know what to expect."

That's less than comforting.

I follow Nik to the back corner. Everyone else in the room is doing something. Eddie has a top hat stuffed under his arm, counting something inside. Gus tunes his saxophone and Mitch his trombone while Tommy sets up a snare drum. Etta and Gayle stretch their legs out in front of them on the floor and pull at their toes. Ben and Pearl direct Eleanor and Gilly on where to stand. James has Chester rolling over to play dead while Pedro keeps digging through the props.

"Can we watch the others first?" I ask.

"The only thing worth seeing back here is Pedro's juggling." Nik flops down on the floor and unfolds the paper. "The rest is mainly a lot of bickering. The real practice isn't until they get on stage, and even then no one bothers using their magic until show time. It's too exhausting otherwise."

Pedro holds up three wooden pins and reaches in for more. My curiosity piques. "Can he really juggle more than three?" One of the farmers' sons used to juggle empty milk bottles during breaks. He couldn't do more than two and more shattered than didn't.

"Are you trying to procrastinate?" Nik asks playfully.

"Of course not." I settle down beside him, tucking my legs and skirt beneath me.

"Here." He hands me the lyrics. "Read this over first."

Wiping sweaty palms on my lap, I do as he says.

SOMETIMES MY DREAMS *are haunted by a sweet symphony. The darkness takes hold and once again, I wake in agony.*

When we met, our future, how it shone. It now seems so long ago. How could we have known our fates were already sewn?

A secret garden in my heart blooms. Under the twinkling sky, I feel you beside me. The fantasy hides our bitter doom.

The fairy tale, my only light. I'll see you again, my love, when stars are bright.

"WHAT DO YOU THINK?" Nik asks.

Tears burn my eyes and I drop the paper. This has to be a joke. Haunted dreams? A shining future ripped away? The memory of a starlit sky shining above Christian and me the night of the dance flashes through my mind. Fate is back to playing cruel tricks on me.

"I can't do it. I'm sorry. I… can't."

Pushing off the floor, I rush back the way we came. The world is a dark, swirling mass of evil, ready to eat innocents at every turn. My mother was right—fairy tales aren't real. I want to go back to my little corner of the universe and never leave it again. If I can get to the docks, some captain might take pity on me. They don't have to be going to Holland. I just need to get on the same continent.

"Where are you going?" Nik rushes in front of me.

"Home," I say in a shaky voice. "To find someone willing to help me get home."

He shakes his head. "I can't let you do that."

"You can't stop me," I snap.

"Canary," he says in a warning tone. Then his face relaxes and his voice softens. "You're right. I can't stop you, but rushing off to that part of the city is dangerous. There's no telling who you'll run into."

"Fine, I'll go to the police and talk to a different officer," I shout. "They'll *have* to help."

"What do you want them to do, Canary?" His voice is tired. "If they arrest Walter, will that change things for you?"

A hot tear rolls down my cheek. "He deserves it."

"He does, but even if he's behind bars, you'll still be here. They'll want you to testify at his trial which will only keep you here longer."

It isn't about getting justice against Walter, although I would love to. It's about getting home. I miss my mother and Christian. I miss my tiny bed and the sight of the windmill behind my house. The cool breeze. The aching back from a long day's work. Everything. I miss everything.

"I need some air." I rub my forehead and walk away from him. The lyrics don't matter but surviving this does. "Let me know when it's our turn. You can set the tempo; I'll try to match it. It'll be fine." *Hopefully.* I'll do my best to make it a success anyway. Right now, I need some space from the craziness of the last few days, including Nik. "I'm going to sit outside for a bit."

"Do you... I mean..." Nik licks his lips and lifts his chin. "Stay out back so no one hassles you, yeah?"

"Okay." I take uncertain steps toward the back door and stop halfway there. *What am I doing?* If I go out there alone, I'll have a panic attack. Well, a more severe one. "Actually, can you come with me? No talking though."

Nik doesn't say a word. He simply presses his lips together tightly and saunters after me into the alley with his hands clasped behind his back.

The sun beats down on the concrete; I don't remember it being this warm when we arrived. Pressing my back against the brick wall, I slide to the ground and ignore the stench of hot garbage. This is a mistake. I must be losing my mind to have let Augustine talk me into this. *No.* I'm just that desperate. That naive. Life never prepared me for this. Why would it? I lived in a happy world where nothing bad ever happened—nothing I was old enough to remember, that is. The danger my mother warned me of was nothing but a bedtime story. I thought she was being overprotective because things like this never happen in our town. Maybe in other places, but never in my own backyard.

A sob breaks in my throat. When I get home, I'll never question my mother again. I'll do anything she says and be glad of it. Everything except leave Christian. That is, if he takes me back. And I'll never, ever sing again, even if I'm alone.

"You," a woman hisses.

I press myself against the wall and my eyes widen at the sight of a plump woman standing over me in a woven dress. Her face is so like Walter's, I'd know her without having seen her before. I cast a look over her shoulder, searching for her son. Why didn't I just stay inside? I'll sing the song. I'll sing it a thousand times if I get the chance.

"Irena." Nik steps between us and holds his hands out in front of him, blocking the entrance. "What are you doing here?"

"Me? What is *she* doing here?" she demands.

"Ask your son," I snap.

"You were told never to come back," Nik says without missing a beat.

"I'm here for my wages."

"Fine. Augustine is in the office. Be quick."

One second Irena looms over me, the next only air and a lingering scent of powder. I blink. Nik still blocks the doorway with a tick in his jaw. *Magic.* Walter told me his mother was able to... transmit without seeing her location but seeing it happen—*believing it*—is different.

"Is she alone?" I ask.

"Yes." He turns, holding a hand out to help me up. "Are you okay?"

"I think so."

"You sure?" When I stand and nod, he chews his bottom lip with a vacant stare. "Let's kick them off the stage and give things a go."

"That won't go over well with Theresa."

"Nothing ever does."

"I'm scared," I whisper when we reenter the dark theater. I'm not sure if I'm admitting to being afraid of Walter, his mother, or singing on stage. Each one is battling its way to the front of my mind, demanding I be more terrified of it than the others.

"I know," he whispers back, squeezing my hand. "I've got you."

CHAPTER 10

"Whenever you're ready," Nik says. He had wheeled a large black piano into the center of the stage after asking Jackie, Theresa, and Will to let us give things a try. As expected, Theresa threw a fit. Or, as Will put it on his way backstage, she cast a kitten. Nik poises his fingers on the ivory keys.

Sing the song, I tell myself. *Sing it and go home.*

I smooth the paper with the lyrics between my hands. The seating area is invisible with the bright lights shining on the semicircle stage. The darkness sends fear trickling down my spine. I squint into the abyss and feel someone looking back. They can't be though. Everyone is practicing their own act backstage and Nik told Irena she'd find Augustine upstairs.

I swallow and force myself to turn away. I have to learn this song, earn money, and get out of this place before paranoia rules my life.

"Can you play it once while I listen?" I ask.

Don't look back. Look at the words. Listen to the music. Don't turn around.

Nik's fingers dance over the keys. The music is sweet and light, tickling the senses. It's different than I expect, given how depressing the song is. As the melody continues, it lifts a weight from my chest, chinking away at the bitterness. I had meant to read the lyrics and figure out how to pace them with the melody, but I'm caught up in the essence of it. It washes over me, carrying me to another place, far, far away. Somewhere bright and happy. The song isn't sad, but hopeful. Something bad happened to rip the lovers apart, but they have a promise to see each other again. Even if some nights are filled with nightmares and the memories hurt, their love is still a treasure worth hanging onto.

When it ends, I float back down to reality. Nik stares at me with his unreadable expression and I shift dab the moisture from the corner of my eyes.

"Well?" He raises his eyebrows. "Do you approve?"

A smile cracks, spreading across my face. I more than approve. I desperately want to sing this song, to let myself be swept away in the spirit of it. Tonight I'll dream of Christian, and perhaps he'll dream of me, too.

"It's amazing," I say. "*You're* amazing. You play so well."

"Thank you." He runs a finger down the length of the keys. A fire ignites behind his eyes and his cheeks flush. I can tell he loves it as much as I do, and I can't help but wonder if he's missing someone too. "Now, what will we do with it?"

I bite my thumbnail. I've never created my own song before. He's given me the foundation, but so much of it lies in my hands. "Can you play it one more time?" I ask. "I'll try something."

Nik stretches his fingers, smiling across the piano at me, and strikes the keys again. I fill my lungs with air and wait for my opening. When the music picks up an extra note, the first line slips across my tongue.

Sometimes my dreams are haunted by a sweet symphony. The darkness takes hold and once again, I wake in agony.

I wait a beat, glancing up at Nik. He holds my gaze, his face alive with excitement, and dips his head in approval.

When we met, our future, how it shone. It now seems so long ago. How could we have known our fates were already sewn?

Fate is cruel. I understand that now, but it doesn't have to be the end. There's always hope.

A secret garden in my heart blooms. Under the twinkling sky, I feel you beside me. The fantasy hides our bitter doom.

I pause again, shaking the feeling back into my fingertips. I can almost feel Christian holding my hand in his car that night—his strong fingers intertwined with mine as he asked me to go with him to the garden party. The party where our lives should've changed for the better.

The fairy tale, my only light. I'll see you again, my love, when stars are bright.

I laugh as Nik plays the final chorus, ending the song. It wasn't my best but it released something in me. Singing, *really* singing, broke down a wall I didn't know I built. Nothing existed for those two minutes on stage outside of Nik, the music, and myself. All the stress, all the worry, I buried deep inside fled somewhere behind the red curtains. Out here I was free, if only for a few minutes. I can't remember why it ever scared me. Purposely keeping my voice locked up around others seems so silly now. It doesn't take anything away—it gives me something: Peace. I want more.

"Wow, Canary." Nik leans back on the stool and his mouth turns up in a lopsided grin. His eyes are slightly glazed. "I had no idea you could sing like that. I mean, I heard you sing for Augustine, but that was nothing like today."

"I can do better," I say. "It was just my first time."

A laugh falls from his mouth. "Give yourself a little credit."

I stick my tongue out at him. "I just know I can do better. I can feel it."

"All right, then. Let's try starting it here instead." He plays the beginning again and stops when he thinks I should join in.

"Yes." I round the piano and step closer to him. He hasn't mentioned my magic, just my skill, which I'm surprisingly grateful for. Maybe all Symrics sound good to the people they affect. *Did I affect him?* He seems fine. I decide to take the compliment at face value and am eager to try again. "And maybe I should stretch out the part about the garden?"

"Maybe. Let's try."

I DON'T KNOW how many times we go through the song before we agree on the timing. My jaw aches and my throat is raw, but I haven't felt so alive since the kidnapping. I pull in as much oxygen as my lungs can hold and collapse into the side of the piano, laughing. It's amazing.

A line of sweat beads along Nik's upper lip and his sleeves cling to his arms. His smile matches my feelings exactly. "That's it," he says. "If you sing it exactly like that this weekend, I guarantee you'll get a standing ovation."

My cheeks burn. A standing ovation is too much, but I can only hope that's all that happens, the extra security nothing more than a precaution. Nik's eyes have gone from glazed to glassy and there's a definite change in the way he's looking at me, as if he's star struck. He seems to pick up on my discomfort—either my expression changes or because he's an Amplifier—and his gaze shifts away.

"What do you guys think?" he calls.

I spin around to see the rest of the troupe peeking around the side of the curtain.

"Brava!" one of them yells.

"Indeed." Augustine pushes through them with her cane. "Very inspiring. You'll soar right to the top as our new headliner."

I breathe in through flared nostrils. The only place I will be soaring is across the Atlantic on the fastest ship money can buy. If she puts me as her headliner, she thinks I'll be around longer than I will but I won't burst her bubble yet. Maybe just deflate it a little. "I'm not sure I'm the right person to end the show. Maybe a more permanent act should have the spot?"

"Don't be silly. Now, come," she says. "I have someone waiting in my office who wants to meet you."

My stomach drops and any joy I felt a moment before vanishes. "Irena?" I whispered to Nik. "Do you think she wants us to work something out? For her to come back? I can't do it. I can't face that woman. What if she wants Walter to come back too?"

"Augustine wouldn't do that to you. Especially after that performance," he reassures me. He tries to hide it, but I catch the glimmer of doubt on his face. It isn't fair he can sound so sure at the same time he looks so suspicious. "You'll be fine. Go on before she gets in a lather."

"Wait for me at the bottom of the stairs?" I plead. If I need to make a quick escape, I want him close by.

"Of course."

I scurry across the stage and the group breaks apart to let me pass. Theresa moves just enough so her arm scrapes against mine. "Scag," she hisses.

I'm too nervous to care what that means. I have to concentrate on the mystery person Augustine is leading me to. She limps her way down the hall much quicker than I thought she could move and I skip to catch up.

"Gus," she yaps as he passes us. "Find us an additional two men to guard the stage."

"Yes, ma'am."

Two additional men? How much danger does she expect? None of the others here acted violently after listening to the song over and over…

Glancing secretly at her, I see the true depth of the lines on her face. She must've been beautiful once but the years have taken their toll. Hardship can age a person faster than years. Even if Jackie hadn't told me about Augustine's husband, I can see she's lived through something tragic. It's the same look my mother has; only I have no idea what happened to my mother. I learned a long time ago to stop asking about her life before me.

"After you," Augustine says, ushering me up the steps. "First door on the right."

The wooden stairs ascend at a slant, groaning under my feet. Behind me, Augustine grunts with each step. My fingers skim the brocade wallpaper, helping me keep my balance, and I focus on the light filtering from the door at the top. A shadow passes across it and I hear feet shuffling against the floor.

"Go on already," Augustine says between gasps. "We're not getting any younger out here."

I inhale and step over the threshold. A small desk, littered with paper, commands the middle of the room with a black safe nestled in the corner behind it. Four leather arm chairs with dark lacquered arms sit facing each other but the room is otherwise bare. There's no sign of the person waiting for us but I know they were here a moment ago.

Something hard knocks against my heels and I jump aside.

"I'm not looking to wait in the hall," Augustine says, tapping me with her cane a second time. She stumbles into the room and, when she shuts the door, unveils a man standing at a bookshelf.

He's obviously well-to-do in a maroon dinner jacket made of velvet. A gold band with a square ruby hugs his right ring finger as he lifts a crystal decanter of amber liquid. His thin salt-and-pepper hair is carefully combed and thick, round glasses rest on his nose. "John Chamberlain," he says in greeting. "Sole patron of the Nova Troupe."

Pouring three drinks in crystal glasses, he slips the

decanter to the back of the shelf and places thick books in front of it. He strides across the room with two steps.

"Lina Holt." *Sole hostage of the Nova Troupe.* I take the glass he offers gingerly, unwilling to give up an ounce of awareness around these people. Maybe when I get home, I'll drink myself into oblivion, but not before.

"Don't worry," he says with a wink. "We're far from dry. The authorities will never know."

"Authorities?" He says it like it's supposed to be a comforting. All it does is make me wonder why I should want them here. I mean, I do, but only to report my kidnapping. "Did something happen?"

"The coffin varnish, dear." Augustine sips her drink. "Prohibition's been around for a decade now."

"Coffin varnish?" I glare down into the glass, confused. Nothing with a name like that can be good for me so I set the drink gently on the desk. It doesn't matter if it's illegal—I don't want it.

"Adorable." Chamberlain snorts. "I watched you today. Your voice is splendid. Truly. People will come from all over to listen to you, and there's no doubt they'll be addicted in a single night. I fear I already am."

I press my arms tight to my sides as he chuckles. Someone had been watching from the dark after all.

"Sit, please." He flops down in one of the chairs, unbuttoning his jacket, and yawns. "Auggie told me about your situation. How are you enjoying New York? You probably haven't seen much of it staying in Jersey."

Knowing what happened, his first question is how I'm enjoying my time? Something is seriously wrong with these people. Are girls kidnapped so often in these parts that it doesn't upset them anymore? If that's the case, I'm doomed.

"I can't say I've been having much fun," I tell him coolly. "I was ill at first and now finding a way home is taking up most of my time."

"Quite right." He leans forward and touches my knee. "How careless of me."

I scoot my feet to the side, crossing my ankles, and his hand falls away. There's a moist spot on my skirt where his palm sat. I'm going to believe it's condensation from his ice-less glass instead of sweat. "Madam Augustine, you said there was a phone here. Who should I speak with about making a call?"

"The phone, yes." She hobbles over to sit beside Chamberlain. "I asked after it earlier and it's being repaired. It should be back in a week or so."

In another week, my letter might beat the call. I want to talk to Christian now. To tell him I'm safe, I love him, and to please get me home. I want to ask him to tell my mother I'm okay and make sure she's taking care of herself. Grief tugs at my core and I swallow against my dry mouth. Mostly I want to know for sure help is on the way.

"You should remedy that—the part about not having fun. I know nothing about fixing telephones." Chamberlain laughs at his own words and leans forward. "I would be happy to show you the sites."

I'm sure he would, but nothing about him makes me feel comfortable enough to go. It takes all my will power not to jump out of my chair and run. "I'd prefer to focus on the show," I say carefully. If I anger the troupe's patron, I might find myself out on the street just as easily as angering the owner.

He laughs. "All work and no play?"

"Traumatic experiences have a way of knocking the enthusiasm out of a person." I bite the inside of my cheek. "I'm much too homesick for tourism."

Madam Augustine tsks. "John is offering you a privileged view of the greatest city on earth."

"It's very generous," I say, grinding out the words. I'm sure there's nothing generous about it. "I just don't think it's the right time."

"Lina," Madam Augustine starts.

"No, no. It's fine." Chamberlain touches my elbow. "She's been through a lot and I'm sure she feels pressured to get her song ready. Although, if I may, it's already enough to impress the crowd in a place like this."

Madam Augustine stiffens in her chair. The slight to the theater is subtle but not lost on either of us. It certainly isn't something I'd expect to hear from the patron of the troupe. He should have more faith in their talent and the audience they draw.

"It has to be perfect," Augustine says. "Not simply good enough. If we want the troupe to excel, we need to set our goals high."

"Quite right. That settles it then. We'll leave the sight-seeing for another time." Chamberlain studies my face. "How are you getting on with the Romani? Auggie says he's been looking after you."

"Nik?" I scowl at the sudden change of topic. "He's been very kind to me."

He grunts. "I'm sure he has. He's a dangerous friend to have, especially for someone like you."

"He doesn't seem very dangerous." I glance at the door, envisioning my escape. Nik's waiting for me at the bottom of those stairs to save me, should I need it. He may be hiding something but it doesn't mean it's something bad. Everyone has secrets. He seems a safer choice than Chamberlain, in any case.

Chamberlain stands and offers me his hand. "Well, it was a pleasure to meet you tonight, Miss Holt. If you'll excuse us, we need a moment alone, but I'm looking forward to your performance this weekend."

I skirt around him as fast as possible without touching him. "Goodnight."

He opens the door, his attention lingering below my

face, and I force myself not to bolt from the room. My mother's voice runs through my head: *Hold your fear close, lest someone use it against you*. It's a little late to listen to her advice but it's better than discounting it. Once I hit the staircase, I drop the restraint and thunder down the steps. I slam into Nik at the bottom and stumble back.

"Whoa," he says, steadying me. "Where's the fire?"

I squint up the steps to see Chamberlain looking down at us.

"Oh. *Him*."

"He said you're dangerous," I whisper.

Nik's jaw tightens. "Did he?" It isn't a question.

"Besnik Sala, it's been awhile," Chamberlain calls. "Join us."

His hands tighten slightly around my upper arms. "I'll pass, thanks."

"I wasn't asking." Chamberlain disappears from the top of the stairs.

Nik takes a long shaky breath. "Go on," he says. "They're getting ready to load up the cars now. I won't be long."

He trudges up the steps with a stiff back, his suspenders tight against his shoulder blades. With the clunk of the door shutting, I head back to the practice room. My elbow burns where Chamberlain touched me and the goose bumps refuse to shrink away. The last person that gave me a feeling like that was Walter. In the future, I'll be avoiding John Chamberlain at all costs.

"There she is." Gus switches his saxophone case to his other hand and lightly punches my shoulder. "Aren't you the cat's meow?"

It sounds like he's giving me a compliment so I mumble a quick "thanks" and look over my shoulder at the empty hallway.

"I mean, Madam Augustine said you could sing but *murder*! Symrics are the real deal. I understand what Walter was thinking now."

My gaze snaps to him. "What?"

"I didn't mean it like that," he stammers.

Mitch nudges him. "I think he's trying to say you may save us after all. We don't have any shows booked in Chicago yet and we're out of here in two months."

I blink quickly, trying to process the information. Two months is longer than I thought, but I told Christian I was at the Whitman Boarding House. If there's any sort of delay, help might come too late. The money shouldn't take more than a week to arrive once he gets my letter. It leaves plenty of wiggle room but my nerves still prickle.

"Right, well…" I look over my shoulder for Nik again. "I hope I can help before I leave."

"Come on, Gus," Mitch says. "Tommy's holding the truck."

Gus winks, hefts his saxophone, and leaves me at the

edge of the room alone. Someone else is watching me but I don't have the courage to look up. I have no desire to repeat the disaster that was breakfast and I'm ninety-percent sure Theresa's the one shooting daggers at my forehead.

Something warm and wet touches my leg. I leap aside to find Chester staring up at me with a wagging tale. "Hi there." I bend down to scratch his head.

"Hi."

I flinch at the sound of Jackie's voice and keep petting the dog. "Hello."

"I don't have long before Theresa comes back." Her red skirt skims the floor as she kneels down next to me. "But I just wanted to say I'm sorry. I don't actually agree with her although it must seem like it. It's... I *have* to be on her side, you know?"

Not really, but I can't cast any stones. I'm desperately doing things I never expected. "I understand. You have to work together."

"It's more than that."

"I get it." Partially, anyway. I intruded here and got Irena fired. Theresa's anger feels personal, and maybe it is, but it isn't worth talking about.

Jackie opens her mouth but shuts it before saying anything. She pats Chester's head and stands. "I just wanted to say I'm sorry."

I turn to watch her leave and Nik is standing in the

entrance with his arms crossed. Anger practically wafts from his skin. I give Chester a final scratch and stand. "So, your name is Besnik?" I ask, unsure what else to say.

"Yeah." He shrugs. "But just Nik."

I stare, trying to figure him out. "Is everything okay?"

"Fine." But his cheeks are flushed and his jaw clenched. He doesn't force me to tell him anything so I don't want to push him, and besides, nothing here is any of my business. For one brief moment, he meets my gaze before stalking out of the room. I'm left feeling like I was punched in the stomach.

If Chamberlain can do that to Nik in two minutes, I don't want to know what he would do to me if I upset him. I grip my skirt in fists and back toward the crate of props, keeping an eye on the doorway. My heart pounds as I lean over the side. It doesn't take much digging to find the string of brightly-colored scarves Eddie stuffed up his sleeve. I unknot the green one at the end with shaking fingers and tie it around my thigh.

If I have to run, I'll be ready. Food, clothes, something to cover my head in case I need a disguise. The broken phone is too convenient—I need a backup plan in case Christian's help doesn't come fast enough.

CHAPTER II

Sweat trickles down the back of my slip, my mind still stuck in the nightmare. It's the same one as the night before and the night before that. A solid five nights of wind, mud, and a black-eyed Walter. At least I haven't screamed out loud again. I hope. No one has come running anyway. Part of me wishes I did cry out so Nik would've been there when I woke up. The darkness of the room is too much like the trunk to be alone in it. Not as confining, but walls don't matter at night. They used to. My house was safe, but now even that doesn't offer any comfort.

I stand in the hallway, the blue quilt from the bed wrapped around my shoulders, and wish I thought better of it. It's not too late to turn around, to go back and sleep with the light on, but I want to be near something alive. Tomorrow is the big day. With the first real performance looming and the realness of the dream hanging over me, I'm trying hard not to make a break for it. Every second I stand here, staring at the line of light under Nik's door, the fact that I have nowhere to go seems less and less important. I need someone to ground me. Someone tangible instead of a memory.

Raising my knuckles, I rap softly on the wood. Something scrapes against the floor, a chair maybe. I wait and wait, but nothing happens.

"Nik?" I whisper hoarsely. "Are you awake?"

Still nothing.

He's been a phantom since Chamberlain called him to the office at the start of the week, sleeping through breakfast, breezing into practice for a couple run-throughs, and then disappearing again. Every sentence he's spoken consisted of one to three words and he hasn't looked me in the eye in days. Jackie's avoiding me too. The same with everyone else unless Theresa's occupied on stage. I've been trying not to take any of it personally but it's not easy.

I'm lonely, I want to say to Nik's door. *And scared. Please let me in.* But he doesn't so I trudge back to my room, hugging my blanket tight. I flick on the lamp and jump back onto the bed with silent tears flowing down my face.

THE MURMUR of the crowd drifts into the dressing room, feeding my nerves. Six square mirrors are propped up on a built-in table that runs the length of the room. Silver makeup containers and hair brushes litter the surface. Light fixtures stick out of the wall with a bare light bulb hanging over each space. Behind us, feather boas and a variety of hats hang on hooks. I perch on a wooden stool at the end of the table and try to breathe through an assortment of perfumes.

The other girls yell to each other: *pass the rouge, what time is it, has anyone seen my other shoe—no, the blue one.* No one pays me any mind while they focus on themselves. My gaze drifts between the mirror and each of their faces, comparing our appearances. I tried to copy their makeup, but I'm not sure how well I manage. Where their blue eye shadow is classy, mine looks more like a clown. My eyelashes clump and the berry-colored lipstick is too stark against my skin. Between the heavy layer of foundation coating my face and the lace dress, I look like a stranger. Maybe if I pretend I'm actually this other person, it'll be easier to get up there and sing.

"It's show time," Nik says in the open door.

Pearl claps her hands twice and adjusts the collar of her heavy wool coat. "Hurry, Eleanor. Your father wants you to say your lines again before we go on."

"Again?" the little girl whines, following her mother out.

The other girls file behind them, clinging to each other with giddy smiles, but I stay seated. Nik and I are scheduled last so there's awhile to wait. Maybe I should pin my hair up while I sit here instead of leaving it loose. I turn back to my reflection and hold it off my neck but it makes the bad makeup more obvious.

Jackie pops back in. Her red hair is slicked tight against her scalp and the feather skirt swishes around the beveled doorframe. "There's a place we can watch without being seen, if you want." A flicker of surprise flashes as she sees my face, and she rushes to my table. "Close your eyes."

I hesitate, then do as she asks. Her fingers skim lightly over my lids followed by quick, jerky movements over my lashes.

"There," she says, and steps back.

I look in the mirror again. The shadow is lighter, blending into the crease of my eye, and the clumped lashes are fanned out. Not as well as hers, but it's better. "Thank you."

"Jackie," Theresa barks from the hallway.

"I'll show her where to watch," Nik says, meeting my gaze. He's dressed in a black jacket with tails. His hair is slicked back, enhancing the angles of his face. I can't seem to look away, although I want to. He holds out a hand for me to take. "We'll have to be quick so I can get behind the piano to open on time."

I stay firmly in my seat. My nerves are already fraying and seeing the crowd will only make it worse.

"Don't you want to see it?"

The magic. Of course I do. But…

"Canary," he prods.

I lose the battle with myself, the chance to see real magic outweighing my fear. Nik smiles when I jump out of my chair and leads me through the theater to a platform.

"Hold onto the ropes." He winks and, as soon as I'm clutching two of the four ropes, he uncoils one hooked to the wall. With swift tugs, he hoists the platform up using a pulley system. I gasp as it rises higher and higher to look over the scenery, hidden from the crown by the valence.

A man I've never seen glances up at me from a planked walkway suspended in the air and smiles. My stomach twists violently. I'm at anyone's mercy up here… But he shifts his focus to his work, pulling levers and ropes and whatever else.

"I'll be back," Nik promises and hurries to the piano hidden behind the now-moving curtain.

A hush falls over the theater as the red velvet reveals the first act. Nik plays an upbeat song. Jackie and Theresa swirl, Etta and Gayle somersault, and the twins prance with Chester at their heels. Sparks fire off the floor, cascading back down in a rainbow of colors, and the crowd *ooohs*. The sense of wonderment swells, and I glance at Nik. His fingers fly over the keys as if he isn't extending any extra energy, but there's no doubt that he is. I'm caught up in the excitement as much as the audience seems to be. Though the emotion is entirely different, the underlying notes are the same, almost like a signature. I wonder if mine gives the exact same impression no matter what song I sing.

Before I realize the opening is over, Nik is already off the stage. Gus, Tommy, and the other band members have taken over the stage, blasting jazz through the building.

Nik's magic is the only constant through the show. He glances up at me between acts to offer a reassuring smile, maybe during the acts too, but I'm too enthralled by the stage. Lights float in the air like fairies and each tap of a heel brings a splash of color up from the wooden stage. Eddie's magic act is *real*. Golden butterflies fill the air and burst into glitter that rains down onto the audience. Then Ben and Pearl take the stage with the twins to do their comedy skit to a boisterous crowd. I've been looking forward to their illusions the most.

The platform jerks, and I scramble to grab the ropes. "Sorry," Nik calls quietly. "We're next."

My heart thunders in my chest. Already? After all of those acts? I'll ruin the entire experience for the audience. Why go out on a bad note after so much talent?

"Are you holding up okay?" Nik asks when the platform hits the floor again.

I shake my head.

"Lina?"

"What?"

"I hope you aren't heated with me. I know I've been busy lately. It's just, there are some things you don't know about, and..." He shrugs. "I think in protecting you from it, I've made you feel abandoned."

I fidget with my curls. Protecting me from what? What else could there possibly be? But I don't have that right to demand answers. What he does is none of my business. "I'm fine."

Lies.

When kids poked fun at me for my past, I held my head up high because I have a mother that loves me. When classmates laughed at the dirt under my fingernails, I laughed along with them because that's what puts food on our table. When they insinuated Christian was using me, I ignored them because I felt his love for me. The truth is that I cried myself to sleep every time they said those things.

I cry every night now too, but there's no consolation for this. No positive side to look at. As of this morning, the theater phone is still out for repair, and I have no way of knowing if Christian's received my letter yet. All I can do right now is keep stockpiling necessities.

"I just miss home," I say when Nik continues to stand there in silence.

He takes a step closer. "We'll talk later."

I nod simply because it's the easiest thing to do. It can't be much longer that I'm in his life—in any of their lives. If there are no delays and Christian wires the money right out, I'll be home by the first frost. I hope my mother can put aside her prejudice long enough to let him reassure her I'm safe. She'll beat him with a frying pan before he can get a word out if my luck is any indication. Or maybe they'll actually bond while I'm gone. She'll need someone to lean on; it may as well be someone else who misses me as much as she does. If he does… I have to stop assuming he wants me back in his life after I called things off.

Gayle and Etta stand behind the curtain, wiping the sweat from their faces with cloths by the time we make our way up the steps to wait. Their tight glittering one-piece suits border a line between revealing and glamorous.

"You look great, by the way," Nik whispers in my ear from behind. My cheeks burn and I rub my hands over the dress. "Are you ready?"

I jump. "Maybe." *Not at all.*

"Do it just like we practiced. Ignore the crowd." He smiles encouragingly. "You can do it, Canary."

"The first time is the most terrifying," Gayle adds. She rubs a smudge of black mascara from under her eye. "You're voice is absolutely berries. They'll love you."

Berries? "How many people are there?"

"Enough," Gayle says.

Etta snorts. "Maybe three hundred. Three-fifty tops. It's not the best start to the season."

Gayle cringes. "Last year we ended with five hundred. It could still get better."

"We'll survive," Nik reassures her. "Start with three, end with six, as long as we perform well enough."

"Always a dreamer, this one." Etta smiles with a mouthful of crooked teeth."Maybe with you, he'll be right." I open my mouth to tell her she's wrong when she grabs Gayle's arm and drags her away saying, "This strap is cutting into my shoulder something fierce."

I turn to watch them weave through stagehands. There's more life to the theater with everyone rushing around, more than I realized from my lofty viewing spot.

"I'm not sure I'll survive this," I say. Another week suddenly seems like a lifetime.

"Sure you will," Nik says. "It's just one song. After we take our bow, it's done until tomorrow."

My fingernails dig into my palms. "I don't mean the performance, but thanks for reminding me we have to do this again."

The crowd applauds on the other side of the curtain and chaos erupts around us. Two men hoist a rope, and pulleys squeak, sliding the curtain across the stage. Ben, Pearl, and the children scurry around the side of the painted park scenery. Two more men wearing faded jackets wheel the piano to the middle of the stage and Nik stretches his fingers.

"The curtain will open as soon we're in position." He takes a deep breath and lets it out through his mouth, motioning for me to do the same. I don't. "Just like we practiced."

My shoes are suddenly made of lead, and I move to take my place in front of the piano. Nik's fingers hover over the keys with his eyes closed, just like every day at rehearsal. The pulleys squeak again and my heart threatens to explode. This is happening too fast. Wasn't I just sitting in the dressing room? Tied up on a ship? Dancing with my other half? I'm not ready. I can't do this.

My feet shuffle backward. *Don't run.* Running solves nothing. Bolting out the back door will only land me in a worse situation. I *can* do this. It's not any different singing in front of hundreds of people than it is singing to an empty theater. Except all the people will be focused on me. Watching, waiting, for me to mess up. Expecting me to give them something worth paying for.

A lump forms in my throat. I look back at Nik. His eyes are open now and dancing with excitement. The red curtain in front of me moves and fear snakes its way through my veins. Each nerve is on fire. It's the most intense, terrifying thing I've ever experienced. Staying on my feet when there's nothing but air between the audience and the stage is a miracle.

Most of the theater is shielded by the same darkness as before but, with the extra lights at the edge of the stage, the first few rows of faces are visible; the rest exist only as a sensation. Hundreds of heads point in my direct and I fight the urge to look back at Nik again.

The first familiar notes ring out and I focus on a red light in the back. It's too late to turn back now. Rushing off the stage is the only thing more mortifying than staying on it. So, when my cue comes, I let the words take over. The lyrics flow out almost effortlessly; my mouth remembers them on its own. I allow my body to go numb to everything but the vibrations in my chest.

The words pour out like a second breath and the air shifts. The crowd is deathly silent. I sense their rapture almost immediately. It's weighty and warm, like a heavy blanket and a cozy fire in the dead of winter. The feeling intensifies with each verse. They want the comfort, need the security, of whatever magic I'm spinning. I'm terrified of myself but also energized by their reaction.

When the curtains swish together, every inch of my skin tingles with excitement. I did it. I really did it. The song went by so fast there wasn't time to worry about messing up. Nik scoops me up in a hug, a whoosh of air escaping my mouth. The cheer of the crowd roars in my ears. I laugh and hug Nik back.

"That was even better than before," he says, leading me offstage.

The rest of the troupe dashes across the back of the stage, struggling to keep out of the workers rushing back and forth. Augustine leans on her cane just beyond the hubbub, complimenting everyone as they pass. She pats the twins on the head. "Lovely, lovely," she croons. "Another wonderful show. Well done. And you." She latches onto my wrist. "John and I would like to see you in the office. Head up, won't you?"

I pause. Did she think it wasn't good enough? Being kicked out now, when I've come so far... I need to survive one more week to be where I told Christian I would be. "I'll change and be right there," I say.

"Nonsense. John bought you that dress. He'll love to see you in it close up." She pats my cheek and turns to Nik. "Take the final bow and then load up."

Nik lets go of my hand, leaving me cold as I head for the stairs. I look back halfway there, expecting to see Augustine behind me, but I'm alone. She hasn't moved an inch and neither has Nik. I can't hear their exchange over all the commotion but his face is tight, her eyes narrow. He points a finger in my direction, then hers flies up to hover an inch from his face. Blood colors both their cheeks and, for a moment, I think Nik will slap her. Instead, he turns on his heel and storms toward the dressing rooms while everyone else lines up on stage.

Augustine moves down the hall, her cane leading the

way. "What are you waiting for?" she snaps. "He's expecting you."

My heart pounds three times for every step I take. To think, I was nervous before my act. The way Chamberlains beady eyes stared the last time, enlarged by his lenses, makes my skin itch. *One more week.*

I hurry to the office door and rap my fingers against my thighs as I listen to the thump-thump-clack of Augustine coming up behind me.

Chamberlain swings the door open, beaming. "The woman of the hour."

I force a polite, toothless smile in return and look over my shoulder, hesitating on the threshold. Augustine isn't the biggest comfort in the world, but she's better than nothing at all. "Good evening, sir."

"The old bat isn't giving you a hard time, is she?" he whispers. "She was pacing around here all afternoon. I thought her hip would give out before she stopped."

Old bat? Augustine is at least ten years his junior. "No," I say shaking my head. "I thought it would be polite to wait for her."

"She'll be here shortly. Come sit. Make yourself comfortable."

He stands aside and I have no choice but to squeeze past him. My bare arm skims his velvet sleeve and I dart further into the room. He leaves the door open which helps keep the nerves at bay, and digs out the hidden decanter.

"A drink?" he asks. "To celebrate."

"No. Thank you."

"You were wonderful." He pours himself a glass. "That dress fits like a glove."

I fold my arms around my abdomen and move my fingers over the lace, feeling certain that's exactly why I don't love it. I dislike it even more now that I know he financed it. It doesn't matter if Jackie picked it out, only that it's from this man.

"Madam Augustine told me tonight that you bought it, or I would have thanked you before." I force pleasantness into the words.

"No thanks necessary. Auggie told me with a little shining up, you'd be a star. I'm sure you were fine in your old clothes but a little polish does wonders. No one wants to watch you sing in a flour sack." He laughs. I hold my breath. My mother's dresses are made from old flour sacks. It cost more than we could afford for mine not to be but she insisted. "Ah, Auggie. There you are."

She shuffles into the room and plops down on a chair, fanning herself. "I've never heard such applause before." She takes the glass Chamberlain offers her. "Keep it up and we'll be performing at the Palace in no time."

"I'm glad you enjoyed it," I say. "The other acts were great too, I'm sure."

"Right you are," Chamberlain says. The two share a guarded stare. "Sit down, Lina."

"I really should be getting changed," I say. The last time I sat next to him, he didn't know enough to keep his hands to himself. "I'd hate for anything to happen to the dress, and I'm rather exhausted."

Chamberlain swirls his glass. "That should be my line. I haven't stayed up this late in years, but I couldn't miss your first performance." He leans over the desk and fishes for something on the other side. "These are for you."

A bouquet of red roses wrapped in white paper land in my arms. I exhale under the surprising weight. The light scent is pleasant, but the weathered hand on my arm stops me from enjoying it. "I can't accept these."

"Don't be ridiculous," Augustine snaps. "Didn't your mother teach you any manners?"

My cheeks burn. My mother taught me many things, including respect for elders. She also taught me I don't have to remain in a situation if someone is making me uncomfortable—to trust my instincts about people. "I didn't mean... I just have nothing to put them in," I improvise. I want to get out of this room. I'll take as many flowers with me as I have to in order to make it happen.

"Of course," he says. "Where was my head? There will be a vase waiting at the boarding house by the time you get back."

I swallow a groan. "That's very kind."

"You deserve it." He sets his glass down and picks at a lock of my hair. It takes everything I have not to shy away. "Have you reconsidered my offer to show you the city?"

"I have." My nostrils flare. "And, while I thank you for thinking of me, I'd rather not. There are rehearsals and–"

"Your song is fantastic. Someone as pretty as yourself needs to get out and enjoy what life has to offer." He steps back, his gaze wandering places it shouldn't. "I don't want to press you, however. Perhaps next week."

I stay silent, clenching my jaw tightly. Next week I should be long gone, and if I'm not, I'll keep putting him off until I am.

"Right then," Augustine says. "Off you go."

She doesn't have to tell me twice.

I bolt down the stairs as fast as I dare. *Please let the phone be back from repair on Monday.* Otherwise, I might have a breakdown. One that there's no way to recover from.

CHAPTER 12

I shield my eyes from the sun peeking down the alley behind The Den. My bones ache, my head throbbing, after another long, sleepless night. Eddie holds the door open for me, and I skip the last few yards when Nik pops up beside me.

"Come with me," he whispers in my ear, then turns to Eddie. "Cover for us?"

Eddie's lips turn into a lopsided grin, and he backs inside, letting the door swing shut behind him.

Nik takes my hand and pulls me around the theater to the street. "Nik?" My voice wavers. "What are we doing?"

"Do you remember the day you got here?" He slows his pace and releases my hand to smooth back his hair. "You asked for my help, but I couldn't give it to you then. When we got to the boarding house, I promised you, despite how it looked, that I would. I tried with that cop but..."

How could I forget? It was the second worst day of my life, falling just behind getting kidnapped in the first place. It was the day I nearly gave up on humanity. It was also the day someone finally believed I wasn't crazy, and when I realized crazy is a relative term.

"I remember," I say.

Nik rubs the back of his neck. "I know it looked bad when I took you to the boarding house, but Walter didn't send word anyone was with him. Or, if he did, no one told me. I had no idea what to do. I want to explain why it was a dilemma for me, but not today." He turns down an alleyway behind a tall white-stone building and knocks on a wooden door at the back. "No one can know about this."

I tilt my chin and look at him from the corner of my eyes. I'm not sure what's on the other side of the door but, judging by the anxious look on his face, I either want it desperately or not at all. "Okay."

A man in a black suit swings the door open and motions us inside. Gel plasters his light hair against his head, parted on the side. He scans us as we pass, and a wave of heat slams into me from the small black and white kitchen.

"Be quick," he whispers to Nik.

"Thanks, Pat." Nik hurries along a wall with eight steel ovens nearly twice my height. Flour coats the tables on my left and the warm, homey scent of bread fills my sense. I breathe it in and hold the comfort close.

When we turn into a tiny windowless office, barely

big enough for the desk inside, I'm tingling with anticipation. Nik breathes heavily as he shuts the door behind us.

He reaches around me and lifts a black candlestick telephone. My heart thuds, a thousand drums drumming in my chest. "Does your mother have a phone?" He lifts the receiver to his ear and spins the zero on the dial.

"No." My voice quivers. "Christian does. Christian Van Buren."

"I need to make a long-distance call," he says into the speaker. "Yes." He pauses for what feels like an eternity and my fingers go numb. "Christian Van Buren in..."

"Leids," I whisper.

"Leids, Holland." Another pause. "There's a Lars Van Buren," he tells me.

I jump at the familiar name. "That's his father."

"Yes, that's the right one. Thank you." He hands the phone out to me. "You have two minutes before we have to leave."

My hand shakes as I hold the cold, heavy cone-shaped metal to my ear. What if he's angry? What if he doesn't want to speak with me? A shrill ringing echoes in my head, ending with a soft click and a woman's voice saying, "*hallo?*"

I lean on the desk to stop myself from falling over. "Mrs. Van Buren?"

"Yes. Who's calling?" she asks in Dutch.

"Lina." I pause, waiting to see if she reacts like she did

at the garden party, but silence crackles through the line. "Lina Holt. Christian's—"

She breathes into the phone. "I know who you are."

Tears flood my eyes, spilling over. "Did Christian get my letter?"

"A letter? He hasn't mentioned one. Is everything all right? You sound upset."

I sound upset? It feels like I'm speaking to a different woman entirely. Surely my mother went to them when she couldn't find me, but Mrs. Van Buren is so calm.

"I was kidnapped. I'm in New York." I cover my mouth to muffle a sob. How can she not know? "May I speak with him?"

"Kidnapped? My gracious. Are you hurt?"

"I'm… safe."

"Christian is attending a party at Cornelia Jonckheer's this afternoon."

My whole body lurches forward into the desk. "He's at a party?"

"His engagement party, yes," she says in an airy voice.

"Engagement?" I squeeze the phone with a sweaty palm. "Christian's engaged? To Cornelia Jonckheer?"

"Of course."

My vision tunnels, my chest cracking apart. "I… Has he mentioned me at all?"

"Not since you did the smart thing and left him." She

sighs. "I have to join the celebration; I'm late as it is. I'm glad to hear you're safe."

"But—" The line clicks. I hold the receiver away from my ear and stare at the black steel. Christian didn't tell her I was missing. He's been too busy with Cornelia Jonckheer. I want it to be a terrible lie, but surely his mother isn't *that* cold-hearted. Tears run down my cheeks, racing toward my jaw, scalding. The receiver slips from my fingers.

Nik dives, catching it before it hits the desk, and sets it back in its cradle. "I'm sorry, Canary. I thought this would help."

"I did too." I scrub the tears from my face. At least now I know not to wait for his help. That I'll have to go through with my own plan. "That was Christian's mother."

"That's great, isn't it?"

"He wasn't at home." I hiccup. "He was at his engagement party."

"Ah, Canary." He scratches the back of his head. "I'm sorry. Maybe there's an explanation."

I can't imagine what Christian could say to explain away his silence. His engagement. He was hours away from proposing to *me*. He never mentioned Cornelia before. Unless… Unless he accepted the end of our relationship with ease, and, if so, did he ever love me at all? I can't breathe. Everything appears sharper, colors darker. *Oh, God. I can't breathe.*

"We have to get back," Nik says.

I nod and the room spins a bit. "Nik, I… Tha—"

"Don't." He flinches and backs away. "Don't thank me. I should've done this when you first got here. I haven't been able to forget the way you looked when you came off that ship." He opens the office door and leads the way back through the kitchen before I can say anything else.

Pat waits by the door, staring at a pocket watch. When he notices us, he stuffs it in his pocket. Nik stops so close their arms touch and a flash of silver passes from Nik's hand to Pat's.

"It's strong stuff," Nik warns. Pat inclines his head and swings the door open for us.

CHAPTER 13

A week goes by. Then another. Two long weeks without a repaired telephone at the theater. Christian may not care, but my mother will. I sent another letter to let her know I'm alive in case Christian's mother didn't mention my call, and promised that I'm trying to get back to her. The green carpet bag hidden beneath my bed is stuffed with canned goods in case my escape calls for spending any time on the street.

I wander behind the troupe in Central Park, listening to them laugh, with my eyes focused on Augustine's back. She wears a gray waist-length knit cardigan over a blue dress despite the humidity and a matching bumper hat as she limps along the edge of the stony path. She told me the letter was mailed right out, just like the one to Christian had been. I sigh.

"Careful, Canary." Nik grabs my upper arms from behind and steers me around a pile of horse dung.

I pull from away from him. Before our first show, he said we would talk but he's been around less and less. And now, during practice, someone is always watching us. It's usually Chamberlain but sometimes Augustine or even Theresa. I don't know what Nik's secret can be but I know he has one.

"Thanks," I say.

Nik's lips quirk up but the smile doesn't stay. Dark circles paint the skin under his eyes and the lids droop with fatigue. "Don't mention it." His thumbs hook under his suspenders. "Gus would never let you back in the car with that on your shoes, and it's a long walk back."

We fall into step with each other, and I chew on the inside of my cheek. "You've been busy lately. Did you find yourself a girl?" It would make sense, and I could stop feeling like I did something to make him want to avoid me.

He throws his head back and laughs. "I wish."

"Disappearing late at night and not coming back until dawn?" I smirk. "I've been there. You can't fool me."

Stepping in front of me, he walks backward. "There's no girl."

I cock my head, my hair frizzing around my face despite the copious amounts of product, and raise my eyebrows. "Then what are you up to?"

His eyes dart to the side, and he turns to walk forward again. "How do you know I don't come back until dawn?"

It's my turn to look away. I would love not to know his comings-and-goings but it's hard to ignore. Sleep comes and goes in waves, and there's not much to do other than stare out the window all night. At exactly eleven, Nik walks off the porch and around to the side of the boarding house every night. Minutes later one of the trucks— always the International Harvester with its tall, boxy red cab and wooden bed—rumbles to life and headlights illuminate the otherwise quiet street every. Around five in the morning, the truck sputters back down the street, and he drags himself into the boarding house looking like he's about to collapse. I could set a watch by the routine.

"I don't sleep well," I say.

He rubs at his cheek with a crease between his brows. "Can you not mention it to anyone?"

"I won't." I glance at Augustine again as she turns her head to examine a large oak. It's getting harder to believe her about the telephone. Surely someone, somewhere, has one I could use. I only need a minute to try again. "Can I ask you for a favor?"

"Not here." Nik leans down to whisper in my ear. "I've been warned to keep my distance from you, but we can sneak away later."

My eyes snap to his face, my jaw dropping. Remembering his expression after Chamberlain called him to the office, I don't need to ask who warned him. That's when he started avoiding me and a few days later he began his late-night disappearing act.

I nod and he releases a breath before hurrying forward to walk with the guys.

"Right here," Augustine says. The troupe slows to a stop near a rocky area with a patch of grass in the center. A few slim trees offer a small amount of shade against the noon sun. Augustine rubs her hands together. "Let's settle in and have a good time."

Mitch and Eddie race toward a tree across the grassy turf. "Faster, Mitch," Etta calls after them. Gus, Pedro, and Tommy lunge forward and the girls cheer them on too. The twins join the fun with Ben and Pearl jogging behind them. James slaps Nik's arm and takes off. Will yells, "wait up" before bouncing over the rocks. Gayle, Etta, Jackie, and Theresa link arms and mosey away from the footpath. I watch it all through a veil, a cloudy haze separating me from them. Then I'm alone with Augustine.

"A lovely day," she comments. "It's good to get away from the theater, don't you think?"

"Yes." I cross my arms over the pink bow at my waist and try to calm the butterflies in my stomach. "Madam Augustine, I was wondering..." I hesitate. Asking her about the letter will sound like I don't trust her word. I don't, of course, but I don't want her to know that. "It's been a while now and the theater phone hasn't been repaired."

"These newfangled things are a tricky business."

By now, I think it's safe to say it's a lost cause and a new phone might be the cheaper way to go. "My second letter should have reached Holland by now."

"I should think so." She puckers her lips, watching the rest of the troupe chase each other. "Don't worry, dear; you're welcome to stay as long as you need to. It's good you like the stage so much."

I blanch at her statement. The stage is strangely addicting; I can't deny it. The thrill of everyone watching is both terrifying and energizing. After each show, the applause sends chills down my spine but, as much as I find myself enjoying it, I want to leave it behind forever.

Theresa pulls Jackie close and whispers in her ear. Jackie glances in our direction and nods. They walk away from the group, arm-in-arm. What nonsense is Theresa telling her this time?

I search for Nik, wondering how long I'll have to wait to get away, and find him trailing Pedro up the side of a boulder.

"I'm king of the world," Pedro shouts.

Nik swings a leg on top of the boulder, his worn calf-skin boots dangling over the side, and smiles down at me. He nods for me to join the others but I don't know how. I've never been good with large groups of people.

"Lina," Pedro calls. "Don't be a fuddy-duddy."

Nik motions me forward again, but I shake my head.

Etta jogs back toward me, her mousey brown curls bobbing, and grabs my hand. "We don't bite."

"Theresa's the only one with a taste for flesh," James adds with a wink.

Gayle shakes her head. "One day she's going to hear you talking about her like that and then you'll be sorry."

"Ah, she's scrappy. I can take her," he says.

I search for Theresa but she's disappeared with Jackie so I let them pull me, uneasy, into the fold.

AN HOUR LATER, Jackie and Theresa are still gone and the rest of the troupe sprawls out on the rocks, gasping for breath. I can't remember the last time I've felt so free with anyone other than Christian. My chest constricts at the thought, my smile fading. It doesn't feel right to have fun when my mother's worried sick and Christian has the ability to assure her I'm fine. Instead, he's attending parties with his fiancée.

"And then." James snorts. "Then, thinking he's this great cake-eater, Eddie tells the girl working the counter—"

"Drop dead." Eddie kicks out at him. "Right now."

Mitch roars with laughter, slamming a dark fist into Eddie's arm. "Kiss off. He's finally getting to the crunch."

Eddie punches him back with red cheeks. "Dry up, the lot of you."

Nik touches my hand, and I startle. "Come on," he mouths.

Climbing to my feet, I stretch the kinks from my knees and ankles. Nik leads me down the backside of the rocks, away from the men as they roar with laughter. He holds a finger up to his lips and points to Augustine. She leans against the tree with her mouth hanging open, and a snore rips through the air. I suppress a laugh.

He smirks and loops my hand through the crook of his elbow. I lean into him, taking the comfort he offers, and we walk in silence. His skin is warm beneath my fingers, his muscles solid. I wonder if Cornelia is touching Christian like this right now.

Nik's hand slips over mine, and I realize I had been squeezing his forearm. "Sorry," I mumble.

"You okay, Canary?"

I nod.

"It's okay not to be," he says.

"I know." But I had to be. I had to keep a straight head on my shoulders to get back to my mother. Dwelling on it won't help so I ask, "What did you give Pat yesterday for letting me use the phone?"

Nik opens his mouth but shuts it without answering. His Adam's apple bobs. "Don't worry about it. Nothing important."

"How hard would it be to use it again?" If I call the police station, they'll undoubtedly get word to my mother.

Nik stops dead in the middle of the path. His face pales, the cords of muscle in his arms flexing.

"If I can't, that's fine. I'll find another phone."

He grinds his teeth. "We should go back."

I follow his gaze to two men walking straight for us, their heads bent in conversation. They wear worn trousers and shirts stained with soot. The closer they get, the more Nik's muscles strain. I'm not sure who they are to Nik, but I don't want to see him hurt, physically or mentally.

I tug his arm but, despite his wanting to leave a moment ago, he seems frozen in place. "Nik? Come on."

"What do we have here?" one of the men says from a few feet away. "Nikolai, isn't it?"

"Don't say a word to them," Nik warns me.

"Nah, that's not it," the second one says. "Besnik. Goes by Nik."

"Yeah, yeah. That's it."

Nik steps closer, shielding me with the side of his body. His voice is low and gravelly when he says, "Fellas."

"Hear you're plunking away at the piano these days." The second man sneers.

"I'm keeping myself busy."

"I bet you are. That fancy suit you wear on stage how you lured this fine young face to the park on her own?"

Nik's knuckles pop one after the other beneath his thumb.

The first man laughs, and they step around us. "Careful this crumb doesn't chisel you, sweetheart. He's a real grifter."

When they're far enough away, I tug on Nik's arm again, desperate to return to the safety of the rest of the troupe. "What was that about?"

"Nothing." He pulls his arm away and shoves his hands in his pockets. "It's nothing. We should…"

He starts off in the direction we came without finishing the sentence. His back is tight, his clammy shirt clinging to the line of his spine. I sprint after him, and he shortens his stride so I can keep up. We don't speak along the way. The few glimpses I stole of his face each revealed something different. Anger. Humiliation. Sorrow. But as we approach the rocky area where the rest of the troupe continues to lounge, it becomes a mask of indifference.

"There you are," Pedro yells. "Why'd you split?"

My heart stops when a figure moves beside the tree Augustine was sleeping under. Chamberlain offers her a hand up, a fedora perched on his head. Sleep still pulls at the corners of her eyes, and they exchange hushed words. I smooth down the front of my dress, then my hair, and try to steady my breathing.

Will comes up beside us with a hot pretzel. "There goes the rest of the afternoon."

"Ah, Lina," Augustine croons. "You must've gone for a walk."

Chamberlain turns, pushing his glasses up his nose, and smiles. His eyes flick over Nik, his face falling slightly before he catches himself. "You're flushed, Lina."

I pat my cheeks with the back of my fingers and I feel sick. "It must be the heat."

"Would you like a drink?" He produces a flask from inside his jacket and comes to stand beside me.

"No." I glance to my right for Nik's reassurance but he's halfway across the stone with Will. "I'm fine, thank you."

"I respect your determination on the matter." Chamberlain slips the silver bottle back into his pocket. "However, there's something I'll no longer accept *no* for."

I hold my breath, waiting. Dreading.

"For now, how about a little song, hm?" Chamberlain runs a tobacco-scented finger over my lips, and I force myself not to recoil. "I missed the last show and need a little taste."

CHAPTER 14

With endless days of rehearsals and an eighth show under my belt, I've finally earned a free day. And, by free day, Augustine means she's finally forcing me to make good on the promise to see New York with Chamberlain. Her promise. Not mine.

The two of them shot holes in each of my excuses the day in the park until Augustine gave up and agreed on my behalf. It's important to keep the patron happy for both our benefit, she said. Maybe she's right, maybe she's not; I don't have it in me to argue. I barely have enough energy to wake up in the mornings after the crushing blow Christian's mother dealt. But I have to pull myself together because I can't stay here. It's time to lay the final brick in my plan. If I'm going to escape, I have to be smart about it.

Sitting in the back of Chamberlain's red Ford, I press myself against the door and breathe carefully through my teeth. The scent of tobacco clings to the interior, making me nauseous. His weathered hand rests too close on the black leather seat next to me, ready to pounce at the slightest opportunity. I refuse to uncross my legs in fear of accidently brushing against him. His visual scrutiny is more than enough contact, but the circulation to my calf cut off ten minutes ago.

When his driver, a wisp of a man with a white beard, pulls along the edge of a wooded area and stops the car, I stiffen. It's a stark contrast to the steel city on the opposite side of the street where more towering buildings stand.

"Stay here," Chamberlain tells the driver. "We'll only be gone a few minutes."

Chamberlain scoots out of the car, and I narrow my eyes at his narrow back. I want to lock the door before he can come around to my side of the vehicle, but I force myself to sit still. Barricading myself in the car with his driver won't resolve anything but getting a layout of the city before I run away might do some good. When Chamberlain opens the door and offers his hand, I accept it. I shiver at the touch, his fingers icicles in the heat. *Let go, let go, let go.*

Today I'll play along. I'll survive this outing because there's still hope buried under all the pain. Christian has abandoned me, that much I understand, but within a few days, I'll tell myself *today is the day.* And now I'll know where to go.

Chamberlain tucks my hand in the crook of his arm

and his bony elbow pokes at me through the velvet. "I'm glad you decided to come," he says. "It's a real treat."

If by *treat* he means *torture*. He may try to come across as a gentleman, but I'm not buying it. There's something wrong with this man. I know it, Nik knows it, and deep down I think Augustine knows it, too. Earlier, she watched me leave with a tired expression, telling me to have fun, but keep my wits about me. It's not a glowing recommendation, if you ask me. Especially coming from his friend.

"I'm glad too," I lie.

"There's far too much to see in one day, so I chose a few interesting stops. You'll have to let me know if I'm tiring you out." He pats my hand. "We can come back any time to see more."

I keep my breath shallow, trying not to let my anger, confusion, and hurt spill over. The only one getting tired today will be him, the old buzzard. Whatever he shows me today will be the extent of my New York experience.

"Look," he points through the trees. "There she is."

I squint in the direction of his finger but don't see anyone he could be talking about. The few men sitting on posts near the water are too involved with their own conversation. "Are we meeting someone?"

He chuckles, dropping his arm so mine falls at my side, and stands behind me. His hands find my waist and he twists me an inch. Goosebumps prickle my skin, and I set my jaw. *Don't vomit.*

"The Green Lady," he rasps.

The Statue of Liberty stands proudly in the distance. I shudder at the sight. She may be a sign of freedom to millions of people, but not me. I'm a prisoner here, trapped an ocean away from home with nothing more than a small sliver of hope and an increasingly flawed escape plan. The only time I want to see this statue again is when I'm sailing away from it.

Chamberlain's face turns stony. "You don't like it?"

"She's lovely," I tell him to keep the peace. The sooner we move on, the sooner this will be over.

He stares off across the water. "Do you see that? In the sky?"

Billows of smoke rise from industrial chimneys across the water. I'd have to be blind to miss it. "Yes."

"They're burning coal."

The stacks reach up, yawning wide into the gray sky. "It would appear so."

"Do you know where coal comes from, Miss Holt?" His fingers tighten on my waist.

"It's mined." I peer sideways at him to see if that's enough of an answer. I don't know the first thing about mining coal.

"It is." He inhales slowly. "Most of the coal here comes

from *my* mines and business is doing well despite the economic situation."

"You're a coal baron?" The fact that he has money was never in question but the source of his income was a mystery. It's nice to know it's legally acquired anyway. "Impressive."

"Fortunately, I was smart enough not to invest my fortune. Cash never spoils."

"I see."

He makes a low noise and turns away. I roll my eyes, keeping my gaze on the giant statue. He must've expected a much larger response, but I'm not affected. Knowing the Van Buren family opened my eyes to one thing: money doesn't make someone better. It simply makes them richer. It's one of a thousand other things defining who a person is, and it's never something to base a friendship on. Not that Chamberlain's after friendship. In fact, I'm fairly certain he's the type of rich man my mother warned me about—the kind she thinks Christian is.

The kind he is. It's hard to reconcile the Christian I know with what he's done.

I follow Chamberlain back to the car and, once inside, he snaps his fingers. The driver pulls back into traffic, leaving the park behind. My body feels heavy as the city swallows us again. This place is overpowering in every way. I don't know how people live here. Even if the parks are lovely, the buildings cover everything else in shadow. The noise of people and traffic is constant. It's maddening.

"The Chrysler Building." Chamberlain leans over me, his voice light again. "They just finished it a few months ago."

The building looms so high that I can't see the top from inside the car. Sun glints off thousands of windows and I shade my eyes. The architecture is magnificent; massive and strong yet elegant. "Wow." And I mean it.

"It's taller than the Eiffel Tower," he whispers. I cringe away from his stale breath on my neck.

I've never been to France, but I imagine it's true. There can't possibly be anything larger than this. It nearly reaches the heavens. "It's like it was built for giants."

His finger traces behind my ear, down my jaw line. "It's comprised of many levels," he says. "Naturally."

I grip the door handle. The tangy taste of blood blossoms between my teeth as I bite the inside of my cheek. "Of course." Somehow I manage to keep my voice level. One more move and I'm jumping out of this car, moving or not. There are limits to what I'll do for a roof over my head.

"How about a song, my sweet girl? Just for me."

I clench my jaw tightly.

"Come now. With all I've done for you, it isn't right to

keep me wanting like this. We need the audience begging for another dose of Symric magic, but not me."

"I should save my voice."

"The rest of the troupe is well satisfied with daily practices," he practically whines.

Chamberlain's fingers slide down the front of my throat and I shiver. "You say that as if I can keep them from listening."

"Do you see those people?" He lifts his hand from my skin. "There."

I tear my gaze away from the building to see a man and a woman sitting on the sidewalk. Their legs are tucked close so they're as out of the way as possible. A bit of dirt smears their faces, and their clothes have seen better days, but it's the look on their faces pulling at my heartstrings. Sadness. Loss. Desperation. These aren't like the people I know back home, tired after a long day of hard labor. These people are broken.

"What happened to them?"

He waves dismissively. "If I had to venture a guess, they lost their jobs and couldn't make rent."

I want to look away but can't. This isn't the first time I'm seeing the effects of the depression; Nik took me in the midst of it when we went to the river, but it's the first time I recognize what I'm looking at. Men carry signs asking for employment and children walk down the street with holes in their shoes. In Holland, there were whisperings of the economy in America but it's not the same as seeing it first-hand. It never is.

I suck in air. "How awful."

Chamberlain hums. "If Auggie hadn't agree to let you stay on, that would be you."

My jaw drops. If *she* hadn't agreed? She asked me to stay, not the other way around. "Mr. Chamberlain—"

He holds his hand in the air. "Spare me the righteous speech. It's a benefit to everyone that you're here, including myself."

I twist to look at him. "How does it benefit you?"

He scowls. "I'm the troupe's patron. Of course, it's good for me if there's a star act. Vaudeville is having a hard go of it so anything that helps Auggie keep things going. I promised I'd look after her when she became a widow." He rubs at his nose. "She had no one else to turn to, like you."

"So you helped her." I wonder what his help cost Augustine and a sense of dread creeps over me.

Chamberlain grips my knee with stiff fingers. "There are precious few things in life money can't buy. For example, a son to inherit my empire."

Blood freezes in my veins. "I'm not sure I understand what you're implying."

"I need a legitimate heir." He shifts closer. "And a wife young enough to give me one. All the better if she has special gifts to pass onto my children."

I want no part of him or the show or his stupid coal, and I'm not stupid enough to let this go any further. Let him be offended and pull support from the troupe. It makes no difference to me, but my self-worth is another thing. "Stop the car."

The driver stiffens in his seat. "Sir?"

Chamberlain's stare digs into me and the sharpness sends me shrinking into myself. "Stop the car," he repeats with clipped words.

The car rolls up to the curb, and I grope for the handle.

"Where are you going?" His fingers tighten on my leg.

"I'll walk back from here." I shove the door open and stumble to sidewalk. I'll figure out where I am eventually but there's no way I'm getting back in the vehicle with him.

"Lina," he calls after me.

My heels pound against the concrete. From the corner of my eye, I see the car circle around to follow and I break into a run. People leap from of my path as I barrel around the corner and a siren blasts in the distance. I pump my legs faster. Fear sweeps over me, though I've done nothing wrong. Leaving before a man can make unwelcome advances is smart, not illegal. But he's rich. Another thing the Van Buren family taught me is when you have too much money, it's easy to get your way. Mr. Van Buren's attempt to pay me off can't be the first time he's bought someone's cooperation. There's a chance my mother is the first to tell him no though.

After a few turns, I stop, gasping for air. There's no sign of Chamberlain behind me, and I don't want to get myself more lost than I already am, if that's possible. I look up at the towering buildings and raise my fingers to my lips. They all look the same and I can't see beyond them to the next street. I can't remember the address to the boarding house to ask for directions, but if I find the river, I might find the bridge Nik and I were near. From there maybe I can sort things out—it's only a few turns. Once I get in the neighborhood, someone should know the house by name.

"Excuse me," I say to a woman. "Which way is the Hudson River?" She points to the left without breaking stride. At least I'm starting off in the right direction. I can only hope Chamberlain doesn't cause any trouble for me. *Fat chance.* He's probably on his way to complain about me to Augustine now.

"Lina?"

I jolt, looking around for who could possibly know me here, and see a woman waving frantically across the street. It takes a moment to recognize Jackie under her wide brimmed hat. My shoulders sag with relief.

"Cross over," she yells.

I hesitate. She's my ticket back to the boarding house, but we haven't had a chance to really talk since the day she apologized. Theresa isn't anywhere to be seen, so I'm confident I won't be tossed to the wolves, but there's a strong possibility it will be awkward.

I wait for a car to pass before dashing across the street. "Hi, Jackie."

"What are you doing here?" she asks brightly. She's wearing a loose royal blue dress with pleating beneath a wide band hugging her hips. "I thought you were spending the day with Mr. Chamberlain."

"I was." I look over my shoulder again to make sure he isn't nearby. "He was… I left."

"He got handsy, didn't he?"

A raw, creeping feeling slithered down my spine. "It probably wasn't the best idea to jump out in the middle of the city."

"No, that *was* the best idea." She shakes her head. "Perverted old rummy. I can't believe Madam Augustine made you go with him. If you call the boarding house, one of the guys will come pick you up. Really, they won't mind."

"Call? There's a phone?" My pulse hammers. There must be some kind of confusion; she can't mean the boarding house. Maybe the repairman finally fixed the one at The Den. "At the theater?"

"No. No one's at the theater today."

My vision tunnels. "There's a phone at the boarding house?"

Jackie blinks, her brow creasing. "Of course there is. It's in the alcove across from the dining room. Who told you there wasn't?"

I bare my teeth, a heat flushing through my body. "Augustine."

Jackie frowns. "I don't know why she'd tell you that. Haven't you phoned home? I know long distance is really expensive but under the circumstances…"

"Not yet," I clip. I promised Nik I wouldn't tell about the call. I don't know why Augustine would lie to me, but I don't like it one bit. After throwing me at Chamberlain, I shouldn't be shocked. I need to breathe, to think, before I make a rash decision.

"What are you doing here? Is Theresa with you?" I ask to change the subject.

"Goodness, no. She won't help with promotion."

She holds up a stack of fliers with *The Den* in big block letters. Beneath, a few of the bigger acts are listed. My name, in letters twice the size of the others, is at the top. They're marketing me as *Little Lina*. My nostrils flare.

Jackie splits the pile in two. "Do you want to help? The sooner we're done, the sooner we can get out of here."

"All right." I take one of the stacks, eying my stage name. I'm sure it wasn't Jackie's decision so I swallow my disdain and, for the first time, I'm glad Theresa thinks she's too good for something. "I just hand them to people when they walk by?"

She nods. "We usually hang them around town but Madam Augustine wants to get the word out about you. You ditching Mr. Chamberlain might work to our advantage. If the public sees you out here looking this cute, maybe they'll be more inclined to come."

"I wish she wouldn't use me as a selling point. I'm only staying until I have enough money to leave," I admit. I'll have to cash in whatever Augustine owes me. I'm not sure it will be enough yet but anything is better than nothing. "It makes me feel... I don't know. Indebted, maybe."

Jackie smiles at a man passing by and holds a paper out to him. "Don't think of it that way. If things go right, we'll get noticed before you're gone. We only need a foot in the door."

I pass a flier to a couple. "I hope you don't take this the wrong way, but I'm surprised you called out to me today. You didn't have to. I wouldn't have seen you otherwise."

She winces, her cheeks flushing. "Theresa's difficult if you don't agree with her."

"I got that impression." *When she turned an entire group of people against me for no reason.* Well, everyone except Nik. He doesn't seem to care about Theresa but someone else ensured his distance. "I swear I'm not trying to steal her spotlight. I wouldn't even be on stage if I didn't have to."

"I know, and I think she knows too." Jackie laughs nervously. "But, the attention I showed you is why she took things to such an extreme; we got into a fight about it after she saw you on the porch that day. She's convinced I'll find someone else. It happened with her last girlfriend so I suppose she assumes it will happen with me too."

"Girlfriend?" I look over at her, about to ask if she means dance partner, and pause. Her cheeks blaze and the look she gives a passerby lacks her genuine smile. "You're together?"

"I thought you knew. Nik didn't tell you? Oh God, I thought he did."

I shake my head. Theresa isn't worried about a temporary singer. She's worried her lover will leave her for the new girl.

"Please don't tell anyone," she says in a low rush. "Madam Augustine knows, and a couple others, but not everyone would approve."

"It's not my secret to tell," I assure her.

Minutes pass where we concentrate on the fliers. It's not my place to give her relationship advice, to tell her she deserves to be treated better, when my own love unraveled so easily. I had placed hope in Christian too and look where it got me. Nowhere fast, leaving my heart a shattered mess. Every breath aches in my tightening chest. I take a steadying gulp of air—I can't think about him right now.

A woman rushes up to us, shouting and dragging a man behind her. "It's you!"

"I… um…" I look to Jackie for help.

"It is! You're the singer at that vaudeville show. Can you sing a little something now? My husband doesn't believe me when I say you're going to be bigger than Ruth Etting."

Her eyes are wild with desperation, and I'm suddenly aware of all the others watching the scene. A real crowd has gathered without my noticing. There are no muscle men standing between us for protection here, though I'm not entirely convinced they would make a difference. The men and woman look on with lustful eyes, inching closer. I press against Jackie's side.

"I don't think that's a good idea."

Her fingers latch onto my arm. "Just a few notes?"

My patience for this day is about to break. The only thing keeping me from screaming is the growing closeness of the crowd.

Jackie shifts so I'm partially behind her and holds out a flyer. "You're welcome to come see the show."

A multitude of voices rise up, drowning out the woman's reply. She doesn't take the paper from Jackie, but reaches for me. Other hands follow. They scrape at my skin and dig at my clothes. There's tugging and screaming. A scuffle breaks out somewhere, but all my brain registers is the word *sing*. It sounds as if there are hundreds of voices instead of the dozen or so pressing in on us.

"Run," Jackie shouts, and yanks me away from them all.

I'm too dazed to do anything but allow her to lead me down different streets. The crowd follows. A few break off at a time, and the last man is only thwarted when Jackie shoves our way into a small café on a corner. When he walks past the window, bewildered, we both breathe a sigh of relief.

"Jackie?" I turn toward her, clutching the fliers I still carry against my chest. "What's the best way to book passage on a ship?"

She tucks her hair back into place while studying the people on the street. "I imagine going straight to the ticket office."

Which shouldn't be too hard to find.

"Are you okay?"

I nod. "Just a little shaken up, I suppose."

"We should make tracks before anyone else notices. Here—" She unpins her hat and sets it on my head. "Let's shake a leg."

"I'M STARVED," Jackie groans. Her arm links around mine as we head back to the boarding house hours later. "They better save us some dinner. Mitch says there's been nothing left when Nik gets back late. Poor fella must be wasting away."

I inhale to speak, then let the breath out. She might know what Nik's been doing, but I can't bring myself to ask. He kept her secret so it's not right to ask her to tell his. "They might save some for you," I say. "They probably think Chamberlain is feeding me caviar on a silver spoon tonight."

"Gross." She laughs, and I join her.

Later, when we get to the porch, I step away. "I'll wait here for a few minutes in case Theresa's still awake."

Jackie sighs, but doesn't argue. "It was nice spending time with you today."

"You, too."

"I'm sorry you had a scare. Symric magic is no joke, huh?" She tries her best to sound cavalier. According to Nik, her magic is common, though I disagree. The ability to manipulate light to create the splashes of color beneath the dancers' feet is remarkable. "See you tomorrow."

I give her a small wave. "Goodnight."

She disappears into the house, and I lean against the siding, rubbing my eyes. I'll sleep like a log tonight. *Maybe. Doubtfully. I'd like to.* First, I have to figure out a way to booby trap my room. I don't know why I didn't think to do it before. Walter can come back at any time, and now there's Chamberlain to watch out for. I can't venture to guess what he's capable of.

Maybe I should try calling someone else tomorrow if the phone is back at the theater. Someone can get word to my mother and—*the phone.* I leap away from the wall. Augustine doesn't know I know the boarding house has one and she'll never have to.

Everyone should be asleep by now, except Jackie, and I'm sure she won't tell if I use it. I inch the screen door open, slip inside, and tiptoe down the hall. I've never used the side door next to the kitchen, so I figure the alcove must be there since I haven't seen it before. Something creaks near the staircase and I pause to listen. When it doesn't happen again, I resume creeping through the house.

I slide into a tiny nook and stare at the device sitting on a round table. Never having made a call before, I lift the receiver and hold it to my ear. "Hello?" I whisper at the telephone. Nothing. *How do I work this thing?* Nik made it look so easy.

The screen door creaks open and I freeze. It's Walter or Chamberlain; it has to be.

I peek out of the alcove and shrink back as a shadowy figure steps off the porch. He's not overweight like

Walter, or frail like Chamberlain. I squint through the dim hall. *Nik?* He's leaving early tonight.

"What are you doing?" I murmur to myself.

Before I can talk myself out of it, I put the phone down and hurry after him.

CHAPTER 15

The heavy tarp covering the back of the slatted truck turns the bed into an oven. I huddle against the cab in a pool of sweat without any idea where we're going or how long Nik's been driving. He's up to something and, while it's none of my business, I want to know what's going on. I won't pretend it's right to follow him but I don't regret sneaking back here. I should, but I don't.

Curiosity kills the cat.

I hold my breath as the truck rolls to a stop and press myself as far back as possible. *Now what?* I can't just wait here where nothing is visible. This whole thing will be a waste of time if I get out too early and he sees me, but if I get out too late, I won't see which direction he went. I roll onto my stomach and inch to the side of the bed. Poking my fingers around the edge of the tarp, I create a peephole. Trees. Lots of trees and the corner of a building but nothing identifying.

"Hey." A man's voice comes from a few feet away, and

I duck back down. My heart pounds, thinking I've been caught. "How's it going?"

"Fine," Nik answers in a tight voice.

Gravel crunches right beside the truck and I drop lower.

"You all right with two stops tonight? My other driver bailed."

"Why?" I hear the hesitation in his voice.

"There's been some trouble on the other side of town. *Prohis* raided a couple joints." A soft chorus of chinking glass mixes with the man's rough voice. "Nothing to worry about. These are staying local."

Feet shuffle around to the back of the truck and my heart slams against my ribcage. Nik can't see me back here, but more importantly, the other man can't. Whatever this is about, I've changed my mind. I don't want to know. Nik's business is his business and I don't have any right snooping around. Nothing good can come from meetings after dark, especially ones that mention *trouble* and *nothing to worry about*.

"Maybe we should lay low for a few nights," Nik says. "Let the heat die down."

The man laughs. "Scared?"

"Cautious. I'm not keen to find myself in the big house."

"Relax." He taps on the side of the truck. "Open her up. I'll grab the other cases, and we'll get you loaded."

A set of feet crunch away from the truck, giving me what might be my only chance. Nik may be mad but he won't hurt me. I don't know anything about the other man. I scuffle down to the end of the bed. "Nik," I whisper. The tarp freezes mid-roll. "Nik, wait. I'm in here."

He peers in at me with wide eyes. "Lina?"

"I'm sorry."

"What are you doing?" he asks in a hushed voice. "How did you even… Have you lost your mind?"

"Yes." I swallow a lump in my throat. *I absolutely have.*

He looks over his shoulder. "Get back as far as you can. Don't make a sound, whatever you hear."

I scurry against the cab again and a gust of fresh air rolls over me as Nik opens the far end. A wooden crate lands with a thud, making the truck bob, and he shoves it against my side. Then another and another. There's barely enough space left for me to breathe. The corners dig into my skin, scratching at my stockings, but I don't move a muscle.

Boots crunch toward the truck again. "Six go to the usual stop," the man says. The truck bounces when more weight is thrown on. "The rest go here." Papers rustle. "The password tonight is prom-trotter. Ask for Tony."

"Got it." Nik pulls the tarp back in place and ties it down.

Locked in a tight, dark place, unable to move, my heart threatens to go into cardiac arrest and I pinch my eyes shut. This isn't the trunk. Walter isn't anywhere near me. Nik's driving and I'm here for my own safety. This is a truck, not a ship, not a trunk. It's not. Everything will be okay. It *is* okay. There are no locks and no drugs. This isn't the same. Nik's not Walter.

The tarp lifts above me and I wince. Nik stands on the rear tire well, looking down at me with fire in his eyes. I hadn't even felt the truck move.

"Mind telling me why you're hiding back here?" he asks.

I can't answer. My vocal cords refuse to cooperate. He reaches down to help me climb out from my slice of space. We're parked on the side of an empty stretch of road. The air is much cooler out from under the tarp and my teeth chatter. Nerves might play a part in it, too. The second my feet hit the ground, Nik lets go and hurries to cover the crates again. *See.* It's okay. I'm fine.

Nik turns to me, pulling the newsboy cap off his head, and runs a hand through his hair. "I thought you wanted to go home. Not an early grave."

"I—"

"We can't stay here," Nik says as he climbs behind the wheel.

I hurry in the passenger seat. "What is all this?"

"I need a minute," he says carefully. "I'm trying very hard not to be angry."

I bite down on my bottom lip. "I'm sorry. You said we

would talk then you got me to a phone and started ignoring me again. I just want answers."

"He would've bumped us off, you know." His voice is raw. "He handpicks his bootleggers and if he thought I was trying to sneak you in his barrel house, we'd both be goners."

"What is it? In the crates."

"What...?" Nik glances over me with a mixture of anger and confusion. "Hooch. What else would it be?"

"Hooch?"

He heaves an exasperated sigh. "Alcohol."

"Alcohol?" I blink rapidly. "Isn't that illegal?"

His chest jerks with a quick exhale. "Lina, if it were legal I wouldn't be smuggling it around in the middle of the night."

"But why would you be chosen for that?" A pianist in a vaudeville show isn't exactly prime outlaw material.

"Lord." He rubs his face and groans. "There's so much you don't know. I want to tell you but they watch me like a hawk."

"No one's watching now," I say.

"No, but I'm dropping you off at the edge of town. I can't take this stuff anywhere near the boarding house."

"Just take me with you. You can explain everything on the way."

He shakes his head. "I'm not going to be responsible

for getting you arrested. You have a mother to get home to."

I shrug and look out the side window. He's right though—I can't go to jail. "Why were you arguing with Augustine after our first show?"

"Lina." His hands tighten on the steering wheel. "Tomorrow, okay? If I say anything, I'll have to say everything and there's no time. I hoped you'd be gone before you had to worry about it, or at least, I'd be in a better place to help you but… tomorrow."

"A better place than what? The boarding house? Vaudeville?" I twist to face him and point at the crates. "Better than doing this?"

He rubs his face again. "You don't give up do you?"

"My mother says I'll squeeze water from a stone someday." It doesn't feel true now. I've been living in a corner for weeks. "I don't feel like *me* anymore," I say quietly. "It's like I'm living behind a glass wall and I can't break through."

Nik rubs his chin. "You've been through a lot. You can't expect everything to just fall back in place."

I don't things to go back to normal, not right away, but I thought once I was safe, it would get better. I'm not feeling particularly safe though. Augustine and Chamberlain expect me to be grateful, and I am, but not so grateful I'm willing to give up the last bits of myself, as tattered as they are. Between Walter, the troupe, and now Christian, my mother will be lucky to get back a lucid daughter.

"It's hard to stay positive when I'm by myself. No one talks to me." I hold back a groan. Even I hear the desperation in my voice. I'm not this person. "Actually, I left Chamberlain today and spent time handing out fliers with Jackie. It helped but tomorrow things will go back to the way they always are."

Nik pulls the truck over to the side of the road, the first row of houses a few yards away. "Tomorrow, okay?"

I look out the window at the dark streets and have no idea where the boarding house is amongst them. Fear gnaws at the back of my brain. Dark. It's so dark. Things hide in the dark. Things like Walter.

"Go straight until you get to the white house with ivy growing up the porch. Turn left and keep going until you see the boarding house. It will take about twenty minutes. Don't talk to anyone and walk as fast as you can without looking suspicious."

"Nik." My voice catches. Admitting I'm afraid of the dark is harder than I thought.

"It's relatively safe—safer than coming with me at any rate."

Relatively. Great. If I don't go, he'll sit here all night before he takes me with him. We haven't known each other long but there's no questioning his solid deter-mination.

"Tomorrow?" I ask.

"I promise." He reaches across the truck and shoves the door open."Go back and get some sleep."

I barely remember what sleep is anymore. For me, it's lying down inside a torture chamber and waiting for the pain to start. Sometimes it doesn't even wait until my eyes are closed to send the nightmares. Shadows crawl out of dark corners, inching along the room, leaving me curled into a ball, weeping. If those few hours when exhaustion wins count as sleep, I'll get right on it.

"Be careful," I say, slipping out of the truck.

He nods. "You too."

I wait until the red glow of the tail lights disappear before moving. Part of me can't believe he left, and another part is glad he did. If the people getting the deliveries are as bad as he claims the supplier is, he's doing me a favor.

The clicking of my heels against the sidewalk echoes around me. In all the time staring out my window, I never realized just how quiet the neighborhood is at night. I hug myself and inhale the warm breeze as it kisses my skin, letting it carry away my fears.

The ivy-covered porch comes up at the end of the block and I turn down the next street. *Halfway there.*

Movement flickers in my peripheral vision. It was large enough to be a person and came from the road I just turned off. I freeze but the street behind me is still.

I turn my back to the corner and shiver. I'm not wrong. Someone's there; I feel them watching me. I know I've thought it a thousand times, starting when Christian dropped me off after the dance, but I was right then. Walter was there. I walk faster, listening hard for footsteps behind me. *Relatively safe.* The shadow could've been someone that lives in one of the houses. Maybe they're watching me through a window to make sure I'm not up to anything. I should be out of sight by now though.

A tree creaks in the yard to my left. Forget trying not to look suspicious. I break into a run and don't stop until I'm on the porch of the boarding house. I swing open the door and leap inside. My lungs burn with each breath as I peek out of the sitting room window. Nothing moves save the gentle sway of branches. I wipe the sweat from my forehead with a shaky hand and back toward the staircase. I'm really losing it. If I wasn't destined for an asylum before, I will be soon if things keep going the way they are.

Better an asylum than dead.

I scramble up the stairs to my room and pull the dress boxes from beneath the bed, eyeing the ratty carpet bag hidden behind them. *The day after tomorrow.* That's when

I'll leave. After I talk to Nik, I'll ask him where the ticket office is and make a break for it. Digging out the twine that was tied around the brown paper boxes, I kneel in the middle of the floor and knot the short pieces together to make a rope.

CHAPTER 16

"*O*omph."

My bed shakes as something heavy hits the floor. I bolt up, adrenaline surging, and swallow a scream.

"It's just me," Nik grunts from the floor.

"You scared me to death." I blow out a breath and slump against the wall. My pulse isn't ready to settle down, still convinced I caught danger in my trap. At least I know it works. "What are you doing in here?"

He sits up, rubbing the side of his head. "Inspecting the floorboards. As one does."

"Sorry." I lean over and pick at the twine tied to the leg of the bed. It was a challenge to figure out what to attach the other end to. There was only enough to reach straight across so I had to drag the table away from the window.

"Is that a trip wire?" His voice is higher than usual.

"No." I huff because it clearly is. "Fine. Yes."

He laughs and mumbles something in another language. Whatever it means, he's obviously amused.

"They don't lock the door downstairs. Anyone could come in." I drop the twine and cross my arms, heat flooding my cheeks. "I would've warned you if I knew you were going to barge in here at the crack of dawn."

"The lock's broken, and it's a safe neighborhood." He stands and brushes himself off. "I am curious though. What were you planning to do if I were someone else?"

I scowl at him. I hadn't thought that far ahead. Jump over them before they could stand back up, probably. At least I wouldn't be caught unaware.

"Okay, okay." He presses his lips together but I see the smile fighting to be free. "Come on."

"What?" I squint out the window. Rehearsals don't start until noon today. Judging by the pale light outside, it's barely six.

Nik looks down at his shoes. "I promised you answers so get dressed and meet me downstairs."

I groan and fall back on the mattress. Sleep is an elusive creature, but I desperately want to know what he has to say so I push the blankets off and swing my feet to the floor. The grin he gives me before leaving sends a fluttering to my stomach.

The last time I felt anything similar was with Christian, and he's thousands of miles away, probably dazzling fellow socialites and planning his wedding to Cornelia Jonckheer. I exhale and shake the thoughts from my head.

Besides, I want to know what's going on here and there's only one way to do that: focus. I throw on the blue dress and spend a few minutes making myself presentable before going down to meet Nik.

He waits for me at the foot of the stairs with a large wicker basket in his hand. "What's that?" I ask.

He holds a finger to his lips to silence me and motions me outside. "Augustine's been into the absinthe again." A loud, crackling laugh streams from the dining room and we both stifle a chuckle "She thinks she's the only one awake," Nik whispers. "We've got until dinner before she notices we're gone. That stuff knocks her out for hours."

"We can't skip practice," I say when we hit the gravel at the bottom of the porch. "She'll kill us."

Nik speed walks down the street, not slowing until the boarding house is out of sight. "Don't worry about Augustine," he says. "Let her yell. What else can she do?"

If Augustine wants to punish us, she'll find a way. There might be a secret dungeon in the cellar for all I know. "Where are we going?"

"You'll see. It's not far." He reaches out nervously, looping his pinky around my index finger. "I may never have things in place before you need them to be and you deserve the truth before it's too late."

My blood runs cold at the seriousness of his voice. I'm not sure how much more I can take. "Why do I have a feeling I won't like our conversation today?"

"You probably won't, but you're better off knowing." He veers off the road and onto a dirt path. "It's possible we're trespassing."

Lovely. More illegal activity.

Nik stops in front of a rundown shack with broken windows and overgrown shrubs. He steps gingerly over fallen bits of wood and disappears behind the building. There's no way I'm following him back there.

"I think I'll turn back," I call.

Nik pops his head back into view. "You're missing out."

"I'll take your word for it."

"Come on," he pleads. "Trust me."

No.

But, against my better judgment, I do. If I'm smart, I'll never trust anyone again, ever. I will, of course, but at least I recognize the fault in myself now. I wince and pick my way through tall grass, careful not to step on any of the old boards or rusty nails hidden beneath. Nik steps through a slit in a rotting wooden fence. I follow.

On the other side, I stop mid-step. Bright pink climbing flowers cover the backside of the fence and tiny white petals dot the grass. A cluster of sunflowers grow near the back of the small enclosure and, from this side, it looks as if ivy is holding the shed up.

"What is this place?" I ask.

Nik shrugs and pulls a blanket from the basket. "I found it one day when I was looking for a bit of privacy."

The rest of the world is gone here, blocked out by nature. It's a little piece of home in a foreign country. I wish he'd shown me this before, but I can't blame him for wanting to keep it to himself. We barely knew each other—we still don't—but since the first time we practiced our song, I've felt connected to him. Somehow, he seems to understand in a way no one else does. Maybe it's because we both want something we can't find here but whatever the reason, I don't want to let it go until I have to.

He kneels on the blanket and reaches into the basket again. "Don't expect anything extravagant."

I sit beside him and kick off my shoes. The dew soaks slightly through the blanket beneath me. Tucking my feet underneath my legs, I peek inside the basket: a couple hunks of bread, two apples, and a small cheese wedge. My heart aches. "I ate this at home almost every day."

"Was your mother a good cook?" he asks.

"No." I laugh, remembering how awful her *hachee* is. Although, I've never had anyone else's stew—maybe it's supposed to taste like that. "But mostly, it's what we could afford."

He hands me a piece of the bread. "We survived an entire month on bean paste and cabbage once. Two months later, my mother begged my uncle to loan her the money to send me here."

For a chance at a better life, he told me. Being so wrapped up in my own problems, I forgot. "Have you heard from your mother lately?"

He shakes his head. "I don't really expect to. Not after —" He stops. "After I failed so miserably before even stepping foot on American soil."

"Failed?" I lower my brows.

"I guess we're going to get right down to it, huh?" He scratches the back of his head and looks away. "This isn't easy to talk about, but it's important you understand what you're dealing with here."

I lean back on my hands to watch him. A haunted expression spreads across his face, and I grip the blanket to stop myself from reaching out. "Okay," I say quietly. "My curiosity is piqued."

He jerks up straight, tossing his apple back into the basket. "I'd really rather not tell you this part—"

"You don't have to," I interrupt.

"I do," he says slowly. "I hope it doesn't change your opinion of me. Assuming you have a good one, that is." He gives me a wisp of a smile. "You did just catch me running booze."

"And then you made me walk home alone in the middle of the night." I don't mean it, but a flicker of regret passes over his expression. "I'm joking. Your past won't change anything." Unless it turns out he's also a kidnapping psychopath.

He grimaces. "When the ship my sister and I came here on docked, police came on board. One of the first-class passengers had their jewelry stolen. I don't know who did it, but the woman pointed her finger at me. I was seen running down the corridor at the time of the burglary, which was true, but only because I was lost and didn't want to get caught on the wrong floor. I was hauled off to prison and convicted."

"Without any evidence?" I ask a bit too loudly.

"It was their word against mine. There was no adult to keep me in line, I was fourteen and barely spoke English at the time. I did two years for it."

"That's terrible. Couldn't you amplify their compassion to help?"

"I can only amplify an emotion that's already there, and all they felt was anger toward me."

I can hardly judge him for something he didn't do, but the courts did… So many people turning a blind eye to my kidnapping makes more sense now. "I'm sorry."

He shrugs it off. "My sister, Flori, came to see me once. She wanted me to know she was continuing on to our friends in North Carolina and would wait for me there."

"Then why are you still here?"

"I had to earn enough money to get there first so I took a job at a factory." He picks one of the tiny white flowers and tosses it into the grass.

I wait for him to continue but he's quiet, plucking flower after flower. "What happened?"

Finally, he draws a steady breath. "About a month into the job my coworker, Charlie, asked if I'd drive him to the bank. His knee was acting up so it was hard to drive himself, he said, and he needed to withdraw some cash. Obviously, I assumed he meant from his account, but he robbed them. When he came running back to the car screaming for me to go, I thought someone else was in there with a gun so I did. It didn't take long for me to realize what he'd done and that I was an accomplice. With my prior record, I couldn't exactly explain it to the police. They don't like people like me to begin with and would never believe I'm innocent. I think Charlie knew about the time I served and that's why he asked me, thinking I would be okay with it." He pauses again. "Anyway, I got out of the car and ran as fast as I could before I could take the rap."

I look down at my lap. If I didn't know him, it would be hard to believe he knew nothing of his coworker's plan, but he has more character than that. He might not mind breaking the prohibition laws, but I would never peg him for a thief.

"I'm so sorry, Nik." I reach for his hand. There are small calluses there I never noticed before, but they're not so rough they grate against my skin. "Why don't you go find Flori now? I'm sure she misses you."

"I stopped writing her last year. I was too embarrassed that I let myself get in the same situation a second time." He squeezes my fingers. "I should've known better than to trust Charlie. He wasn't exactly a standup guy."

I inch closer to him and stretch my legs out so they're parallel to his. "That's ridiculous. How could you have known?"

He goes quiet again, tracing the checkered pattern of the blanket. A black and white chickadee lands on the fence near the sunflowers and wiggles his tail. It must be nice to be so free. To take off into the great big sky and go anywhere. If I had wings, I'd never be still. I'd see the world but it would be of my own choosing, and I'd always go home in the end. I'm sure Nik would too.

"Nik?" I ask, breaking the comfortable silence. He makes a low noise. It feels wrong to ask—his admission being so huge—but there has to be more he hasn't told me. "Is that what you wanted to tell me?"

"No." He sighs. "Charlie was shot a few days later by the police but they never found the money. He must've hidden it somewhere or given it to someone to hold. I have no idea."

"Oh…"

"And, now that I've got you wondering where this is going." He gives me a small smile. "Chamberlain saw me getting out of the car that day."

I gasp. "And he didn't turn you in?"

"He wants the money, and he doesn't believe I don't know where it is. If I hadn't agreed to work for Augustine, he would've had me thrown back in prison."

"What does Augustine have to do with it? And what does he want the money for? He's a coal baron."

Nik's soft laugh holds no humor. "No matter how rich he is, he'll want more. That's who he is—never satisfied. He forced me to take a job with the troupe so he could keep an eye on me. It was pure coincidence that I had magic—the plan was to keep me away from the others so I never found out. Like that's possible." He snorts. "Anyway, he expects me to lead him to the cash one day. If I try to run, he assumes it will be for the money."

"I'm going to meet every existing lunatic before I get home, aren't I?" I shake my head. "Does Augustine know he's blackmailing you?"

"She doesn't care what Chamberlain does as long as he keeps giving her financial support." His finger loops beneath my chin and turns my face toward him. "Augustine uses people to get what she wants. She preys on the less fortunate and people with something they wish to hide. If she knows your secret, you're trapped. Jackie and Theresa, me... you. Everyone in the troupe has a reason to stay. Besides magic, that is. Hiding in the open, in a show, might be the only safe place to use some of our gifts."

Reality slams down on my head like an anvil. I knew Augustine wasn't helping me out of pure compassion, but

I didn't expect her to be so calculating. I should have. She threw me at Chamberlain to keep him happy while I drew in a crowd for her show, and I've yet to see a single red cent. She has me in the palm of her hand with no intention of letting go.

"Oh, God." I lean forward and try not to give into the spinning sensation. "I'm never getting out of here, am I?"

Nik swivels, resting his hands on my arm. "You need to leave before she knows you're onto her. The troupe goes to Chicago in less than two weeks. If she thinks you're suspicious of her or that you plan on leaving, she'll do everything in her power to keep you."

"I *am* leaving," I blurt. "Tomorrow. I've got a bag full of food and a change of clothes already packed in my room. I stole a scarf and a pair of sunglasses from the theater to disguise myself. All I need is to find the ticket office, and I'll be on the next ship home."

"And money?" he asks. "You have money?"

I cringe. "I'm going to ask Augustine for my wages tonight."

"Do you still trust me?" he asks, his voice raw.

My stomach twists into a tight knot, squeezing. I'm going to be sick right here in the grass. "Of course I do."

"Then don't ask Augustine for anything." He leans back and tips his head up toward the sun. "Because I have a plan too."

"A plan?" A throbbing starts behind my eyes. *Don't cry, Lina.* There's a plan. "For what?"

"Getting us both out of here. Why do you think I risked those late-night runs? It pays well." He cracks his knuckles one at a time. "First, I have to get rid of my tail, but after that it shouldn't be too hard—"

"Your what?"

"They have me followed—"

"Someone's been following you?" My breath catches, my pulse banging in my ears. I spin around to face the shed. "Now? Are they here now?"

"No, no." He touches my cheek, guiding my face back toward him. "Everyone thinks we're at rehearsal, remember? It's safe."

Pressure pulsates behind my forehead. All those times I thought I saw a shadow, heard footsteps, or felt someone watching me, they could all be true. I'm not crazy. I cover my ears with my hands. How many times have I been in danger and pretended it was all in my head? From the first day, someone's always been there. I fight the black spots dancing in my vision and let his eyes ground me.

"Sorry. I just..."

"Don't apologize."

A sob worms its way to my chest. The last thing I want is to breakdown now. I'm still saving my big moment for after this nightmare is behind me. "I didn't want to give up on Christian, but everything just seemed so impossible for us. I had a weak moment when I left him, but I never thought he would abandon me like this."

"He's an idiot."

"How can he just leave me here?" I blurt, hot tears finally spilling over. "Even if he never loved me, even if he's engaged to someone else, how can he just *leave* me here?"

Nik winces. "I wish I had an answer for you."

It's not hard to understand, actually. So many people saw it coming. Now he doesn't have to be the bad guy for breaking things off. My kidnapping gave him an easy way out, and he'll even gain some sympathy. Who wouldn't want to comfort a heartbroken heir? Cornelia wasted no time at all tying herself to him. All he has to do is pretend I never wrote or called and he's free.

"Don't let him drag you down," Nik says quietly. "Keep being strong. You're a survivor, Lina Holt. You'll have the opportunity to give him a slap, I promise."

I'll give him more than a slap. I sniffle. Christian isn't worth another one of my thoughts. "Did you really risk going to prison again with the bootlegging to get us out of here?"

He pauses. "I've watched Augustine take advantage of a lot of people, but I can't let her do it to you." He scrubs his hands on his pants. "Wait until the next show. Augustine will give me what I'm owed after that, and we can leave together."

Another show. I'm not sure I can wait that long, not with everything I know.

"You might have to wait days for a ship to leave," he adds. "With my wages, I can help you get the ticket and find lodgings if you need them before I get on a train to North Carolina."

"Why?" I ask before I can think better of it. "Why do so much for me?"

He opens his mouth but he says nothing as his gaze drops to the blanket. Then, "Call it atonement for not helping you when I should have." His lips quirk. "Besides, you've grown on me."

Goosebumps prickle my skin. If Nik can go through everything he did and still be strong, so can I. "Okay. One more show."

Nik lets out a breath and lies down on the blanket. "Let's eat."

I laugh, feeling almost giddy at the thought of escape, and pass him an apple from the basket. "So, where did you get the scar on your eyebrow?"

"You noticed it?" His finger traces the small line. "When I was ten, Flori thought it would be funny to shave my eyebrows while I was asleep."

"Oh no."

He smirks. "Well, in her defense, I did cut one of her pigtails off with a pair of shears."

"Your poor parents."

"I'll say." He chuckles. "This one—"

Nik pushes up on his elbows and I freeze. His face is so close I can see each fleck in his light green eyes. The air thins in the few inches between us, drawing me closer. He glances at my lips and just as I'm sure he's about to kiss me, he draws a sharp breath. A flush creeps up my neck, but I can't tell if it's relief or disappointment coiling inside me.

"We should get back," he blurts, hopping to his feet.

CHAPTER 17

However awful the truth, knowing Nik had my back allowed me to sleep soundly for the first night in forever. All thoughts of Christian, of home, seem to have vanished from my mind, and I ease onto the floor of the practice room. I *will* get back to Holland, but to do that, I have to focus. Zero in on the right-here-right-now.

Chester crawls into my lap, and I scratch behind his ear. His nails dig through my skirt while he gets comfortable. I don't mind—the affection is nice after dealing with Theresa's death stare all day. When his head rests on my arm, his breath hot against the crook of my elbow, I want to hug him tight. Maybe I can talk my mother into getting a dog. Something big that can protect me.

I lean my head against the wall and run my fingers across Chester's wiry fur. Before long, his head tilts and he goes limp against me. The smallest snore rises from him, and I grin.

"Hey," Will shouts. He rushes through the doorway,

huffing as if he just finished running a race. "Something happened."

Props clatter to the floor as the troupe crowds around him, pummeling him with questions. I lift Chester from my lap and strain to hear Will speak over the voices when the room erupts with cheers and shrieks, bouncing and hugging.

"Did you hear that?" James grabs Etta, swinging her around, and laughs. "We did it," he yells. "We did it."

Nik slips inside, skirting around the excitement and stands beside me with a solemn face. "This is bad."

"Why? Everyone seems happy. What's going on?"

"We booked the Orpheum." He crosses his arms and studies everyone celebrating. "Chamberlain got someone to watch the show last week."

I lick my lips. "That's good for them, isn't it?"

"For them, yes." He gives me a pointed look. "The troupe leaves for Chicago a week early. The next show at The Den will be our last. We won't have time to leave after the performance."

"I can't go to Chicago," I whisper. "My deal with Augustine was to stay on in New York."

"This is the *Orpheum*." He rubs his chin. "If we go to Chicago, we'll never get out."

Three loud bangs cut through the merriment. Augustine stands in the doorway, slamming her cane down, beaming. "Congratulations," she cheers. "We're finally achieving our dreams." There's a round of applause. "Enjoy yourselves tonight because tomorrow we'll work on beefing up your acts. Lina." She crooks a finger in my direction. "Office, please."

A few glares shoot in my direction but they're mostly too excited to care I'm getting special attention. Except Theresa. Any trace of a smile disappears from her face. I'm truly sorry she isn't responsible for the newfound greatness. I'd give anything for it to be her glory instead of mine.

Nik touches my arm, holding me back. "She can't suspect anything."

"I know." There are still holes in the plan, ones we thought there was time to fill, but she'll smell the mere idea of it if I'm not careful. "She probably wants me to apologize to Chamberlain for jumping out of his car. She needs his money more than she needs me."

I wish that last part was true but his money never booked them a huge gig before.

Nik glances at Augustine over my head. "You better hurry."

"Wait for me?" I squeak.

"Of course."

I purse my lips and start for the stairs, unsure how I'll force out an apology. Chamberlain doesn't deserve one and Augustine knows it. She has to be aware of Chamberlain's intentions, but his advances are likely good news to her. It's another way to keep me around. To secure her source of money. Why wouldn't I jump at such an offer? I frown at her back. Because, unlike her, I'm not a fortune hunter. My mother taught me to value myself and, unlike other lessons, that one stuck.

"Hello, dearest." Chamberlain guides me through the office door by the elbow. "Isn't it wonderful? The Orpheum is a real treat."

There's that word again. *Treat.* I'm not sure he understands the meaning, but I bob my head in agreement. "Everyone's very excited." *Almost* everyone.

"It's all because of your angelic voice. You must be very proud."

He sips his glass and I wonder who delivers their alcohol. Are they in a bad place like Nik? I swallow, looking away. "Thank you, Mr. Chamberlain, but I can't take the credit alone."

"Yes, yes." He presses my elbow until I follow him further into the room. "The others have some merit. And please, call me John."

If the troupe is as mediocre as Chamberlain seems to think, it can't be worth the investment. I've seen them, heard them, and they can hold their own without me. They drew a crowd before I showed up and they'll draw one when I'm gone. A theater isn't going to book an entire troupe for one act.

"Sit," Augustine says. "I'd like to discuss something with you."

Here it comes. My fingernails dig into my palms and I sit, rigid, on the edge of the chair. "If this is about the other day, I won't apologize."

Augustine and Chamberlain exchange a quick look before laughing.

"You're a real live wire." Chamberlain clears his throat. "No, that day was my fault. I should've taken your situation into consideration before speaking ill of the less fortunate. Although, in the future, you'll need to control your temper and use better judgment."

My jaw clamps down until my teeth hurt. Two back-to-back insults and judging by the smug look on his face, he doesn't even realize it. If he only knew how much fury I'm holding back from them, he wouldn't be telling me to control my temper. I focus on my breathing. In and out. Steady. Calm. I won't win against them in a head-to-head battle so I have to bide my time. One day, maybe two, is all Nik and I have.

"Then, you want to talk about Chicago?" I ask in my most relaxed voice possible.

"Chicago?" She puckers her lips. "What about Chicago?"

I square my shoulders and clasp my hands together before my nails draw blood. I have to be careful how hard I press the next issue. "About my wages before you leave.

I'm not sure how much I've made, but even if it's not enough to book passage home, it's a start." I had to do it. Not asking would be strange since our agreement was for me to stay on in New York.

Augustine laughs again, her hand clutching the arm of the chair. "Wages? You haven't covered your expenses yet."

Expenses? No one mentioned expenses… I summon every ounce of my courage and plow ahead with the act. If I'm careful, she won't suspect anything. "You said all I had to do was ask for it."

"Yes." She taps her fingers over her lips. "Which is still true. Once you pay back what was spent on you, there's nothing to keep you from collecting. You have new clothes, a room, food, and there was that doctor we called in when you fainted. You won't be making a profit until next season at the earliest."

Heat creeps up my spine and explodes at the base of my neck. *Manipulative* is too kind a word to describe her. Had Nik not filled me in, I would be dumbfounded. I wish he'd told me sooner. We could've worked together long before this. "It will take me a year just to repay the cost of the lace dress alone."

"That one was rather expensive." She fiddles with the top of her cane. "Be glad I'm not charging interest. I know you're in a bad place."

"A bad place?" My voice rises. *Calm down.* Remain

compliant with just enough anger to make it believable. Our escape depends on it. "This was your plan all along, wasn't it?"

Chamberlain's hand covers mine. "You sound like an ungrateful brat, dear."

"Ungrateful?" My laugh is more of a high-pitched shriek. The words keep coming and I can't stop them. "My chances were probably better with Walter than the pair of you. At least he was upfront about his intentions. You're just using me to get people addicted to your show!"

"I have enough trouble with employee attitudes," she snaps. "I won't tolerate it from you too."

I glare at her, my mouth hanging open. If anyone has a right to a bad attitude, it's me. Others here might not have a lot of options, but they *have* options and that's what counts.

"Now, we've discussed things." She motions to Chamberlain. "It was brought to our attention that you weren't at practice yesterday, and we feel it's necessary you don't go off on your own anymore."

"And by that, we mean anywhere with Mr. Sala." Chamberlain pats my thigh. "It isn't good for a lady's reputation."

"Or your fair skin," Augustine adds. "I haven't once seen you wear the hat we gave you and I can't very well put a lobster up on stage."

A wave of fire washes over me, sweeping away the lies I'm supposed to humor them with. "You can't tell me where to go or who to be friends with. You're not my parents, and I'm not your property."

I move to stand but don't make it more than an inch off the chair before Chamberlain's fingers dig into my shoulder. I suck in air as sharp pain radiates down my arm.

"You'll learn to bite that tongue, or I'll cut it out," he warns.

"Really?" I narrow my eyes, feeling much braver than is likely good for me. "Go ahead. Cut it out. I can't sing without it."

His grip tightens, and I clamp down on the inside of my cheek to stop from crying out. "Once I'm your husband, you'll learn I have no tolerance for disobedience."

"Husband?" A laugh bursts out before I can stop it. "Now I know this is a joke."

Augustine moves quicker than I've ever seen before. Her hand lands on my cheek with a crack, stinging my skin. "You'll marry him, or you'll be on the street without a red cent."

"I'd rather be on the street," I hiss.

I tear my arm away from Chamberlain. If they hadn't gone too far before, they have now. I fly out of the room and down the stairs before they can utter another word.

Marry him? He's off his rocker. Bolting from the car in the middle of New York City should've kicked the idea out of his head. They can't force me to the altar and if they try I'll tell the world what's happened to me. It doesn't matter if there are consequences for me. Bile rises in the back of my throat. There would be problems for Nik though.

I slam into Theresa's at the bottom of the stairs, sending us both straight into the wall. We fall to the ground in a heap. My body slumps across her lap but my head bounces off the floor. Lights dance in my vision.

Theresa shoves me aside with an ear-piercing shriek. I scramble to my feet, grabbing at the smooth wall to keep myself from tumbling back down.

"What the hell are you doing?" She cradles her elbow. "Trying to ruin our big break?"

"No," I mumble. Her face is blurry.

"I bet you were." She steps so close I feel the heat radiating from her. "You were trying to break my legs so I couldn't steal your thunder. And I will, you know? Our new act will be—"

"What happened?" Jackie skirts around us and pulls Theresa away from me. "I heard screaming. Are you okay?"

Theresa leans into her girlfriend and watches me. "My elbow," she whimpers.

"Theresa, I'm sorry." I crush my eyelids shut to stop

the hall from spinning. It doesn't work. "I was going too fast and didn't see you there." In my defense, it's impossible to see around the corner when you're on the staircase, no matter how fast you're moving.

"A likely story," she snaps. "You've hated me since you got here."

I've hated her? We haven't spoken a word to each other when she got it in her head to set everyone against me. I'd say as much if I thought it would help the situation but it most definitely wouldn't.

"Hey now." Nik slides an arm around me. "That's enough."

"Always sticking up for your little whore, Nik," Theresa shouts. I blanch at her insult. "She just drove me into the wall. How is that my fault?"

"It's not, Terr. It was an accident," Jackie says gently.

"Whose side are you on?"

"Come on," Nik whispers. He leads me down the hall, away from the building argument, and into an empty dressing room. "What happened?"

"I ruined everything." I wrap my arms around him, desperate and afraid. What if we can't get away now? "They made me so mad, I couldn't keep quiet."

He leans back to scan me over. When he's apparently satisfied I'm okay, he asks, "Did you tell them we were planning to leave?"

"No, of course not."

"It can't be that bad then." He guides me back into the hug I so badly need. "What did they say?"

I hesitate. He should know but I don't want him rushing up to the office to beat Chamberlain to a pulp. It'll be a one-way ticket to prison. "If we're going to leave, it has to be now." I lift my head and look him in the eyes. "*Right* now. Chamberlain proposed. Well, he didn't pose it as a question exactly, but we have to get out of here."

Augustine bursts inside the empty room. Her lips are pressed so thinly, they've all but disappeared as she glares at us from beneath lowered brows. "The cars are ready."

Nik pulls away, leaving me cold. "We're coming."

That's it; the window for escape just slammed shut. But there are more ways to rid a house of vermin. I ball my hands into fists. Tonight my sleeplessness will be put to good use.

"Soon," Nik mouths when Augustine turns her back.

I nod, my head throbbing with the motion. Sooner than he thinks.

CHAPTER 18

My mother told me the only things I deserve are the things I earn. Well, dang it, I've earned this money ten times over. If Augustine hadn't tried to play me I might've cut my losses and left without taking my share, but she lied from the beginning. She probably never mailed my letters either. If I didn't talk to Mrs. Van Buren, I would still be waiting for help but now it's time to save myself. Which is why I spent last night moving about the house, memorizing every loose and creaky floorboard in preparation for a silent escape.

A fast-paced melody from Gus's saxophone drifts up from the stage. I spin the heavy dial on the office safe slowly, my palms coated in sweat, and wait to feel a slight catch. I may have underestimated how difficult cracking the combination would be. Luckily, Augustine is still at the boarding house with her absinthe so I have more time before anyone notices I'm gone.

My knees absorb the vibrations of the floor as the band rehearses below, and I strain to hear if anyone is coming down the hall. I wouldn't put it past Theresa to send someone up here to spy on me, or to come herself in hopes of catching me red-handed. The manager was lurking around earlier too, but I haven't seen him in a few hours.

"Come on," I growl quietly and slam my palms against the cool steel. "Open."

I breathe heavily through my mouth, fighting back angry tears. There isn't enough time for this thing to be so difficult. I wipe my palms on my blue skirt and resume spinning the dial. Why couldn't Augustine be forgetful enough to need the combination written down? There's a slight hitch in the smooth motion of the knob and I jerk back before I pass notch nineteen. Two more to go. The first one only took fifteen minutes.

I massage my temples, battling the remains of last night's headache. Getting no more than an hour of sleep didn't help the pain, nor did it help plan something as dangerous as this. With twitching fingers, I lean in and turn the dial to the left.

A soft clunk rises above the music. I leap to my feet and press my back to the safe as if it could hide what I was doing. "Nik?" I exhale. He leans against the closed door with wide eyes. "What are you doing up here?"

He sprints across the room. "I could ask you the same thing."

"Don't worry about it." I glance over my shoulder at the safe. With his history, the last thing he needs is to get roped into this part of my scheme. His involvement comes later.

He narrows his eyes. "You're trying to break into the safe, aren't you?"

"What?" I laugh but it's too high-pitched to be believable. "I'm just looking for something I left here."

He crosses his arms and a piece of gelled hair falls out of place. "Really? What?"

"My..." I exhale sharply. "Just go back to rehearsal and pretend you never saw any of this."

"Like that's possible." He scowls, his nostrils flaring. "I'm not letting you go down this path. Augustine may not be here today but that doesn't mean you won't get caught. What do you think will happen when they find the safe is short?"

"Recount it." I force a smile. It doesn't matter to me what they do. We'll be long gone before they get a chance to go over the books.

"If you steal their money and run off, you'll be pointing the finger at yourself better than anyone else ever could. And trust me, they *will* be pointing. And not just at you."

A stone settles in my stomach. I doubt Chamberlain will overlook his money being taken. Especially not by someone he's blackmailing. That makes it all the more important that we don't waste any time getting out of here.

Nik steps around the desk. "You're asking for trouble, Canary. Come downstairs and forget about all this." He holds out his hand, but I don't take it. "Trust me. This isn't a path you want to go down."

"I know it's not," I hiss. "But I have to do something. Chamberlain wants to marry me, remember? I'm—"

The floor creaks outside the office and we both freeze. When the knob turns, my heart plummets, my feet rooted to the floor. Nik takes a step away with wild eyes. Chamberlain stands in the hallway in his velvet jacket and black pants. A fedora hangs from one hand. With the other, he pushes his round glasses up his nose, blinking behind the thick lenses.

"Miss Holt." Surprise laces voice. "What are you doing in here?"

I open my mouth but no words come out. What reason could I possibly have to be in the office? And with Nik of all people.

"I can't let you do it," Nik shouts at me. He steps in front of me and raises his eyebrows, pleading silently for me to go along with him. "You can't marry him."

"Nik," I shriek. "What—"

He grabs my arm, squeezing. "I know you think it's a good idea."

Chamberlain slams the door shut. "What is this?"

"You really burn me up, Chamberlain." Nik turns to

face him. "I knew you were entitled but proposing to a girl young enough to be your granddaughter?"

"Remember your place, Mr. Sala. Remember what I can do to you," he replies calmly.

"How could I forget?"

Chamberlains eyes flick over Nik's shoulder to mine. "It sounds like you're reconsidering?"

I nod, too stunned Nik threw me to the wolves to do anything else.

"Out," he barks at Nik. "Now."

Nik walks around the sitting area with squared shoulders. The silence weighs heavy as he leaves, freezing me in place, and when he slams the door behind him, the wood shudders.

I hesitate, cursing Nik, and motion to the desk. "I was looking for your address to pay you a visit this afternoon. Nik followed to stop me." There's no choice but to play along now.

Chamberlain tosses his hat on a stack of papers and unbuttons his jacket. I step back, my jaw tight, and fight the urge to fly out the door after Nik.

I'll strangle him for this.

"I'm here now," he says. "What would you like to speak with me about?"

I swallow hard and force a smile. An engagement is something I should be glad about. *Happy. Be Happy.* This is supposed to be one of the greatest days of my life and if

I want to get out of here without Chamberlin sensing the lie, I have to act like it. "About last night," I say. My voice wavers. I sing—I don't act and he's surrounded by people who can do a daily basis. My deception will be paper thin. Dropping my gaze, I hope he mistakes my flushed cheeks for embarrassment instead of my rising outrage. "I'm truly sorry for my reaction. You caught me off guard and I apologize."

"Well," he mumbles.

He pulls the books away from the hidden decanter and fumbles with a glass, nearly tipping it over. It doesn't take long before he recovers enough to pour himself a drink and step up beside me again. "I must take partial blame. I thought my intentions were clear, but I underestimated how innocent you are. It must have given you quite a shock."

I place a hand on his sleeve. The red velvet is sandpaper beneath my fingers. The trick to lying is to stick to the truth as much as possible, especially if you have to make it up at the last second. "My mother warned me men sometimes take advantage of girls."

He places his hand over mine. "Your mother is a smart woman. However, I'm far too old to be playing games. There are things I need in life and I'm getting up in years."

"Mr. Chamberlain," I start.

"John, please."

"John." I yank his name from my throat. "I have to admit, I'm nervous. It's a big commitment."

He laughs. "The thought of marriage makes all young girls anxious. Especially if the man is much older, but I assure you, you will want for nothing. Anything you want will be yours. I understand it's a hard concept to grasp but I have enough money to buy you a new dress for each day of the year. Jewels. A room full of pianos, if you wish it."

I look down to hide the flash of anger on my face. Why would I need a constant supply of new dresses? And I've never played a piano in my life. "Thank you," I say.

TEN MINUTES and a thousand promises later, I exit the office as Chamberlain's fiancée and storm into the practice room. I'm so angry I can barely see straight as I scan the room for Nik. I find him at the back, behind Pearl and Ben, talking to Tommy. They lean over a sheet of paper and Tommy snaps his fingers in quick succession.

"Gus should have a solo," he says.

I grab Tommy's fingers before he can snap again and glare at Nik. "Can you give us a minute, please, Tommy?"

"Sure thing, Dollface." He backs up, winking at Nik. "Don't be too hard on the lug."

I stare Nik down, not speaking, until Tommy's a few

feet away. His expression is tight, his eyes dull. "What was that?" I whisper. "Are you dipping into your nightly deliveries? Is that an added perk of your night job?"

"Hush." He looks over his shoulder. "Don't say that so loud; you aren't the only dry person in here. Besides, I quit the day after you followed me."

"Swell," I screech. "So what's your excuse then? Temporary insanity? It seems to be going around."

He steps closer until he's an inch from my face. I want to step back but my pride won't allow it. "You're welcome," he says.

"Yes to the insanity then?"

He presses his lips together and takes a shallow breath. "It was the best excuse I could come up with."

"If that's your best excuse, I'd hate to see your worse."

"Listen, we were alone in the office." He steps closer and lowers his voice. "If we didn't have a good enough reason, something to distract him, the first thing he would've assumed was the truth. Only instead of thinking I was trying to talk you out of it, he would've thought I was the mastermind."

His eyes burn into mine and I see the truth there. He panicked like I did, but he was able to recover in time to save us both. It doesn't change the fact that Chamberlain is upstairs planning our nuptials as we speak.

"I'm not going to marry him," I say. "I won't do it."

The corners of his mouth lift in a bitter smirk. "Canary, if I thought you were, I'd kidnap you myself."

"I'm glad it's so easy for you to laugh about this." I push past him, blood boiling, and storm from the practice room.

"Canary, wait," he calls. "*Lina.*"

Ignoring him, I move faster, desperate to be alone somewhere I can scream.

CHAPTER 19

The silence of the boarding house pulses in my ears; each groan in the walls twists my stomach a little tighter. Everyone's been asleep for hours. Everyone except me. Any moment now, the grandfather clock downstairs will chime four times and it will be time to go.

Bong.

I take a long, shaky breath. Pushing the covers off, I fling my feet to the floor, still wearing a pair of nylon stockings. I shake out the skirt of my pink dress and pull my hair back into a messy braid.

Bong.

My heart threatens to pound out of my chest. It was a mistake to try stealing from the safe, but a mistake I would make again. If I could do things over, the only thing I would change is the end result. Chamberlain's arrogance made my lies easy for him to believe but there's absolutely no way I'll go through with the engagement. Penniless or not, I'm leaving now.

Bong.

I grab my shoes from under the bed and tiptoe to the door. I'm leaving the supplies—they'll only slow us down. We'll have to move fast for this to work. My hand shakes as I reach for the handle.

Please let Nik agree to come along. My anger from earlier at the theater is forgotten. In fact, I'm grateful. Without the push, I might have kept delaying until I had money and I'll likely never have any here. I'll go on my own if necessary but I really don't want to.

Bong.

It's officially four. I inhale, holding the air in my lungs while I slip into the hall. *I can do this.*

I creep across the hall to Nik's room and slip inside without knocking. Silence is essential when making a getaway. If I learned anything by sneaking out to meet Christian, it's that.

With Nik's curtains shut against the full moon, I spare a moment for my eyes to adjust to the darkness of the room. When they do, I make out his outline beneath a dark sheet. He's lying on his side, facing the wall, with one bare arm on top of the covers.

Please be wearing pants.

"Nik," I whisper. He shifts but his eyes remain closed. "Nik. Wake up."

He grunts and rolls on his back. "It's morning already?"

"Get up, would you?" I shake his shoulder until his eyes fly open.

"Lina? What are you doing in here?"

"We're leaving." I squint around the dark room until I find the blue dress shirt he wore earlier crumpled on the floor. Snatching it up, I toss it in his direction. "I can't stay here anymore. It's been too long already and things have gone too far."

The bed groans under his weight as he sits up and the sheet slips around his waist. Heat blossoms in my cheeks at the sight of the toned muscles in his chest and stomach, but it's the large wing tattooed over the left side of his chest that holds my attention. He hurries to pull a sleeveless white shirt on over his head, then slips the dress shirt on over it. "Have you thought about this?" he asks in a rush. "We haven't even checked the ship schedule yet."

"It's all I've thought about." I ball my hands into fists against a shudder. "There's no other choice. I'm leaving now before Augustine or Chamberlain can stop me."

"Mind turning around?" He leans over the bed and grabs his pants. I spin to face the wall, my blush spreading down my neck, and fabric rustles behind me. "All right."

When I turn around again, he's pulling suspenders over his shoulder. "I know it's dangerous for you to come. Chamberlain could turn you in and the authorities would be on your tail, but you can't stay here forever either. You want to leave too so why not now?"

"Why not," he echoes. He kneels beside the bed and presses on a loose floorboard. It shifts and he picks it free, reaching into the hole. A moment later, he has a handful of neatly folded bills inside a silver clip. "I should still have enough without my pay to get us both a train ticket."

My breath catches but I don't want to make assumptions. This whole plan might crumble without him. "Does that mean you'll come?"

"Well, I'm not going to let you run off on your own." He shoves the money in his back pocket, grabs his shoes, and stands. "We'll go to Grand Central and take the first train to North Carolina. We can stay with my sister until we figure things out."

"North Carolina?" That's further away from Holland than New York is. It seems counterproductive to run in opposite direction.

"Just for now." He hurries around the room, grabbing his jacket and hat. "I know it's not where you want to go, but if I'm going to leave, I have to get straight out of New York." He meets my eyes in the dark. "I can't stay. They'll find me."

There's a gleam in his eyes, both nervous and excited, and I can't bring myself to take it away. The important thing is leaving—my final destination doesn't have to be the same as Nik's. If I'm with him, I'll be safe long enough to earn passage home. *Really* earn it, not dig myself deeper into trouble.

"I'll get you home as soon as I can," he adds. "I swear it."

I nod. "Okay. Let's go."

He smiles, letting out a breath, and cracks his bedroom door open. After peering into the hall, he steps out with me right behind. We slink along the wall. My palm runs over the textured wallpaper, feeling every bump and groove.

The top step creaks under Nik's weight and we both stop. "Let me," I whisper. My heartbeat echoes in my ears, making it impossible to hear anything as I slip in front of him. "Step where I step." I move slowly, supporting some of my weight with my hands against the walls, and step in certain places on certain stairs. Some I skip completely, just like I practiced.

Finally, we reach the landing and I breathe a sigh of relief. I step toward the door and pause. The screech of screen door slipped my mind. "Should we go out through the kitchen?"

Nik shakes his head. "We'll hit loose floor boards between here and there, and then the back door is just as bad. If we open it slowly and just enough to get out, we'll make it."

I'm not so sure about that. Screen doors are tricky.

Even opening it slowly, the spring will make a popping noise. But no one ever came running when Nik crawled in and out for his bootlegging runs so there's a chance. He has more riding on this than I do—prison is a lot worse than marriage to Chamberlain. If we're caught, I'll still have a choice. They can drag me to an altar but they can't make me say *I do*. Nik won't be given an option about jail.

For every second the door inches forward, it seems like a million of them pass. I hold my breath and glance between the door, the hallway, and the staircase. Finally, Nik presses himself against the doorframe and ducks onto the porch. He's wider than I am, so it's not surprising how easy it is to slip out after him. It takes Nik another minute to shut it behind us then he jumps to the lawn to avoid the stairs. His socked feet land quietly on the grass and he turns with his arms held out, dropping his shoes. I throw mine down beside his and jump without a second thought. Nik catches me under my arms, setting me gently down beside him.

Taking a second to shove our feet into our shoes, we sprint across the lawn and down the street.

We don't slow down until sweat pours down my face and my lungs scream. He seems to be holding up better than I am with only slightly labored breathing. It sounds like I'm dying.

"We can't stop," I wheeze. The prick of watchful eyes burn at my back, but when I turn, the street is empty.

Nik bends down and grabs his knees, gulping air. "I know."

The boarding house is behind us but it's not enough. We still have to make it to Grand Central before dawn, which seems nearly impossible now that we're out here. The walk home with Jackie took hours, and we weren't far from the station. Even if we continue at this pace without stopping, it will take at least two hours. I steel myself to run again because there's no choice.

I wipe my forehead with the back of my hand. "Do you know the way?"

"Yes."

We reach for each other's hand at the same time and take off toward the bridge leading to the city. Our pace is slower this time and more manageable. There will be plenty of time to rest once we're on our way to North Carolina.

I UNDERESTIMATED THE JOURNEY. Instead of two hours of running, jogging, and stopping for air, it takes nearly three before Grand Central Station is in view. The white building rests between two taller ones but it's by far more appealing with its massive arched windows, decorative columns, and elaborate clock. The mere sight of it makes me want to collapse right there in the street. My throat burns and my muscles quiver, but we made it. The sky is already bluish-gray and we can't risk missing the first train. I lock my knees and try to still my quaking body.

"You okay?" Nik rasps.

I draw in air like I've just spent an eternity under water. "I will be as soon as we're on the train."

We stagger across the street and through a set of glass doors. The brilliance of it makes me stumble. Arched windows, polished stone staircases, and a golden orb with four clock faces over an information kiosk. It's more like stepping into a palace than a train station. Nik tugs me toward the ticket windows before I can take everything in.

"The next one leaves in forty minutes," he says.

"So long?" Really, I'm glad it isn't longer.

"By the time we buy tickets and make our way to the terminal, it will feel like no time at all." He sounds confident but he's blinking rapidly. His pupils are blown wide and he keeps darting glances at the exits. I press closer. "Why don't you get cleaned up while I go up to the counter? It might be better if the teller doesn't see us together," he says gently. "In case anyone comes asking."

"Good idea." I pause, gathering my strength to make the short walk to the washroom.

"I'll wait over there." He plucks a curl off my temple

and points to rows of double-sided wooden benches with a few weary looking travelers. Small suitcases with worn edges and a round hat box sit by their feet. An older woman clings to a leather travel bag with gloved hands.

"Okay." I sink my teeth into my bottom lip to direct the pain away from my legs.

Everything seems to move slowly through my haze, but I manage to make my way to a white porcelain sink. The cold water I splash on my face steals my breath, but doesn't help shake the fatigue.

My gaze drifts up to the girl in the mirror. I barely recognize myself looking back. Gone are the soft edges and playful spark in my eyes. I'm broken. But, I'm not alone and I'm safer than I've been since Walter took me. Even if someone discovers we're missing this very moment, the chances of them finding us on time are slim. I pat my hair into place the best I can and splash more water on my neck. It doesn't help much—I still look like a hot mess—but it's as good as it's going to get.

NIK WAITS right where he said he would. Something white pokes out of his shirt pocket as he leans over his knees, his head bent. A warm sensation fills my center. He has done nothing but protect me, even with his hands tied. Maybe I've asked too much of him. If he didn't pay for my ticket, he'd have enough money to live for a few days, at least, regardless of finding a job or his sister. If he had waited just a little longer, a better way for him to disappear might present itself. This may be my only chance but is it his?

"Nik?" I ask quietly.

He slides over so I can sit between him and the armrest. Pulling the tickets from his pocket, he runs a finger over the dark ink. "We have to change trains in Pittsburgh but it gets us out of here."

My body dissolves into a pile of goo when I sit beside him and my legs shake uncontrollably. "Are you sure this is a good idea?" I whisper so the women on the other end of the bench don't hear.

"Am *I* sure? This was your plan." He peeks over at me with a weary expression. "But, yes. I'm sure. We can make it."

"I know we can. But... It's just... I'm not sure it's right to ask so much of you."

"I want to be here, Canary. It's my choice." He leans into me and rests his cheek on top of my head with a yawn. "We're in this together."

This time it's not just a phrase to show he's support- ive. We *are* in it together now and there's no turning back. "Right."

"Don't sound so enthused," he jokes.

I nudge him with my elbow. "If I had to choose anyone to have this adventure with, it would be you."

He laughs. "An adventure, is it?"

I wave my hands, drawing a circle through the air. "One so epic they'll tell tales of it for years and years."

He chuckles into my hair. "I hope our story ends well enough to be told."

"Nik," I say, my voice coming out as a puff of air. I ache for him; for both of us. "You're supposed to be the optimistic one. Leave all the worrying to me. I've become an expert these last months."

He straightens his legs out in front of him. His hands shake as he rubs at his knees. "It might suit us better to be realistic until we're safe."

I swallow against a lump in my throat. Walter will always be looming in the shadows for me. There will always be an Augustine trying to use me and a Chamberlain trying to own me. It's no wonder my mother prefers to stay away from people. People like Christian will never be in short supply and it's too hard to find someone like Nik. It's impossible to know who will hurt you and who will stick by you. One day I hope to tell the difference but for now, I choose to stick with the handsome fugitive with too much kindness in him.

"How much longer?" I ask after a long silence.

"Not long." He stands with a grunt and rubs at his thighs. "We should head to the platform."

I follow him closely, a yawn bringing tears to my eyes. It won't take long to fall asleep once we get moving and it scares me how deep it will be. People can't run on empty forever. They can only pretend to, and I'm tired of pretending.

A cold wave rushes over me, like being dunked in ice water. I know the sensation too well. "Nik?" I press into him and look over my shoulder. "I think we're being watched."

He wraps an arm around my shoulders and peers behind us. "I don't see anyone," he says, but his body stiffens against me.

I shiver. "Are you sure?"*Because I'm not.* The tight look on his face tells me he isn't either.

"I'm sure." We weave around a few men sitting on milk crates and join the line of people waiting for the train to roll up. "We're almost there."

A gaze digs into my back whether we see anyone or not, making it impossible to stand still. It doesn't feel angry, so it can't be Chamberlain himself but one of his employees might be a casual observer. Maybe we're drawing attention for other reasons.

But it feels familiar, unnerving.

Nik leans his face down into my hair and sings. His voice is low, barely audible even to me. I don't understand the language, but I feel the vibration of his abdomen against my shoulder. I close my eyes tight, trying to focus on the song instead of the person behind us. He isn't using his magic, but the melody still soothes me.

"What does it mean?" I ask when he's finished.

He shrugs one shoulder, a smirk on his lips. "It's just a song I remember from home."

The train chugs into the station, sending puffs of smoke into the air. Nik smiles and I can't help matching it with one of my own.

Next stop, Pittsburgh.

CHAPTER 20

A piercing whistle rips me from a sound sleep. I clamp down on Nik's leg, my fingers digging into the rough fabric of his pants, before I remember we're on a train. The car rattles up to the Pittsburgh station with the sun high in the sky and smile. *We did it.*

My feet don't quite reach the floor and the hard bench digs into my spine, but we did it. Slipping out from under Nik's arm, I inch forward and roll my ankles to help get the blood moving again. "We're here." I laugh. "We're really here."

Nik stretches his back with a yawn. Sleep tugs at his eyelids and I know he didn't sleep a wink. He gives me a sly smile and leans closer. "You twitch in your sleep."

"I do not." I scowl at him before laughing. "Why didn't you get some rest?"

"I wanted to keep watch." He peers out the window as a large brick station rolls in front of our window. "I will on the next train."

I stare at his bloodshot eyes and move the loose hair from his face. "You should've slept on this one. Even if we're being followed, there's nothing they could've done here."

He stifles another yawn. "We can both rest after we make our connection."

I lean back, my shoulder brushing his, while the other passengers in our car scramble to their feet and clamber toward the exit. If it means avoiding the crowd, I'll wait to be the last one off. I don't want to be jostled around and get lost or separated.

"Do we have to stop at the ticket counter for our—"

Walter slides in beside Nik and I slap a hand over my mouth to muffle the scream. The shock erases all thoughts from my mind.

Nik twists around and inches back until I'm pressed between him and the window. I grab his shirt beside the suspenders and hold tight. "What the hell are you doing here?" he asks.

"We need to have a chat." Something clicks softly and Nik tenses. "Outside. Now."

Nik grabs the back of our seat and the one in front of us, creating a barrier. "Walter," he says slowly. "Let's be calm about this. There's no need for a gun."

A gun? He has a gun? Stars litter my vision and my blood drains to my feet.

"I'm perfectly calm." Walter slides off the bench as the last passenger steps out of the train car. I see a flash of silver in his hand before he hides the weapon inside his jacket. "Get off the train. Transmitting all of us at once could be messy so do as I say and no one gets hurt."

"Okay." Nik speaks slowly and takes my hand, stepping into the aisle. "Okay. We're coming. Relax."

Walter motions us in front of him and we move toward the exit as the whistle blows a second time. I risk a quick look over my shoulder. The same anger lines Walter's face as the day I made my second escape attempt on the ship. One wrong move and this time I'll get hit with a bullet instead of a fist. I cover my ears against an internal ringing and I stumble forward, knocking into Nik's back. He steps aside, pulling me in front of him.

"Faster," Walter says. "If you're not off the train before it starts moving, I'll do it. I'll blow your brains out."

There isn't a doubt in my mind he's telling the truth so I clamber down the iron steps to the platform with Nik close behind. The urge to run rips through me like fire but there's no outrunning a bullet. Hundreds of people bustle around the station. It makes testing Walter's aim both tempting and horrifying. If he misses us, he'll almost certainly hit someone else, but with so many witnesses, he may not be daring enough to try.

"Don't," Nik whispers in my ear. He holds my hand so tightly my fingers go numb.

That's easy for him to say. I can't let Walter kidnap me a second time. I just can't. I'll bite and claw my way to the nearest security personnel and have him arrested. It's what I should've done the day I arrived but I was stupid enough to believe Augustine.

I may not be able to escape Walter's gun, but I *can* make it so he can't use it. Just like in the barn back home, I sing softly, testing the magic. My voice wobbles with fear as I sing a bit louder. The people need to hear it for this to work.

"Don't sing," Walter hisses.

Instead, I sing louder. Heads turn and people slow to a stop. Slowly, they press closer. A small, victorious smile touches my lips as dozens of eyes burn into me. If Walter fires now, he'll have to transmit to safety which, with any luck, will give us a chance to get lost in the crowd. If we're not shot…

A hand clamps down on my arm. Before I can turn my head to see who grabbed me, the world tilts. I've felt the sensation before on the ship when Walter transmitted us. My stomach wretches when we land hard. We're still in the station, but the crowd is gone.

"Glad that worked," Walter mumbles to himself. He jabs his elbow to the left. "Walk. Look casual. If you try anything else, I'll take you out."

I plant my feet and turn to face him. "Walter, please." I cringe at the desperation in my voice. I was past this with him, past the begging. "Let us go. You don't have to do this."

He steps closer, pressing the gun to my hip. "I said, walk."

Everyone at the station continues about their own business as if my world isn't crumbling. They pay us no mind, swerving around us without a single glance at my face. *Help* sits on the tip of my tongue, but the metal digging into my flesh holds it back. Besides, there's no guarantee anyone will listen. They didn't last time.

Nik propels me forward but I'm not giving up hope yet. It's possible to lose Walter in the crowd if we move fast enough. It can work, I know it can. It would've worked on ship too if there was anywhere to go, but Nik holds tightly, forcing me to move at a steady pace. Tears splash down my cheeks and drip from my chin.

Outside the station we walk beneath a giant open dome with red brick pillars. Cars both unload passengers at the doors and line either side of the parking area. "That way," Walter says. He motions to the right where the sidewalk slants down before turning into stairs.

"Where are we going?" Nik asks.

Walter doesn't say a word. He simply shoves us into a nearby alcove, grabs Nik and I by the upper arm, and his magic flares to life.

It could have been five minutes or five hours that Walter transmits us through the city. The magic is making me physically ill now, and each stretch of walking makes my legs wobble worse than the last. All I know is, with each new secluded spot we find to transmit from, I'm about to lose any chance of getting my life back. Possibly of having a life at all. Why won't Walter just shoot us and be done with it? But torturing us first is more his style, I suppose. A quick kill won't give him much satisfaction, but watching us squirm will.

When we reach a jumble of rundown huts with scraps of metal for roofs, a pipe reaching up from each, and assorted wood patched together for walls, Walter stops. The smell of waste is so overwhelming, I gag. We stand on a giant patch of dirt with wires overhead and the cries of a baby in the distance for what seems like ages while Walter looks for something. I reach over and squeeze Nik's hand for support. He squeezes back.

"It should do," Walter announces. He slips the gun from under his jacket and points it in our direction before peeking in the window of the first shack. He backs up a few paces, looking into the second. His aim never falters.

"In." He pushes the door open. I know without a doubt if we go in there we won't be coming out again. If, by some miracle, I have an opportunity to escape, I won't leave Nik behind. This thing with Walter started with me and it should end with me. "Move it."

Nik guides me forward with a hand on my lower back. I buck against him at the threshold. We can't go in there. *Can't.* If he wanted to talk, we could've done it on the street.

Walter points his weapon at my forehead. "Behave."

I won't cry over Walter. *Won't, won't, won't.* He doesn't get to break me a second time.

Enough morning light filters through the doorway to know someone lives here. Two plates sit on an uneven table and a moth-eaten blanket is folded neatly on a bed, but no one's home. I choke back a sob and scan the room for something to use against him. A pot. An iron. Anything.

"Why?" I ask.

"Why?" Walter shuts us inside with stiff movements, not turning his back on us for a second. "I want everything I was *supposed* to have." Spit flies from his mouth. "A profitable act in the troupe, a place for me and my mother to sleep at night, and food on the table. Everything you stole from me."

I blanch. The only one of us stealing anything is him. He should be glad he's still walking free and if he's living on the street, good. It serves him right.

"Watching you earn the crowd's applause week after week, laughing and enjoying time with *him*." He shifts his aim to Nik. "After seeing you all over your man back home, and how quickly the two of you became attached, I think I misunderstood your character."

"How dare you bring Christian into this?" I lunge

forward but Nik wraps an arm around my waist, holding me back. I pry at his fingers but he holds tight. "Put me down. I'm going to claw his face off."

"Does the truth hurt? You're on your third relationship in the few months I've known you. Engaged to a coal baron now, I hear. Impressive." He laughs bitterly. "Lucky for me, Theresa hates you as much as I do. She knows I've been employed to follow Nik around and when she saw you two sneaking out, was kind enough to send word."

"You've been watching me?" I ask. Whatever he thinks of my reputation is irrelevant as long as I survive long enough to see each of them behind bars. Walter, Augustine, Chamberlain, and anyone connected to them that played a part in this. "This whole time you've been watching me because Chamberlain hired you to?"

"He hired me to follow him, not you. Mostly." Walter rubs his chin. "Don't act like you didn't suspect it. I saw you looking over your shoulder every time you walked outside. Besides, I had to earn a living somehow." He turns to Nik again. "Speaking of money, where is it?"

Nik squeezes his arm around me, and his breath hitches. "That's what this is about? The money Charlie stole? I've told him a million times, I don't know where it is."

"Yes, you do. Chamberlain's tired of waiting."

Nik's eyebrows rise. He drops me back to the floor

and moves to block my body. "I have no idea. I swear. If I knew, he would've had it a long time ago."

Walter steps closer and Nik presses his back against me. "Do you really expect anyone to believe that?"

"Stop." I inch around Nik. "He's telling the truth. What does Chamberlain need it for? He has more money than he could spend in two lifetimes."

"Sharing secrets with your lover?" Walter wags his brows at us. "Maybe I should be asking her where it is?"

"No," Nik shouts. He tries to push me behind him again, but I dig my heels into the dirt floor. "Leave her out of this, Walter."

He smirks and lowers the gun to my chest. Black spots dance in my vision. If my choices are to die now, fighting, or die a slow, painful death married to Chamberlain—and I would—I choose the fighting. I refuse to be anyone's prisoner again.

"I don't have the money," Nik repeats. "I looked everywhere to get Chamberlain off my back, but I don't know where Charlie hid it. I can't ask him; he's dead."

"Too bad." Walter shifts the gun away from me. "That makes you useless. Step away from the girl and we can get this over with."

"You can't shoot him." Panic skitters along my spine. It can't end like this for Nik. He has to find his sister. "He hasn't done anything."

"Shut up." Walter's face turns a violent shade of

purple. "If you speak again, I'll ignore the fact that I'm supposed to bring you back unharmed."

"What are you going to do, Walter?" I step toward him, my anger making me too brave. "Shoot me?"

"Lina, stop it," Nik says through his teeth. He pulls me next to him and holds me there. "No one's getting shot."

A loud bang echoes off the bare walls and the blood drains from my face. I wobble on my feet, but then I see it. The makeshift door barely clings to the entrance, the bottom of it swinging into the room, knocking over the table.

A large figure leaps inside, knocking Walter off his feet. The gun falls from his hand, skidding across the floor, but it doesn't stop him from elbowing the man in the face. The cracking sound grates on my ears, and he falls back with a grunt.

Nik leaps on Walter's back, reaching for the weapon, but Walter's closer. Things happen so fast, my mind scrambles to keep up. One moment, Nik is straddling Walter. The next, Walter's twisting around and a thundering pop rings in my ears. The world slows while I wait to see which one of them holds the gun.

Nik rips himself off Walter and stumbles to the side. Red blossoms on his arm.

"Nik," I shriek. He can't die. Not Nik. He has too much life left to live. He *can't*. "Nik!"

Falling to the floor beside him, all I see is blood. A

bright red stream flows from a hole in his upper arm, staining his shirt and trickling around my feet. "Oh, God. Nik? Nik, say something. Please, please say something."

"Don't move," growls a man.

I whip around expecting to find a firearm in my face, but it's aimed at Walter instead. Somehow, the stranger wrestled it from him, or maybe he carried his own. As long as it kills Walter, I don't care who it belongs to. Walter shifts, rising up onto his elbows.

"I said, don't move. The police are on their way," the man says.

That voice... I know it. My gaze travels from the gun to the man's hand, then past his crisp cuff and up the sleeve of a black jacket. I already know what I'll see before I get to his face.

"Christian?"

His eyes are hard as he stares down at Walter. "Are you hurt, Lina?"

Hearing Dutch again jars me, the familiarity cutting through me like an arrow, and I almost don't comprehend the words. *Christian's here.* How...?

"Lina?" he asks, softer this time.

"Christian." My backside hits the ground. "Wh... How?"

"Don't even try it," he shouts when Walter tries to stand.

Nik groans behind me. I turn, my hands shaking

uncontrollably as they hover over him. I don't know where to touch him or what to do. He's white as a ghost, and there's so much blood. "Nik?" I ask through my tears. "Hang in there."

"I'll be fine." He shifts to sit and falls back, wincing. "But I need a doctor."

"We'll get you there as soon as we can. Hold on."

"You don't learn, do you?" Christian snarls behind me. "Give me an excuse to shoot you. *Please.*"

I don't turn around to find out what Walter's doing. The hot tears spilling down my cheeks don't let me see much of anything anyway. Instead, I stay kneeling in dirt and blood, between Nik and Christian.

The police are on their way.

CHAPTER 21

The stench of disinfectant has stopped burning my nose, but my eyes still sting against it. The countless tears I shed aren't helping the ache. The only reason I'm not crying now is because I have none left. Pressure rolls through my head, and I rest my cheek on the crisp white sheet. Nik's hand is warm and still under mine. I focus on the steady rise and fall of his chest while I wait for him to wake up. He hasn't moved since he lost consciousness on the stretcher. The nurses cleaned him up after surgery but I can't say the same for myself. His blood flakes on my hands, staining my dress and stockings.

"The doctor said you'll make a full recovery," I whisper to Nik. The bullet passed through his bicep, missing anything major. "But I won't believe it until you wake up and tell me so yourself." I sigh and stare over his head at the steel rungs of the headboard.

Christian is here. It feels like a dream. A figment of my imagination. Because he can't be here—not really. It's too impossible. The police separated us for questioning and I haven't seen him since we left the tiny hut hours ago. It's entirely possible I imagined the whole thing due to stress.

Nik's hand stirs and I bounce up on my stool. His lids flutter, fighting to open. Then a sliver of green as he wins the struggle. "Where...?" He groans.

I tighten my grip on his hand, relief bubbling through me. "We're in the hospital. They said you'll be okay."

"Yeah." He winces. "I feel okay."

I fidget with the sheet, running my hands over it to brush out the creases. "It'll take some time to heal, of coure."

He shifts with a grunt. "What happened?"

"You don't remember?"

He rubs his forehead with his good arm. "I think so but I don't understand it."

I don't want to relive the whole ordeal again. The police already asked me a million questions. I'll be happy never to talk about it again, but Nik deserves to know. "Walter was going to kill you. Christian tackled him, and then you wrestled Walter for the gun. He got it first, shot you, then lost it to Christian."

Nik lets his lashes flutter shut and takes a few long breaths. "Where is Walter now?"

"The police took him." I lay my head back down on the bed beside his hip. "I told them everything about the kidnapping and the troupe."*Almost everything.* I didn't mention Nik's history, the blackmail, or the magic.

"Good." His body relaxes. "That's good."

I'm not sure how good it is. The detective told me I shouldn't leave town before Walter's hearing but if I have to, I should be available to travel back. They need my testimony to go to trial. I have no intention of staying here and I definitely don't want to come back. Ever. But that's a problem for another day. Christian's appearance has changed things. I want to leave everything behind which may be cowardly but it is what it is. I'm tired. I hope Nik wants to leave New York behind too because it isn't likely Walter will keep the robbery to himself after everything that happened. And we have to take his magic into consideration. Can a prison hold him?

"So." Nik cracks one eye open. "That was Christian?"

"Yes." A heaviness tugs at my core. Exhaustion and confusion. For whatever flaws Christian has, he came for me in the end. If he hadn't, I'd likely be dead or on a train back to New York with a gun to my head. He deserves a chance to explain his engagement and why he didn't come sooner.

"I'm glad for you," Nik says.

My body tenses. I'm glad too, but I'm not sure if I should be until I talk to Christian. "Don't push me out the door just yet," I say. "I'm not leaving until I know you're going to be all right."

He flips his hand over to meet my grip. "I'm fine,

Canary. Get out of here and forget about me. Start your life again."

"Forget about you?" The air whooshes from my lungs. "I'll never be able to do that."

His smile is faint.

"I'm not going to abandon you in the hospital. End of story. You don't know anyone here, and what if the police come back to arrest you? I'm not leaving until you do and there's nothing you can do about it." I cross my arms and glare at him.

"So tough," he jokes.

The girl I was before is dead. The world looks different—bleaker—now, but somehow I feel stronger for it. I can't find the words to make him believe it; I barely believe it myself but I *am* tougher now. I remember the desperation and the despair of the few months, but not in a tangible way. It's like looking at a photo of someone else. All the horrible feelings are still inside, but they've gone through a filter. Or maybe I'm still partially numb from shock.

"Miss?" A nurse in a white dress and matching cap touches my shoulder. She extends a towel and smiles. "The doctor will be by shortly to examine him. Maybe you'd like to wash up and wait with your friend?"

"I..."

"We'll take good care of him," she assures me. "I'll even sit with him for awhile if you'd like. I have the time."

There are only two other patients in the room and a dozen empty beds identical to Nik's line the wall.

"Go on. Talk to Christian," Nik urges.

"But…"

He taps the IV line running to his good arm. "I'm not going anywhere, Canary. Cross my heart."

I know he'll be okay but I don't want to leave him, not even for Christian. I'm too afraid Chamberlain will send someone to finish what Walter started. Too afraid that, if I ever stop looking at him, I'll never see him again and the thought makes me sick.

The nurse gently helps me off the stool and places the towel in my arms. I shuffle toward the end of the bed, my gaze never leaving him.

"Get out of here. You've been waiting long enough for him." He closes his eyes. "I'll see you later."

I wince. The conversation with Christian won't be easy. I don't know what he knows or where to start. What to say… "I'll be back. Don't move him," I tell the nurse.

She pats my arm and turns her attention to Nik's bandage. "How are you feeling?"

I turn away and hurry to the nearest bathroom.

Goodness, I look awful. No wonder Nik didn't want to look at me anymore. My hair is a twisted rat's nest. The tears left clean streaks down my dusty face. I set to work scrubbing the layer of gray from my cheeks, then turn to the dried blood on my arms. The sink runs red with it. There's nothing to be done about the stains on my dress but at least it doesn't look like I just went through what I did.

I glance at myself again, a far cry from the girl Christian knew, and vomit into the sink. He claimed to love a happy, energetic girl but that's not me anymore. If I was a bad choice for him before, I'm a hopeless choice now. His parents will never approve, even if I want them to, and I'm not sure I do. Going home is one thing, but going home and pretending like nothing changed is another. *Everything* is different.

Sighing, I head back to the waiting room where the police left me—a long hallway off the side entrance with brick flooring and dark u-shaped chairs. Assuming Christian hasn't wandered off he should be nearby. I round the corner and stop in my tracks.

He's slumped over his knees at the edge of a bench. His fingers disappear into messy bronze hair. A small cut on his cheekbone is already bruising. I watch him from a distance, my heart sputtering in my chest. I've never felt so awkward near him before, but I can't stand here staring all day. I move slowly closer.

At the sound of my footsteps, he looks up, saying nothing.

"Hallo." I break the silence in Dutch. It feels strange on my tongue even after such a short amount of time.

Christian pushes silently to his feet. He tosses his dinner jacket aside and with two steps, his arms are around me. I'm held against him so hard my lungs struggle for air but I don't care. I remember the feel of him exactly. The light hint of mint leaves mixes with sweat and if I close my eyes, it's like we're on one of our dates. But the feeling doesn't last longer than it takes to think it. *He's engaged to someone else now.*

"I thought I'd never see you again." His voice is muffled against my hair.

I clutch at his wrinkled shirt and, before I can stop them, sobs wrack my body. I lean into him, fighting to inhale. All my feelings for him, the good and the bad, seep out in the form of tears. I thought the well dried up when I sat with Nik but it feels like a bottomless pit again. I want to tell him I'd given up hope of seeing him too but the words don't come. I can't tell him how much his betrayal hurts. I want to enjoy him—us—for a moment first. Just one.

"Let's get out of here," he whispers.

For every bit of me that wants to stay, I equally want to escape the curious onlookers in the hall. I cling to his hand and follow him outside. I need answers, and more importantly, I need to feel safe again. I want Christian to hold me, protect me, and give me a taste of home, even if it's for a few minutes.

"The detective told me there's a hotel a few blocks this way," he says.

I let him lead me down the sidewalk, silent tears running down my face. It isn't until he's secured a room and we're inside that the tears stop for a second time today. I'm sure I look even more wretched now than I had in the hospital bathroom but I only care Christian's here in front of me. Nik haunts the back of my thoughts, lingering just out of reach. He's in safe hands where he is and, right now, I have to sort things out for myself.

"Do you need anything? Are you hurt?" He holds me at arm's length and scans my body. His thumbs rub against my upper arms, sending chills skittering toward my elbow. "If anyone hurt you…"

"No." I use my palms to wipe the moisture from my cheeks. "I'm not hurt. Not really. You came in before Walter could do anything."

"I don't mean this morning. Were you hurt at all by that man or anyone else?" he asks in a choked voice.

There's being shoved in a trunk, the chloroform, and the ropes tying me to the bed frame. A single punch after my second escape attempt, but no one's laid a finger on me since I arrived. The slap I received from Augustine isn't significant enough to worry him over. The biggest weapon of choice was manipulation. I consider myself lucky, given the situation. Things could've been much worse. There were even moments I was happy.

"Do you remember Walter? From the dance?" I ask, ignoring his question.

"From the dance?" His face darkens as he thinks back. "The man in the barn? That was him? How did he find you? I didn't see a car behind us on the way to your house."

How could I tell him the truth? That magic is real and Walter can transmit. There's no other way he could've followed us.

Christian's brown eyes take me in from head to toe, not missing a single inch, and he skims his hand over my arms, my neck, my cheeks. "God, Lina. I was so worried. I didn't know what to think. You broke things off with me then vanished. I knocked on your door only minutes after you got out of the car to beg you for another chance. You didn't answer and I couldn't see you through the window so I figured you ran out the back. I planned to give you a little time to think before trying again, but your mother practically knocked down my front door the next morning.

"She said you were missing and thought I had something to do with your disappearance. The police looked everywhere for days. I couldn't sleep. Couldn't eat. I swear, every time someone walked into the room, I thought they were going to tell me you were dead. I felt dead myself." He crushes me to him again. "I'm never letting you out of my sight again."

He knew I was gone so soon after it happened and still it took him this long to come. It shouldn't have been such a hard decision for him. "You were so worried about me that you got engaged to Cornelia Jonckheer?"

He pushes me back and takes my face in his hands. "I *what?*"

"Your mother told me." My voice is harder than I intend, but he doesn't deserve to be let off easily. "You were at your engagement party when I called."

"You talked to my mother?" His eyes nearly pop from his head. "*My mother* told you I was engaged to someone else?"

"Did you get my letters?"

Patches of red rise on Christian's face and he draws deep, angry breaths through his mouth. "I swear, if I had, I would've been on the next plane to bring you back. You know I would. My mother never told me you called."

"Okay." I'm too tired to argue. Whether his mother hid them or Augustine never sent them, I'm grateful he showed up when he did. It doesn't change the fact that he didn't deny the engagement. I brush his hands away from my cheeks. "I'm going to take a nap."

"Lina, wait." He catches my hand. "I'm not engaged to Cornelia or anyone else. I don't know why my mother told you that. There wasn't a day that went by that I wasn't out looking for you."

My heart jumps. *Not engaged.* A new wave of tears

burn at my eyes but I will them away. I know why she told me that—to keep me out of the way. How convenient for her that I disappeared after her husband tried to pay me off, but I never realized they hated me so much as to abandon me to the world. Even my mother wouldn't have suspected it of anyone.

"Your mother…" He studies me hesitantly. "She told me. About you."

He can't mean about the magic—my mother never said a word to me about it so why would she tell him? "About me?"

"Being a Symric," he whispers. He watches my face as he says the word, waiting for my reaction. I press my lips together and my chin trembles, but I say nothing. He's giving nothing away to tell me how he feels about it either. Not even surprise.

"How is she?" I ask instead. When I get home, I'll figure out the truth. *My* truth. "My mother, I mean."

"She took it hard. I checked in on her every day. Sometimes twice. She had enough energy to toss a shoe at my head some days, but others she wouldn't even roll over to look at me."

My chest aches, and I bury my face in his shirt. "I don't know anything anymore," I say quietly, my words hollow. "I thought you were finished with me. That my mother was right and I wasn't anything to you." I hiccup. "I thought you left me here."

He tips my chin up. "You can't think that. Not really," he pleads. "You couldn't believe that I would…"

The hurt on his face makes me want to deny it, to tell him I never believed it, but I did. Any hope of him coming to the rescue dwindled away with each passing day until it was crushed completely. In the end, I had to choose between wasting away, waiting for someone I knew would never come, and getting as far away as possible with Nik. I chose the latter. I had to if I wanted to stay sane. Stay free.

"If you didn't get my address from my letter, how did you find me?"

"The…" He drags a hand over his mouth, looking away. "A sailor wrote home about a girl matching your description. He said you tried to jump overboard and your brother was taking you to New York for medical treatment, but it didn't set right with him. His mother saw the image of you I put in the paper and let the police know. I hired a private investigator the same day. It didn't take long for him to find you with your name being on a theater bill. I chartered a plane the second I got his telegram to come get you."

"Oh."

All the doubts I had peel away, one layer at a time, until I know with the same certainty as before that he loves me. No amount of suspicion whispered to me else will ever take root again. I'm a fool to have ever believed it, even under the circumstances. I know Christian and I know how he feels about me. He can't understand the changes forced on me but for this one night, I'll be selfish. I'll pretend I'm the same for a small taste of what we had.

I stretch up on my toes, pulling him down to meet my lips. The world explodes around us and I lose myself in it. Totally and completely. We belong to each other, just as we did before.

"Wait." Christian breaks away. His chest heaves and his cheeks are flushed, but he hesitates as he touches me. "There was a message waiting for me when the plane landed, telling me you were at Grand Central. The detective followed you there. I know I should've made myself known right away, but I had to see..."

"See what?" I murmur, eager to get back to kissing. To forgetting.

His gaze darts away. "You looked so close on the platform. His arm was around you and..."

My face falls. I knew someone had been watching but never would've guessed it was Christian. If only I searched the faces instead of Nik, Walter never would've been able to get to us. "You were watching us?"

He swallows. "I'm sorry. I know it's wrong, but you were leaning into him and I didn't know what to do. It felt like I was losing you all over again, and I had to be sure."

"Sure about what?" I ask.

"That you weren't with him. That you hadn't forgotten me and moved on," he chokes out.

"Christian—"

"I'm sorry. It was wrong of me to spy on you like that, but, God, Lina. It hurt so much. And... and I still don't know so please just tell me. Are you with him?"

"With Nik?" I lean back. Why do people keep implying Nik and I are together? *Because they have eyes.* I shake the idea out of my head. It's not like that, even if it looks like it. "He was the first person to believe I was kidnapped and not insane. He helped me convince Augustine I was telling the truth, which led to my having a safe place to stay. He helped me create an act for the show, which was supposed to help me earn money to get home. Knowing I'd never see a penny, he took a job smuggling alcohol so we could both leave. When I dragged him out of bed to run away before Chamberlain could force me to marry him, he didn't hesitate and bought us both train tickets. We were going to find his sister in North Carolina and then he was going to help me get back to Holland. Nik's the only person I've been able to rely on since I stepped foot in this country and I'll never be able to repay him."

I gasp as I finish speaking. Having it all laid out together, hearing the defensiveness in every word... Nik became more important to me than I realized. The term *friend* feels wrong to describe him. It's not powerful enough but I don't have one to replace it. None that would be appropriate anyway.

"I'm sorry," Christian says. He presses his forehead to mine. "I shouldn't have thought that. It was stupid. You've been through so much and now here I am, accusing you. Can you forgive me?"

I kiss him again, sweeter this time now the desperation is gone. He relaxes into me, satisfied it was a misunderstanding, but I can't shake the tension. Confusion settles over me like a thin veil. Is this wrong? To love Christian but feel so connected to another man? It feels wrong, like a betrayal to them both.

"I love you," Christian murmurs against my mouth.

I wrap my arms tightly around his neck, throwing myself into the kiss. I'll worry about right and wrong in the morning.

CHAPTER 22

I hover beside Nik as he makes his way down the gray hospital steps. Less than twenty-four hours under a physician's care can't be enough time for a gunshot. The hospital staff doesn't think so either, but we can't risk staying longer and having the authorities coming for him.

"Are you sure you're well enough for this?" I ask.

"There isn't much choice." His wounded arm is wrapped tightly against his abdomen with white cloth and each step is painfully slow, but it doesn't stop a smirk from playing across his face. "Don't worry. I know my limits."

"I have to disagree."

He laughs. "I'm just walking to the car."

I glance at Christian where he waits beside a brown Mercedes Benz with a soft top and long hood. Apparently his father keeps it stored here for business trips. My mother will have a stroke if she ever learns I slept in the same room with him, regardless of the fact nothing happened and we had separate beds. I simply wanted him close by. I'll gladly take any lecture she wants to give me about it.

"You have to walk to the car, then into the train station, to the platform, and then sit in a bumpy train car. Who knows what you'll find when you get to North Carolina? You might walk twenty miles just to find your friends moved away and took your sister with them." I swallow a lump in my throat. "Won't you just come with us? We can send for your sister. If Christian's private detective can find me, I'm sure he can find her too."

He reaches out and rubs his thumb against the back of my hand. "You know I can't."

Butterflies fight frantically in my stomach. Once he gets in the car, it's a short drive to the train station, and then he'll leave. I'll never see him again. It's wrong to ask him to abandon his sister but I want to beg him to change his mind anyway. I want to say his sister's survived this long without him and she'll manage until we can get her passage to their mother in Denmark but I can't. No matter how badly I want to, I can't, so I trudge after him to the vehicle and slide into the middle seat.

The engine rumbles to life and Christian joins us behind the wheel. We pull away from the hospital in strained silence. I haven't told Christian why Nik can't stay longer in the hospital but he accepted it, along with everything else, without question. I know they're there, swirling around in his head. Unanswered questions torturing him in an endless loop. But he doesn't ask. Not yet anyway.

When we pull up to the train station, I dig my nails into my palm so hard I draw blood. Christian hurries to open the door for Nik and my pulse quickens, so much so that it's painful. I'm not ready for this.

"I guess this is it," I say, managing to keep my voice steady as I join the men on the sidewalk.

"Wait." Christian looks between us before settling on Nik. "Lina told me how much you've done and how much you mean to her. I'd like you to be a part of this."

Nik's forehead creases in confusion.

Christian inhales, holding the air in, and rubs his hands together before reaching back into the car. "I had an elaborate plan for the garden party, but..." He straightens with a white peony in his hand. The fluffy, delicate flower twirls as he spins it between his fingers. He takes a shaky breath and pushes his hair back.

I take the flower carefully, smelling the sweet-scented petals. "Christian—"

He drops to one knee in front of the train station and produces a small box. "Lina," he starts.

I step back, bumping into the vehicle. *Now?* He's going to propose now? After everything that's happened and what his mother did, how can he still think this is a good idea? "Christian, wait." I peek at Nik. He watches me carefully with the same blank face he had when I arrived. "I don't think this is a good time."

"It's the best time." A ring glints up at me from the box, sparkling brightly under the noon sun. The diamond is held up by a gold, expertly wrought crown. "I've seen my life without you. Now that I have you back, I'm never letting go. Forget all the obstacles; none of them matter. I love you. Will you marry me?"

His last few words are barely audible over the roaring in my ears. A small crowd of onlookers stop to watch us expectantly, smiling and whispering to each other behind their hands. They seem so sure of my answer. Two months ago I would have said yes before he finished the question. The flower falls from my fingers, landing at my feet. "I need a minute."

I bolt down the sidewalk with no idea where I'm going. This city is just as unknown to me as the last so I let my feet move while trying to keep track of landmarks. Hurting Christian is the last thing I want to do but I panicked. His mother, my would-be mother-in-law, hates me so much she would let me be forever lost. There's disapproval and then there's malice. I'm not sure I can marry into that no matter how much I love him. Besides, he has no idea what I've gone through. What if he finds he can't stand me anymore?

I drop down onto a patch of grass at the base of a stone footbridge, the dry grass tickling my legs through my new stockings, and groan. Why couldn't he just wait a little longer? I was more than ready to marry him before the garden party. He could've given me a piece of twine to tie around my finger that day and I would've said yes. Our parents didn't matter then. My mother would've come around eventually. We loved each other and would've made it work somehow.

No. We *love* each other. That's why I want what's best for him, even if it's not me. At a week old, the entire town knew my name—Lina, the baby in the tulips. Now I'll be known as something different and significantly less attractive. How can I chain him to me when his future is so promising?

"You're going to ruin your new dress," Nik wheezes beside me.

My heart leaps into my throat. "You shouldn't be so good at sneaking up on people."

I stand, brushing bits of grass from my bottom. I couldn't walk around wearing bloodstains so Christian bought me a peach stardust skirt and an ivory crepe blouse first thing this morning. It's a nicer quality than anything I've ever owned, including the lace performance gown. It makes me feel even guiltier; I can accept an overpriced dress but not his proposal? *Why not the proposal?*

"Sorry. I wasn't trying to." Nik leans against the bridge, a sheen of sweat on his face and neck. "I told

Christian I'd bring you back. We've been walking for about ten minutes so I'm fairly certain he's having kittens by now."

"Ten minutes?" I cringe.

He shrugs his good shoulder. "I couldn't call it quits before you did."

I cross my arms and study his bandage for signs of blood or pulled stitches but there isn't any. "I would've stopped if I knew you were back there. You're supposed to be resting."

He smiles. "Yes, nurse."

"See?" I raise my eyebrows. His lack of concern for the hole in his arm proves my earlier statement. "You *don't* know your limits."

"Knowing limits and pushing limits are two different things." His smile shrinks, and he takes a labored breath. "You needed to think. It helped, didn't it?"

"Not really." It feels as if I'm suddenly wired wrong. I don't fit in here, but how will I fit in at home? "I'm more confused than ever."

Nik tentatively reaches out and takes my hand, pulling me into the shade under the bridge. "Let's sit out of the sun."

"I don't want to ruin the dress," I say weakly.

He glares at me and plops down, pulling me with him. "Do you want to talk about it?"

"About the dress?"

"Canary." His voice is tired as he leans his head into the wall.

"I..." I huff. "What was he thinking? Proposing like that? Now, after everything. Doesn't he think I might need some time to readjust? To get back to normal before throwing myself into more life-altering situations?"

Nik draws circles on my palm with his middle finger. "You have to remember, he's looking at things from a different perspective. To him, your relationship hasn't changed. It was just frozen in time. If anything, it's made him realize how much he loves you. He doesn't know everything you've been through yet. Right now, he's only thinking he's got you back."

Pressure builds behind my eyes. That's my point: he doesn't know. "Have I changed?"

His head rolls to the side to look at me. "Remember that day at the bridge? You were looking over your shoulder the entire time like you expected the devil himself to jump from Hell and drag you away."

"It seems like forever ago."

"It does." He gives me a wistful smile. "But look at you now. You tried breaking into Augustine's safe and then dragged me out of bed for an *adventure*. You took off in a strange city without a second thought, leaving Christian and I standing there like a couple of twits."

I groan. "I feel so stupid."

"Well," he chuckles. "Two of the three were rather risky but if I were you, I wouldn't regret any of them."

"Even the safe?" I ask.

He wrinkles his face. "Okay, maybe the safe. Chamberlain would've hunted us to the ends of the earth."

"He did that anyway."

Nik's hand stops circling my palm to rest there instead. After a few moments of dense silence, I knock his leg with my foot. "Is Christian angry?" I ask.

"I don't think angry is the right word. He seemed shocked at first, then embarrassed. Hurt, I'm sure." He hesitates, a painful look on his face. "Lina, why didn't you just say yes? I can feel how much you love him."

"I do, but…" I hold my head with my free hand. I'm not sure if it's right to want the same things I did before. It feels like if I do, I'm ignoring everything that happened. It's too confusing. "I'm not sure who I am anymore. I know who I am here, I think. At least I'm starting to, but I don't know how I'll fit back into my regular life. And to go back to his family instead of my own? Not only would I have to learn how to be myself, but I would also need to navigate high society. Then there's his mother. He deserves someone with fewer issues."

"He'll give you space if you ask for it."

I lift the corners of my lips. Christian will be more supportive than anyone if I give him the chance. The warmth of Nik's hand calms me but doesn't help me sort through the jumbled mess in my head. There's a thin line between different types of love and ours is growing slimmer every day.

"It's not just that though," I admit.

There's a short pause before he speaks. "Nothing's more painful than loving someone who doesn't love you back. If you don't love him the same way anymore, you need to tell him. Don't drag it out."

I look over to find him staring intently at me and heat creeps up my face. "I'm..." I pause, embarrassed by how breathless I sound. "It's—"

"Complicated," Nik finishes for me, the same way I finished the sentence for him when I first got to New York. He shifts until he's resting on his knees, facing me. His hand reaches out and cups my cheek with his free hand. "I know."

It's hard to sit still, let alone think. I've never wanted to be close to him the way I do now, and I want it very much. A wave of energy swoops down, inching me closer. I try to fight it but each second he's touching me, the force grows. "What do you think I should do?"

Nik stands and helps me to my feet in front of him. In one step, he presses me against the stone. His face is an inch from mine and his breath hitches. His body is as close as it can be without touching mine. Each place fabric or skin grazes, it sends sparks of electricity through me. I loop my hands carefully around his neck as he stands motionless, his eyes on fire.

"It's okay," I whisper.

He hesitates before leaning in and touching his lips to mine. His magic swirls around me, seemingly pulling me closer. I lean into him. This kiss isn't enough—I want to drown in him. I didn't know I wanted this until now, and I don't want it to stop. But the tender embrace ends after a few short seconds and he steps back with a glazed look.

"I'm sorry," Nik says in a husky voice. "I shouldn't have done that. I just wanted to see if…"

My world centers itself. A fog lifts and the complicated things don't seem so complicated after all. I knew the truth all along but it got muddled up with dozens of other emotions. Beyond a doubt, Nik's the only person that will understand what happened in New York. I'll never love anyone else the way I love him and no one will ever be able to replace him—not if I live to be a thousand —but I'm not *in* love with him. I could be in time, but not yet. Somehow, I know he absorbed every bit of that truth with our kiss in the same way I now want to explore what could be.

"Nik?"

"It's nothing," he chokes. "Marry him, Lina. Live a happy life."

My lips part, my brow low. "I thought you—"

"I do." He kisses one corner of my mouth, then the

other, lingering. "Trust me, I want you more than I've wanted anything. I want to bring you to North Carolina with me and set up a new life. I want to give you *everything*. But I can't offer you stability. I can't promise that you'll be safe or that the law won't catch up to me. We both know the cops will find me eventually if Chamberlain has anything to do with it."

"I don't care about that."

He leans down to my level, fixing me with his bright green eyes. "You should care. *I* care. You deserve more than my mess of a life and Christian can give you that."

I shake my head. It isn't fair to Christian to marry him for safety or comfort. That's exactly the thing everyone thinks I'm after, but I don't care what his money can buy me. I simply want to be happy.

"If you don't want to marry him, don't, but go home. Go back to your mother."

I wince. "It's not fair to use my mother in this."

"Is it fair not to?" he replies gently.

Nik's right. I know he is, and yet my heart feels brittle. His magic swells again. It pulls on the sense of comfort my mother gives, even with all the distance between us. Tears blur my vision, and he wipes them away.

His breath is warm against my ear as he presses something hard into my palm. "This was my mother's, but I want you to have it."

I peer down at the pin. A silver sparrow, wings spread

in flight, glares up with tiny emerald eyes. "I can't take this."

"You don't have a choice." He folds my fingers over the bird. "It's not wholly unselfish, you know? I want you to have a piece of me with you so you'll remember me from time to time."

I breathe in his fresh scent, now tinged with medication, and concentrate on how solid he feels. I don't need a piece of jewelry to remember him. Every time I see a piano or a picnic basket or a bridge, or a dozen other things I don't realize right yet, I'll think of him.

"Sing for me?" he asks quietly.

I gasp. I don't want to sing. I never want to sing again. "There's no music."

"There is up here," he says, tapping his temple with my finger. "Please."

"Okay." I stare at his face a moment longer. *One last time.* I'll sing our song once more. I fill my lungs and begin.

Sometimes my dreams are haunted by a sweet symphony. The darkness takes hold and once again, I wake in agony.

When we met, our future, how it shone. It now seems so long ago. How could we have known our fates were already sewn? A secret garden in my heart blooms.

Under the twinkling sky, I feel you beside me. The fantasy hides our bitter doom.

The fairy tale, my only light. I'll see you again, my love, when stars are bright.

The tears fall without warning. This song belongs to him, not Augustine, or anyone else. It's mine and it's his, and I'm going to lock it away forever where it can't hurt me.

Nik rests his forehead on my shoulder. "Thank you."

For countless minutes, we don't move from each other. I run my fingers through his hair while he taps his fingers against my back as if he were playing a song. If not for the children that run past us screeching, I'm not sure how long we would've delayed our return to the train station. To Christian and our goodbye.

Nik straightens. His face is tight with pain, though I can't tell if it's from his wound or from... this. "Come on," he whispers, and takes my hand.

THE MERCEDES HASN'T MOVED since I walked away, but Christian has. He sits on the ground beside it, his back against a tire, rolling the peony petals over his kneecap. The red spots are back on his cheeks but this time it's not from anger.

"Lina?" Nik whispers hesitantly. "Do you know? Not that it matters, but he's told you what he is, yea?"

I scowl. "Who?"

"Christian." He swallows hard. "I felt his emotions, just to make sure of his intentions, and they buzzed."

I fidget, eager to put Christian's suffering to an end. "Buzzed?"

"The magically inclined give off a slight hum that's different from everyone else, but his is like a beehive. I've only felt anything like it once before, and that was when I met a changeling."

My breath catches, my mouth parting in surprise. *So it's true then.* Mrs. Van Buren has been right all these years. "He doesn't know," I say under my breath. He deserves the truth, but my mind goes blank as I try to think of how to tell him. We haven't talked about magic yet, not even after he told me that he knew.

Nik seems to sense my trepidation and offers a warm smile. "You don't have to tell him today, Canary."

I nod and let go of Nik's hand to walk the last few feet alone. There will be time when we get home. "Christian?" I call, feeling both horribly guilty and lighter than I have in a long time.

"Lina." He scrambles to his feet, bumping his shoulder on the wheel well. "You came back."

"I'm so sorry." I step closer and carefully pluck the flower from between his fingers. I *do* still love Christian which is why I need to be fair. The uncertainty about where our future is heading hurts down to my very core, but our relationship will have to wait until I put myself back together. "I didn't expect that and there are so many things I'm trying to sort through."

"No," he insists. "I'm the one who's sorry. I should've waited until we got home and given you time. And what must you think of my family now? I wasn't thinking straight."

I shake my head, feeling tears roll down my face. "I want to go home before anything is decided."

"Of course. Our plane leaves in a few hours."

Christian hugs me, his arms sturdy and safe—just like Nik said he would be—and that only makes me cry again.

"You've missed your train," he says over my head to Nik. "Let me take you back to the hotel. You can have our room tonight, and I'll arrange for someone to bring you back in the morning."

There's a heavy pause. "I appreciate it, but I think I'll wait for the evening train."

I pull myself from Christian's arms. "Stay. Rest first."

"It's best to go now," he says with a sad smile. I stumble toward him, shaking my head, and he takes my hand with his. His voice lowers so only I can hear. "It's for the best, Canary. Please. I want to get out of this city and put everything behind me."

"Everything?" I breathe.

"Not you," he amends. "Never you. You know that."

My brittle heart sheds a layer. "I'll... walk you to the doors then."

He nods to me, then again to Christian as a goodbye. Those dozen steps up to the station feel as if I'm walking to my own execution. I want to scream *don't go, don't go, don't go* but I have to let him. He needs to go his way and I have to go mine. Our lives are both starting over after being trapped somewhere we never should have been. He's been controlled since he arrived in New York and I won't be the next thing to hold him back. It's time we both fly free.

"Thank you for everything." I'm proud of myself for sounding steady when I feel anything but. "I never would've survived without you."

"Yes, you would have, but you saved me too. I don't know how long it would've taken me to build up the courage to leave if you hadn't come along." He pulls me into a one-armed hug. "I'm going to miss you, Canary."

"Do you think we'll ever see each other again?"

"Maybe." He pulls away and places a lingering kiss on my forehead. "When stars are bright."

A sob falls from my throat. Why did he have to use *those* words? "Goodbye, Nik."

"Goodbye, Lina."

He steps away when I can't and, with one last smile, turns. I remain frozen in place, watching him until he disappears into the station. When the doors shut, I can't hold back anymore.

The tears flood down my cheeks, dripping onto my

dress, and then Christian is there. His arms wrap around me again, pouring his strength into me. I'm not sure I deserve him anymore, but I'm grateful for his understanding. I'm grateful for *him*.

Christian gives me a gentle kiss, wiping my tears with his thumbs, and we walk back to the car. When he's seated beside me, he takes one of my hands in both of his and hesitates. "I know it will take time for you to adjust to being home. I want you to know that I'll be there for you in whatever way you want me to be."

I'm not sure what's best for me yet. There are so many unknowns waiting at home and so few certainties. I want to see my mother as soon as we land. Chances are I won't want to leave her side for at least a few weeks. And I want to sleep in my own bed. I want to sleep for *days*.

But I don't need to have all the answers right now. I squeeze the sparrow pin tightly in my palm. Right now, all I know is that I survived and am stronger for it. I'll decide the rest when the time comes.

"Are you okay?" Christian asks when I stay silent. "Can I do something for you now?"

I smile at him then—a real smile—and feel the first bud of hope. "Take me home."

EPILOGUE

NIK

FIVE YEARS LATER

Escaping New York was meant to free me.

Finding my sister in North Carolina was meant to settle my heart.

And returning to my mother's side was meant to give me a sense of home.

In truth, I've never felt so restless. I sit on the roof of my mother's third floor apartment, my legs dangling precariously down the side of the building, and stare across the sleepy cobbled streets. There's nothing quite like the early morning glow in a sleepy city. Denmark is undeniably beautiful, but it doesn't have what I'm looking for.

A thin man in a suit walks down the street. He looks up when he reaches the front of the building and waves as he does every day after his early morning stroll. I return the greeting, thinking nothing of it, and begin humming the song that haunts my waking moments. My fingers tap lightly on the terracotta roof as I lose myself in the rhythm.

"Excuse me," says the same man who waved.

I jump at the intrusion and find him peering up at me from his window. His apartment is apparently next door to my mother's, though I didn't know it until just now. "Sorry. Am I too loud?"

"No, no. I quite enjoy listening to your song every day." He scoots a chair up to the window and extends a hand. "Hans Andersen."

His statement unnerves me—I thought this was a private moment every day. I lean forward to shake his hand. "Nik Sala."

"What's the name of the song?" he asks conversationally.

I wince at the memory of Lina. The sensation of her voice echoes through me even all these years later, filling me with want. "It's something a friend used to sing."

"Is that why you hum it every morning?"

I blink at him. "I suppose."

"It's beautiful."

"Yes." I smile then. "But not as beautiful as the girl who sang it."

"Ah." He chuckles. "I detect a story here."

"There is," I admit, but not the story he thinks. This story doesn't end with a happily ever after for me, nor for the rest of Augustine's troupe. According to the papers, after Lina and I escaped, a mob descended on The Den, demanding to hear the infamous Little Lina sing. Things got ugly. A riot broke out, a fire ignited, people lost their lives. I still don't know who escaped—only that some did.

"Tell me about the girl," Mr. Andersen says kindly. "I do love a good romance."

Lina.

My Lina.

Except she's not mine. With any luck, she's happily married to Christian by now with a couple of rowdy children in a big country house, but I don't allow myself to seek the truth. Old wounds still ache and there's no point in reopening them. Even thinking her name makes my heart throb painfully.

"She isn't just a girl," I tell him in a hoarse voice. "And it isn't much of a romance, but I'll tell you if you still want to hear it."

He sets his elbows on the sill and settles in. "Please."

Maybe telling Lina's story will help soothe my soul, but I'll tell it differently so it will never lead back to the real girl. I'll tell it the way she deserves it to be told. I stare at the sky where the sun spreads its warmth and begin.

"Once, there was a girl no bigger than your thumb

with a voice of an angel, a sparrow who wanted nothing more than to fly free, and a fairy prince." My fingers resume playing our song on the roof and my mind hears it as if they were piano keys. "To truly understand, we'll have to start at the beginning when a girl, born of magic, was discovered inside a tulip."

ACKNOWLEDGMENTS

As always, thank you to my family!

My husband for entertaining the kids and the kids for being entertained. Nonny for her undying support. My dad for phone calls that keep me sane. My mom for loving this story before it had an ounce of magic. Kathy—maybe I'll get around to that baby story one of these days. Heather for being such a good sister. All my Georgia family—Sherri, John, Jason, Layla, Ovi, and Georgia—it meant the world that you guys visited me in Decatur! Ashley, Michael, and Aiden—next time!

Lindsay and Judy—we've been friends for almost two-thirds of our lives! xoxo

All my writing friends! K.M., Elle, Candace, MB, Sarah,

Kristin, Laynie, Loretta, and Lauren. You're all an inspiration! Write on, ladies!

Oh! And to the lovely elderly couple in that New Hampshire Starbucks back when I edited this. I absolutely eavesdropped on your entire conversation about vaudeville.

Amber R. Duell was born and raised in a small town in Central New York. While it will always be home, she's constantly moving with her husband and two sons as a military wife. Before becoming published, she had a wide range of occupations including banking, bartending (though she's never tried alcohol), and phlebotomy (though she faints with needles). She also volunteered as a re-enactor at the local Revolutionary War fort and worked near shelter cats which led to her previous crazy cat lady status.

She does her best writing in the middle of the night, surviving the daylight hours with massive amounts of caffeine. Her favorite stories are dark with a touch of romance and a villain you either love to hate or hate to love.

When not reading or writing, she enjoys snowboarding, embroidering, snuggling with her cat, and staying up way too late to research genealogy. She loves to travel and has visited more countries than states. Kissing the Blarney Stone and hand-feeding monkeys in the mountains of France will be hard to beat, but that doesn't stop her from trying to find the next real-life adventure.

Photo taken by Melissa L. Dimos

Visit Amber and connect on social media!
www.amberrduell.com
Twitter
Facebook
Instagram

If you enjoyed When Stars Are Bright, please consider leaving a review!

Then check out more books from Amber R. Duell and Crescent Sea Publishing!

ALSO BY AMBER R. DUELL

The Dark Dreamer Trilogy

Book One: Dream Keeper

Book Two: Dark Consort

Book Three: Night Warden

Fragile Chaos

Fragile Chaos

Prequel Novella: The Last Goodbye

DREAM KEEPER BY AMBER R. DUELL

The Sandman is seventeen-year-old Nora's closest friend and best-kept secret. He has to be, if she doesn't want a one-way ticket back to the psychiatrist. It took her too long to learn not to mention the hooded figure in her dreams to her mother, who still watches Nora as if she'll crack. So when Nora's friends start mysteriously dying gruesome deaths in their sleep, she isn't altogether surprised when the police direct their suspicion at her. The Sandman is the only one she can turn to for answers. But the truth might be more than she bargained for...

For the last five years, the Sandman has spent every night protecting Nora. When he hid the secret to the Nightmare Lord's escape inside her dreams, he never expected to fall in love with her. Neither did he think his nemesis would find her so quickly, but there's no mistaking his cruel handiwork. The Nightmare Lord is tired of playing by the rules and will do anything to release his deadly nightmares into the world, even if that means tormenting Nora until she breaks.

When the Nightmare Lord kidnaps Nora's sister, Nora must enter enemy territory to save her. The Sandman is determined to help, but if Nora isn't careful, she could lose even more than her family to the darkness.

Learn more about Dream Keeper
Now available!

A GOD OF WAR SEEKING RESTORATION.

AN UNWILLING SACRIFICIAL BRIDE.

BETRAYAL THAT COULD DESTROY THEM BOTH.

"Every fiber of my being is woven from the rage of mortals."

Theodric, the young God of War, has a talent for inciting conflict and bloodshed. After being stripped of his powers by his older brother, King of Gods, he sets out to instigate a mortal war to prove himself worthy of being restored to power.

"I loved Kisk once; it was my home... But that was before. This is now."

Sixteen-year-old Cassia, like many in the modern era, believes gods and goddesses to be just a myth. Enemy to her country and an orphan of the war, she has no time for fairy tales. That's until religious zealots from Theo's sect offer her up as a sacrifice.

Can Cassia and Theo end the mortal war and return balance to the earth and heavens? Or, will their game of fate lead down a path of destruction, betrayal, and romance neither of them saw coming?

Learn more about Fragile Chaos
Now available!

JADED BY K.M. ROBINSON

Her father failed in his mission to take control from the Commander, a defeat that has cost Jade her life. She will die as punishment. Now she belongs to the Commander's son—as his wife. Knowing his intent is to quietly kill her in revenge, Jade's every move is calculated to survive—until she learns her death ensures the safety of her father and her entire town.

Roan doesn't want to kill Jade, but once his family isolates her from her father and community, his only choice is to go through with the plan. Jade doesn't make it easy as she tries to sway him into falling for her. Each misstep makes him question his cause. Each moment makes every decision harder, but the Commander won't allow him to fail.

One chooses life. One chooses death. In the midst of the chaos, only one will succeed.

Now available!
Learn more about The Jaded Duology at
jaded.crescentseapublishing.com

HUNTER'S TRUCE BY ELLE BEAUMONT

The Big Bad Wolf never killed for fun—he was on a mission.

Little pig, little pig, let me come in. I'll huff, and I'll puff, and I'll blow your house in. We're tired of death, of prejudice and more, if you don't make some changes I'll kick down your door.

When Niklaus von Brandt's mother is murdered by a poacher it moves him to make a change in the kingdom of Abendrot. Once a kingdom founded by werewolves, it is now ruled by humans who have one goal: eradicate the werewolves. In order to protect what is left of his family, he must make an important decision, one that leads him to become an assassin, and the shadow the kingdom murmurs about.

Too bad the royal family has a secret—a secret that Niklaus plans on using to his advantage, and in the meantime he has given King Ansgar three chances before he comes huffing and puffing.

Now available!
Learn more about Hunter's Truce at
hunterstruce.crescentseapublishing.com